Beautiful Liar

A Sisterly Relations Novel

J. Jakeé

Edited by: Val Pugh Love

For free weekly inspirational and motivational messages sent directly to your email, subscribe by clicking the link below...

http://www.authorjjakee.com/

ISBN 978-0-9969366-1-3

WRITTEN FOR Vanessa, Tiffany, Chanel, Damion and Granville.
Your destiny awaits. You got next ☺

ACKNOWLEDGMENTS

While most girls I know grew up practicing the speech they'd give when they received some kind of entertainment award, I was the one imagining what the acknowledgment page of my very first book would be like. I wondered what I'd write and who I'd mention. Would it be funny or serious? Would it be one page or four? I would literally sit curled up on a couch, studying the acknowledgments written by my favorite authors. I would take delight in their personal style and humor. Then, I would close my eyes and imagine mine… my very own acknowledgement page… and, here I am. By the grace, mercy, and goodness of my Lord and Savior, I am here doing the very thing I began dreaming of when I was sixteen years old.

Of course, I have to first give honor and glory to Jesus Christ, not only are you my homie, but thanks to You and only You, I get to know what it feels like to be a "daddy's girl." Next, I have to thank my #1 fan, my mother Yolounda Barlow, who began investing in my dream before I knew it was there. You purchased a journal for me back when I was ten, and I wanted nothing to do with it. Flash forward nineteen years and forty-three journals later, and I can't see myself functioning without one. I'm an avid scribbler like described in Cacoethes Scribendi written by Oliver Holmes. I have to thank her husband, Mr. Otis for investing in my dream by purchasing me a new laptop for Christmas 2014. If it weren't for you, I definitely would have kept on procrastinating.

If it wasn't for Vanessa, I would have given up for the 1000th time. I hope that she is ready for me to give up 1000 more times with the next. Seriously, your unfailing encouragement, sisterhood, dedication and push throughout this entire journey has been such a blessing. God spoiled me when you became my best friend.

My Soror Tiffany who got to know the characters of this book before anyone else. Tiff rode with me when I only had about 1,500 words typed, and she sometimes knew Nola better than I did. You were initially my sister through Alpha Kappa Alpha Sorority Inc. Over time, I've realized that you are also my spiritual sister in Christ, and you may just be my identical twin sister at that… Thank God for you.

I need to thank my cousin Chanel for her gift of persuasion and marketing. Be steadfast and that gift will take you far. Thanks to my brothers Gordon and Damion, and my cousin Granville for their support and belief in me. Thanks to Soror Naomii for proofreading my website, Calvin for being my first unrelated biggest fan, my sorors Trice and Moya, my grandmother, my aunt Missy, my uncle Byrd and my cousin Baron who all encouraged me and made me feel like a celebrity.

I'm also thankful for my friend Gavin. I love you for your artistic mind which is often identical to mine. You allowed me to cry on your ears when I felt defeated and discouraged, even when that sometimes left us falling asleep on the phone. You remind me of how beautiful, how intelligent, and how talented I am at the most unexpected times. Thank you for being genuine. And, I saved the best for last - my baby boy "Ro" and his father. To my son's father, we don't always see eye-to-eye,--especially when it came to completing this manuscript. You knew when I was sleep deprived and on the brink of a meltdown. You would send me to bed, and I would hate you for it, yet I'd wake up grateful and refreshed. When it comes to needing anything, even some peace of mind for the sake of what's left of my sanity, you are never hesitant to be there for me.

Thank You! Thanks, for being a wonderful co-parent and friend. To my son, your existence is the reason why I told myself I will no longer waste time. In order for me to encourage you to follow your dreams, I would first have to follow my own. Here it is. I do this for you baby boy. <3

Beautiful Liar

A Sisterly Relations Novel

These are the stories from the sorors of Alpha Kappa Lady Sorority Inc., The Omega Tri-State Chapter.

Founded: February 8, 1973
Alias: Pretty Ladies of Poise
Colors: Chrysanthemum Pink and Olive Green
Symbol: The Chrysanthemum
Purpose: "To establish and maintain a lifetime of sisterhood, dedication to service, and highly ethical standards."
Motto: "We are our sisters' keepers."

CHAPTER 1

It had been the third morning in a row that I woke up in our bed alone. Engaged… yet abandoned for some floozy on the fourth floor. The fourth freaking floor. I did my usual routine and called to leave him the usual message after he hit the usual ignore button.

I spat through my cellular, "I hate you. Do you hear me? I hate you!"

My soror, Marley, crept behind me with caution. "N-Nola…They… we're about to call you forward."

I snapped, "Jesus, Marley! Can't you see I'm on the phone?" I threw my hand just centimeters from her face. "You need to back up!"

Her nude-colored kitten heels nearly slid across the linoleum floor as she scurried behind the conference room doors. The automation from Trav's voicemail echoed through the lobby of the community center.

To send your message now, press one. To re-record, press two. To delete your message, press three.

My hand shook as I pressed the END button. The rays from the morning sun beamed through the oversized windows, as I paced the floor. A marathon of thoughts raced through my head… *I knew about his cheating… Why am I mad? … My sorors are waiting on me… Smile…Don't let them see you mad… Don't let anybody see you mad. Call again… BE CALM…You have everything… Don't call him again…Get even. Get even. Don't call him again. Smile… Smile. Call him, again.*

My heart pumped and thumped against my chest as I redialed. Being sent to the voicemail again after three rings only exacerbated my wrath.

I boiled, but I exhaled and whispered through the phone, "If I'm pregnant, you can forget about seeing our child. You cheating son of a bi—"

"Soror Nola, we're just about ready for you."

Our chapter president, Gabrielle, held the door open and extended her hand for me to grab. Her warm and friendly smile competed with the sun rays. Her hazel eyes twinkled, as did the crystal buttons on her soft pink suit jacket. And, just like that, I simmered as she led me to my post in front of my sorors.

The large room hosted about ninety of us every second Saturday morning from September through May. I had a weak spot for the women who sat before me, because six years ago, they chose to love and accept me without even truly knowing who I was. They showered me with the honest support and sincere affection that my family withheld. On top of that, they were distinguished scholars, career women, and retirees—a few them were over the age of seventy-five. They were real life examples of what I needed to be, if I wasn't already, and I felt compelled to impress them for that.

Most of us were entrepreneurs, corporate climbers, lawyers, nurses, doctors, educators, and freelancers above the age of twenty-two. Well, except for Marley. She is our baby who graduated high school and college early. She joined the chapter at twenty, just a little over six months ago. Gabrielle selected me to be her mentor. I initially obliged, because Trav had recently proposed and an extra hand with the wedding planning was just what I needed.

Marley's puppy dog eyes studied me as I approached the stage and joined another soror at the podium. I smiled as if it was effortless, and all of my sorors smiled back. Some of them nodded with their hands pressed together, faces full of elation, and their eyes and smiles showing that they were proud of the young woman they thought they knew from mind to muscle.

"Without further delay, we present Soror Nola Victor with the 2014 Soror of the Year glass plaque," Gabrielle said.

Everyone rose and appalled as I posed with Gabrielle and smiled pretty for the cameras. The soror at the mic pulled out a folded paper and read, "If there is anyone who truly understands the meaning of devout dedication to our sisterhood, it's Soror Nola Victor. Her selfless spirit has been reflected through her leadership roles within the executive committee, and through her participation with all of our community service events and philanthropy."

She peeked from the paper and laughed. "Not to mention, whatever she does, she always looks good doing it."

My sorors playfully clapped and cheered mirthfully as I flipped my long hair and slowed-twirled, showcasing my Vera Wang hot pink tulip skirt.

The soror continued, "Soror Nola Victor has also been dedicated to revamping our closing year retreats, making them fun, exciting, and most of all memorable. Since she chaired the Retreat Committee four years ago, our membership retention has never been better! Her work ethic is phenomenal. Her sweet and kind heart is incomparable. Soror Nola, we admire you, we appreciate you, and we love you."

As the room awed, I hugged my soror tightly, hoping I could squeeze some of her positive energy onto me. I approached the mic and tried to shake off the negativity that consumed me.

"Thank you so much, sorors. I feel so honored to be recognized by this chapter. You ladies are my inspiration to do better and to do bigger. With that being said, could sorors Marley and Bailey please join me up here?"

Marley and Bailey looked at each other, confused and caught off guard. Yet, they rushed to the front.

I continued, "In light of doing bigger and better, the Retreat Committee has already decided on this year's location."

I heard Marley whisper to Bailey, "We have?" Through my peripheral, I saw Bailey shrug as I announced with a smile, "Hotel De Relajar. Some of you may have heard of it. It's a spa retreat right here in Delaware. For the first two hours, we will have our leadership seminar. After that, we will have a banquet lunch followed by massages and manicures. My fiancé and I got lucky at the firm just recently, and well, all expenses will be paid by me! How does that sound?"

My sorors stood, cheered, and hugged each other. All of them were full of excitement. Marley and Bailey looked stunned, but neither one of them bothered to question my decision. I watched everyone's reaction, tickled with complete satisfaction. Revenge tasted so, so, so good. Plus, I got to feel like Oprah when she used to do the *My Favorite Things* specials on her daytime television show.

Immediately after the meeting, I tossed on my Dior shades, slipped on my fur, and slid out of the doors without saying good bye.

Marley caught me in the parking lot sitting in my pure white Range Rover. I had just pulled out one of Trav's credit cards and charged $3,685.23 for our retreat through Hotel De Relajar's mobile app. She knocked on my window. Her grey trench was sloppily thrown on, and piece of lint clung to her hair.

"Leaving so soon?" she asked.

I pulled down the window. "It's going to be a busy day for me. What's up?"

"I wanted to apologize for disturbing your phone call earlier, and I wanted to thank you for funding our retreat!"

"You are forgiven, and you can thank Trav for the retreat, actually," I smiled.

Marley pressed her mitten-covered hands together. "He's so amazing, Nola. You're marrying a good one."

I reached over and plucked the annoying lint from her head.

"You blindsided Soror Bailey and me. We can't wait. When January ends, I'll be counting down the days."

"You and I both," I replied as I started up my Range. "Do you need a ride or something?"

Marley's eyes bulged, "Oh no! I drove today."

I started to pull the window back up, "Bye, Marley."

She waved her hands to signal me before I pulled off.

"Wait, one more thing!"

"Urgh. Hurry. It's cold," I griped.

"Church, tomorrow?"

I frowned. "No. You ask me this every single month. My response won't change."

Marley sucked her lips in and nodded solemnly. And then she perked up again.

"Well, just don't forget about lunch Tuesday!"

I stroked my hair nervously and tossed it behind my shoulders. Tuesday. Lunch with Marley on Tuesday was the absolute furthest from my mind.

"I'll let you know, Marley. I have a doctor's appointment that day. Listen, it's cold. I'm tired. I have a lot on my mind and a lot to do. Do you mind if I... I'm gonna drove off now."

Marley shook her head and stepped back.

CHAPTER 2

Sharron, the concierge, was her usually chipper self.

"Good morning, Nola!"

I removed my sunglasses. "Good morning, Sharron."

"I have a package for you. It arrived yesterday." Sharron lifted a box onto her desk. "Looks like shoes."

I shook my head. "Nope. Make up."

Sharron pressed her lips together and smirked, "It's usually shoes. I bet you have a lot of shoes you don't wear anymore. You need to just go on ahead and pass them to me."

I shrugged, "Ok."

"No, but I'm serious!"

"I'm serious, too," I replied nonchalantly.

"You would do that?"

"Yes, crazy girl. It's not a big deal."

Sharron clapped her hands and leaped, causing her curls on her blonde wig to bounce.

"Thanks, Nola! Oh… and…" She spun around to a table sitting to her left and retrieved a stack of envelopes that was placed next to a floral arrangement. "There's one more thing," she said as she handed them to me.

I shuffled through them quickly. Nothing but a bunch of junk mail and credit card bills.

"I had the mail man leave them here just as you instructed."

"Thanks," I said as I motioned to the floral arrangement. "For suite 1020?"

Sharron rolled her eyes and replied, "You know it."

"Lucky wench," I sighed. "He must be away on business."

"Or feeling sorry."

"No… he sends gardenias when he's sorry. Those are tulips. He misses her."

Sharron smacked her teeth, "Well he must really miss her, because he just sent some earlier this week… white roses."

"Wedding anniversary."

"What? Ok… yeah, she must be a good friend of yours."

I ripped the envelopes. "Never formally met her, but I've lived here going on three years. Seen her reaction, and her husband keeps it predictable. The same flowers are designated for a particular occasion."

Sharron stuck her finger in her mouth and pretended to gag.

At that, I said, "I think it's a sweet a gesture. Especially how he does it. You can tell he loves her. He appreciates her being in his life, and accepts her for who she is."

With a look of confusion, Sharron replied, "And, you learned all of this based on the flowers this man delivered? You sure you don't know these people?"

I laughed. "Here. Shred these."
***

Trav was home, and I was surprised. The aroma of bacon greeted my nostrils as soon as I keyed into our apartment. Our dining table held a few dozen red roses and a table setting for two. Pancakes, grits, and bacon were plated neatly. He was naked under his apron, wearing nothing but his Cartier wrist watch, which wasn't so surprising. Trav, a very arrogant and sexual man, was standing at ease with a smirk on his face. He was failing at trying to ameliorate the damage he had caused about a year ago. His dark, perfectly chiseled body glowed as if he had just hopped out of the shower and oiled himself down.

"Is this for me, or am I home too soon?" I asked sarcastically.

Trav wagged his finger and shook his head. "Good, one. That was a good one."

He attempted to help me remove my coat. I threw my hand up and helped myself, tossing the fur across one of the chairs.

"I got your voicemails, Nola. You seemed a little stressed out. So, I did this for you, Queen."

"Oh," I replied sarcastically elated. "You ran from your girlfriend's house to cook me a romantic breakfast? WOW! That's sweet, Trav."

He grabbed my hand, and my ring twinkled and blinked as he lifted my arms before backing me against the wall. His stiffened man-shaft pressed against my waist as he leaned in for a kiss. I turned my head catching his lips with my cheek.

He backed up. "Maybe it's the workload. Maybe it's too much for you to handle. I'm not gonna allow you to put our baby at risk. Take a break from work and focus on becoming a mother."

Trav pulled a single rose from behind his back and stroked my face with it. I swatted him and his rose.

"You're firing me so *L* from the fourth floor can have my position."

Trav looked at his toes, then slowly back at me while rubbing his chin.

He finally replied, "Not firing you. Just a simple suggestion since you're pregnant."

"We don't know if I'm pregnant,"

"You mentioned something about your period…" he said with a look that suggested that he was trying to recall our conversation.

I rolled my eyes. "Irregular periods aren't always a pregnancy symptom."

"Then, why are you seeing your doctor on Tuesday?"

I smirked. "For the same reason you want me out of the office - to cover my bases."

He crooned, "Here we go…"

"You don't give a damn if I was pregnant! If you cared you would be here—" I spat.

"Lower your voice…"

"—The only thing you care about is hiding soon-to-be Mrs. Travis Beaumont from the company, so that you could play around in your little playground."

Trav huffed, "I'm only saying that I make enough to take care of the family."

"And, what if I'm not pregnant?" I challenged, with folded arms.

"You don't need to work, Nola. You don't like to work."

"You're a hoe."

Frustrated with my jabs, Trav threw his hands in the air, slapped them on his head, and blew air from his puffed cheeks.

"Let's be honest with ourselves for once, Nola. Okay?" He droned, "You don't give a damn if I was with another woman."

My lips parted, but I didn't dare deny his accusation.

"All you care about is that sorority, and spending MY hard earned money," he said smacking his chest and putting an emphasis on MY.

"My sorority loves me more than you do. My sorority appreciates me. Initially, no I never wanted your money." *Until you dangled it in my face.* "I wanted you!"

Trav spoke calmly and confidently, as assholes usually do, when he said, "I'm a busy man, Nola. If you can't handle it, there are a sea of women fishing to be in your shoes. I told you this before the first date."

Of course you did, Asshole. "Had I known you were also busy with skanks, I would have never said 'yes' to dating you!" I yelled.

I wanted to crush Trav's balls, so bad. Just grip them from underneath his apron. Instead, I snatched the bud of the rose from Trav's hand and smeared its petals into the floor with the tips of my Louboutin bootie. I stormed off.

"See, you're being dramatic again, Nola!" Trav called to my back as I picked up my package from downstairs and headed towards our bedroom. "Get some rest. Take a nap. You'll feel better afterwards," he said sarcastically.

I slammed our door without saying another word.

CHAPTER 3

"Nola. You're not pregnant. You have gonorrhea."

Four hours later, Dr. Keller's voice still haunted me. Those horrifying words replayed in my head over and over again as I pressed my head against my office window. Outside were shades of cyan and indigo. Downtown Philadelphia was twenty stories below, coated with yesterday's snow. The temperature had to be under twenty degrees. The wind howled giving bundled-up pedestrians a beating with its wintry whip. The sun had seemingly taken a personal day off, tucking its beams beneath the puffy clouds. My heart felt colder than that January afternoon.

Gonorrhea

My saturated eyelashes barricaded tears that weren't allowed to crawl. I took a deep breath and massaged my shoulders. *You're Victor, not a victim!* ...my father would have said. I swallowed hard, smoothed down my pencil skirt, and then my 3ct diamond engagement ring flickered. The sight of it sent me in a rage. I could have broken my hand with how hard I pounded it against the thick glass... *THUD!* After *THUD!* After *THUD!*

I should have felt pain, but I was numb. No one heard my loud banging. Even if they could, most of them would have sat stationary, watching with their mouths foaming of malicious satisfaction. Thirsty for more gossip-tea to sip to go along with their daily cubicle prattle of how I "screwed my way to the top and was granted a promotion solely for being the CEO's future wife" and how I "got my knees dirty to score such a fancy office."

Gonorrhea.

It was a tough pill to swallow—the diagnosis and the antibiotic alike.

Dr. Keller's eyebrows wrinkled with concern. "Do you have any·idea how you contracted it? ...I mean, aside from the obvious."

"My fiancé did this," I replied somberly. I was blindsided by the STD but not the cheating, of course.

A month after Trav proposed, he stopped coming home. On the mornings he returned, I would listen to his mendacious tales of how stressful traveling for work has become, and how he just wished he could stay home with me and cuddle. One night while he slept, there were several missed calls from a number stored under "L". When I called "L" back, she disconnected after hearing my voice. Moments later "L" called and revealed that she was a customer service rep from the fourth floor of the firm. Yep. A basic, hourly paid telephone girl.

It was then that I read the GPS history on his phone and found hotels and restaurants, all of them within a 50 mile radius. *A 50 mile radius!* I immediately created a machination to marry him in spite of my findings, so I could eventually divorce him and snatch everything he owned or even dreamt about owning. I would make his family's business mine. But game over by forfeiture.

This dirt-bag jeopardized my health, I thought to myself as my heart continued to freeze from the rage that was building up inside of me. After Dr. Keller broke the news to me at my appointment, I was flabbergasted and unable to think clearly.

"If you want, we can schedule an appointment now for you both to come in and get him tested," Dr. Keller suggested.

I snatched my navy blue Chanel maxi handbag off of the examination table, and harshly replied, "His penis could rot and crumble to the ground."

I let the trailing sound of my click-clacking Jimmy Choo heels drown out Dr. Keller's voice as she called for me to come back.

"Nola.... Nola!"

I was so gone in my thoughts staring out of the window at nothing in particular, that I hadn't noticed Marley had let herself in my office. She was carrying two plastic bags with platters of Pad Thai and Khao Pad. *Dammit, I knew I would forget about Thai Tuesday this week.* Anyway, it was something she made up months ago when she discovered we worked just a few blocks from each other.

Marley chirped from behind me, "It's beautiful to view, but Lord knows it's a monster to endure. That walk was brutal…Get over here. Let's say grace!"

Before I turned around, I pasted on the biggest smile I could borrow for the next forty-five minutes and hid my problems in the back corners of my mind. I winced when Marley's cold hands clasped tightly onto mine, awakening the pain I should have felt moments ago. Her cheeks were rouge, her nose and ear lobes were a winter-kissed pink, and the turquois knit scarf that I bought her for Christmas clung to her chin and neck. She was a pastor's kid but not at all troubled like the stereotype holds. She rarely did anything without a prayer first.

Marley was a naturally beautiful young girl. She was pretty and book smart, which is why I didn't mind having her around and being her mentor. However, she was also naturally plain, wearing only neutral colors and barely any makeup unless I coaxed her to add a bit here or there. If her hair wasn't pulled up in that awful bun, then it was worn flat like it was that past Saturday, sweeping only the top of her shoulders. Since we were like the sisters that neither one of us had, on occasion I'd treat her to my stylist and doll her up with extensions that resembled my God-given and panache mane.

She dished out our lunch and without bothering to remove her coat, she plopped into the chair opposite of mine.

"Oh! And, please don't get on me about my hair," she begged, patting her messy bun. "It was a rough morning."

Talk about it. "You get a pass today. At least there isn't lint in it," I said.

I reached into my drawer for a stack of napkins that she didn't ask for as usual. She was a pretty girl, but she ate like a warthog. Marley grabbed the napkins and nearly knocked down a framed picture of my baby brother as she pulled her arm back. She was also clumsy.

"So, how's the wedding planning?" was her typical conversation starter, but I hated that she asked today.

My eyes never left my plate as I murmured, "Fine."

"Fine?" She dropped her fork and genuinely asked, "What's wrong?"

"Nothing worth mentioning," I replied, trying to add more life to my voice.

Marley begged, "Aw come on, tell me."

I would never.

I looked her in the eye—because for some odd reason, people thinks it's impossible to lie looking directly at a person. It's not hard to do at all when it's practiced with your father who happens to be a prominent criminal defense attorney.

I told her, "Everything is good aside from a little bit of wedding jitters—normal stuff."

" Already? The wedding isn't for another year... and a half," she said as if she knew I was hiding something.

"The planning—I keep bumping heads with my coordinator. I need to fire her," I lied.

Marley gave me a slow nod. Just as she parted her lips to probably badger me some more, there was a knock on the office door followed by the knob twisting.

It was Trav. Marley perked up at the sight of him. To her and to everyone as a matter of fact, he was perfect. He was tall, dark... very dark, comely, stylish—always clad in Boggi-Milano suits and Hermes ties – and fiscally successful. He was a bossed-up realtor who used to spoil me with attention and affection. He was the same knight who snatched my title of Intern and labeled me lead Marketing Coordinator for Beaumont Real Estate, the soon to be franchise.

Shortly after we began dating, Trav put me in his condo, a high-rise nestled in that famous big blue building that scrapes the central city sky. He supported my addiction to designer EVERYTHING, and he kept me for almost 3 years before he proposed. To most, we were a power couple, but in reality, only he had the power. Without him, I was simply a 28-year-old college graduate with mommy's, daddy's, and granddaddy's money and a little bit of my own. To Marley, I was the epitome of where she wanted to be and who she wanted to become within nine years. However, she had no clue. None of my sorors had a clue.

Marley beamed and said, "We were just talking about you! Well, not you per se but the wedding."

Trav nodded with effrontery, and I nearly spat fire. The sight of him boiled me.

"Marley could you excuse us for a minute?" I asked while rapidly tapping my fork against my plate as a method of anger containment.

As soon as Marley shut the door behind her, Trav opened his arms for an embrace. I tapped my fork and continued to pierce his eyes with my icy stare.

He finally dropped his arms and said, "Well… what's up? Are you pregnant or not?"

"No, I'm not, but I hope L and all these other women know how dirty you are."

"Nola, let's not do this here."

Right then, my fork became a dart, and his head was the target. Unfortunately, he ducked. I leaped forward, reaching for Marley's fork. Our platters crashed to the floor, and he raced over gripping both the fork and my wrist. He squeezed so hard that the veins in my hand rose.

"Have you lost your mind? Do you know what I could do to you?" he spoke through clenched teeth. "You're lucky if I don't choke the life out of you!"

I spit on him. A thick, gooey wad of phlegm smacked him in the area between his nose and the top of his lip. He jerked away almost slipping backwards on Pad Thai.

Trav seethed, "You nasty, cunt!" He wiped his mouth on his sleeve, "YOU'RE FIRED!"

He nearly knocked Marley down as he flew out of my office and charged down the hall. She was alarmed as she stood with her mouth wide open while she watched Trav disappear.

"What in the world just happened?!"

I grabbed my purse and my coat. "I'm driving you to your office."

"Is everything ok?" Marley asked, still trying to make sense of the mess.

"Everything is perfect. Work just has him stressed."

Marley's eyes fell to the Pad Thai mess. She wailed, "But, what happened to my lunch?!"

CHAPTER 4

After I dropped Marley off, I spent the rest of the work day at my favorite Moroccan Restaurant smoking a hookah, stuffing my face with their signature appetizer, and sipping two dry martinis. By the time I got home, I was enervated from contemplating my next move. I had no job, yet somehow I needed to find a place to live, since living with a man whose face I just spit in would be tricky.

Sharron spoke, "Hey, Nola."

Trying to avoid conversation and to keep her from spotting my disheveled appearance, I didn't bother to make eye contact with her this time. With my fur opened, exposing my now untucked and halfway unbuttoned shirt, and my hair pulled into a sloppy high bun, I pressed the elevator button and looked down at my shoes.

I moaned, "Hey, Sharron."

"I have your stuff," she replied.

I threw my head back and groaned as I approached her desk, "I am so tired. I don't even remember what I ordered. How big is it?"

I nearly tripped over garbage bags and boxes as I made my way over to her desk.

"Jees! Someone moving out?"

Sharron raised her eyebrow, and scratched her now wavy and burgundy wig. She spoke through clenched teeth. "Uh yeaaah... you?"

I felt my heart leap from my chest and crash to the floor somewhere in between the gigantic black trash bags. I heard her, but I didn't hear her. When I asked her to repeat herself, it looked like Sharron's lips moved in slow motion.

"All of this is your stuff," she said.

I dropped my maxi handbag on her desk and frantically ripped through one of the bags. Dresses and suits were balled up but on a hanger. All of them were definitely mine. I untied another bag and found more of my clothes and some coats. I opened a box to discover

24

some of my shoes and boots. There were six garbage bags and eight boxes total. My body burned, and my chest rose and fell rapidly. Then, my voice boomed through the lobby.

"THAT BASTARD!" I screeched.

Sharron flapped one hand, and raised a finger to "shhhh" me with the other.

"He has my Vera's, House of CB, and Zimmerman dresses crammed in a garbage bag. IS HE CRAZY??!!" She didn't have a chance to respond as I said, "Sharron, please watch my things while I run up and trash up his place!"

She buried her face in her hands and then dragged her hands down her face. "He changed the locks, Nola."

If my eyes were bullets, her face would have been shot up. I snapped my head back, "What did you just say?"

"I saw him leave with a locksmith," she said quietly.

***

I swapped my heels for my Ugg Boots and loaded my things into the Range. Sharron began helping me before I could even ask.

She stuffed the last bag onto the back seat and asked, "Are you okay?"

I said nothing.

She continued, "If this happened to me, I would have lost it."

I quietly loaded a box into the trunk, then grumbled, "I'm fine."

"Are you gonna cry?" she asked in a sincerely concerned tone.

"I don't cry," I replied frankly.

"You need to. It's not good to hold pain inside. It'll bubble over at the wrong time."

I slammed the trunk shut. "If there were any truth to that, I would have combusted over twenty years ago." I took Sharron's hand. "Thanks for helping me. Here's a tip."

Sharron looked down at her hand. Her eyes nearly popped out of her face when she saw that she was holding onto my engagement ring.

She smacked her gums, stuck out her tongue. "You know Im'ma pawn this, right?"

***

"What do you mean your condo caught fire? Where are you?" Marley asked in a panic.

I calmly replied, "FeliciTEAs."

"Your condo caught fire and you are sitting somewhere sipping tea?"

"I was shaken up and needed to calm my nerves. The good thing is that I was able to get my stuff…" I looked at my loaded SUV, through the large window in front of me, "*all*…of my stuff."

Marley sighed through the phone. "Yes. Glory to God. Where is Trav?"

"Trav is gone."

Marley shrieked, "What?!"

I pulled my phone from my ear to protect my eardrums. "Calm down, child. He's not gone as in death. Gone as in away… for a couple of months. Business. You know how that goes."

Marley gasped, "Ooooooo. So that's why he was so upset earlier. He's gonna miss you!"

Yeah… sure… whatever. I sipped my cherry flavored green tea and slouched. FeliciTEAs was crowded as usual. It was packed with students, avid readers, writers, corporate folks, and anybody who needed free Wi-Fi and that country-styled living room feel. I loved it there and everything about it. The delicious yet becalming scent of premium teas, the multiple sofa and coffee table set-ups throughout the shop, the shelves and shelves of borrowed books along the wall, and the randomly, but maybe strategically, placed wall décor that read, *"Welcome Home," "Sip. Chat. Reminisce,"* and *"Love is*

Unmeasurable" which were all probably meant to make a store full of strangers feel like family.

Marley sighed again. "Sounds like you're having a tough evening. If you need to stay with me for a while, you know you're always welcome."

Marley lived in an apartment out in Delaware, quite a distance from my parents. Although I've only been there twice, I knew staying with her wasn't going to be an option. She lived like a freshmen college student with lights on in every room—even on a sunny day—mix match table and glassware, and clothing thrown every which way. No thanks! Plus, the thought of having to live with my mentee was depressing. *She was my mentee* - not a good look!

"Thanks, but I have it under control."

"Yeah. I guess I am being silly. I'm sure Trav has a hotel booked for you already."

I rolled my eyes and said, "You know Trav."

"You are so blessed, Nola."

I rolled my eyes again.

"I pray that God moves in my life as he moves in yours," she continued.

I huffed, "Marley, don't start with the God talk right now. I'm not in the mood."

She laughed. "Tough times are the best times to talk about Him!"

While Marley giggled, a tall man with a knit Eagles hat approached my sofa.

"Excuse me. Can I sit here?"

I shook my head "no" and continued with Marley, "No preaching. You preach even when you don't realize you're preaching."

The man, who was still standing in front of me, looked to the left and then to the right just before sitting next to me anyway. Shocked by his blatant mutiny, I dropped my phone to my lap and snapped my neck back like a 'hood girl would.

"I said you couldn't sit here, Rosa!" I spat.

The man tilted his head… and then he slowly shook it. Still, he didn't budge.

"*Hello?!* You need to move. I'm having a personal conversation with my friend. I'd appreciate it if you respected my privacy."

"Look man—"

"Woman. I'm obviously a woman."

"—I had a rough day. There is nowhere sit, and I'm tired. I don't feel like standing, nor do I feel like having a confrontation. So if you don't mind, I'd like to study my bible."

"I do mind. And, your bible? Are you kidding me? Go to a church! If you're tired, go home!"

The unbothered man flipped through his bible and shifted in his seat in an effort to get comfy. Then he said, "I'm gonna ignore you."

"*Jerk*," I mumbled as I lifted my phone back to my ear.

Marley was still connected.

"Nola! What happened? Is someone bothering you? Maybe you should head to your hotel now. Crazy people come out at this hour."

***

I think my mother was pretty happy to see me. My father, not at all. He stood against the kitchen cabinet with his arms folded and his face wrinkled with agitation. My mom sat at the kitchen table with her chin resting on top of her folded hands. Even when she was concerned, she looked strikingly beautiful. She used to model for catalogs to help pay her way through medical school, and she still had "it." Tonight, she looked as if she were modeling her grey satin pajamas. Her dark thick, long hair fell suavely and draped over her shoulders as if it were a hooded blanket. Her long eyelashes batted as her gaze wavered from me to my father, and then back to me.

"I can't believe he fired you, then kicked you out of the condo all in the same night," she shook her head. "And, he gave you gonorrhea…"

My father groaned, "After all the money we shelled out for that wedding." He pointed at me, "You have a case. Take him to court and get EVERY penny I spent."

My mother exhaled and gently placed her hands on top of mine.

"Before you do anything, you need to figure out where you'll live right now."

My father chimed, "That's what her trust fund is for. She should have enough to find a good house in the morning."

I rose from the table and grabbed a bottle of Riesling from their wine rack. "That's what I needed to talk to you both about," I added as I poured myself a glass.

My mother eyed me, and suspiciously asked, "What, Nola?"

I took a large gulp of the Riesling and swirled it in my mouth allowing myself time to get the words out. My father instantly read my body language.

He pounded his hand against the cabinet and yelled, "SHE EMPTIED IT!"

"Nola… No," my mother moaned.

I said, "Not exactly all of it. There just isn't enough to buy a good house… or rent a good place. And, you know I'm not going to any old neighborhood."

My father paced the floor the way attorneys do, running his fingers through his white hair. His pale face was now red from anger. "Your grandfather worked until it killed him…. and you just blow it…like it's nothing… like it's toilet paper to wipe your ass with."

My mother exhaled, "Nola, I thought you had your spending under control."

"Mom, I tried. Trav dragged me through hell for the past several months. I was so stressed... I maxed his cards, and then I maxed mine."

My father laughed sarcastically, "Stressed. You lived in a building with millionaires. You were practically handed a career. Your wedding was being paid for. You drive a Range Rover paid off by us. Your bank account has never been under $50,000 for more than two weeks with the help of the trust and with the help of us, and *YOU* were *STRESSED*? Do you know that your brothers haven't touched a penny of their inheritance?"

"Hunny, calm down. You need to relax," my mom said in her usual angelic tone.

He spat, "She's a joke!"

I cut my eyes at my father and barked, "Frankenstein, I'm YOUR monster!"

"Don't you DARE blame me."

My mother jumped to her feet, "Walter. Nola. Enough. Dominic is upstairs sleeping. You both are getting too loud."

I sat down and said, "I need to squat here. It'll be temporary— just until I get myself together."

My father shoved his hands into his pockets, still pacing the floor. "You'll never get it together. You were born a failure," he said coldly.

Then, there was a CLINK-CLASH! I flung my wine glass, and shards flew in every direction as it crashed to the floor. My mother jumped back, dodging the shatter.

"Nola!" she cried.

"He's an ASSHOLE! And, why do always you allow him to talk to me like that?"

My father groaned, "No, I'm your ATM!" He turned to my mother, "If she breaks another dish in our house, we're cutting her off. I mean it this time."

He left us in the kitchen sitting silently. Finally, my mother handed me the broom and followed her darling husband upstairs. I sat and stared at nothing in particular as I recalled the events of my day. Trav gave me gonorrhea, yet I'm the one who ended up fired, homeless, and on the verge of being cut off by my parents. What a day…

CHAPTER 5

Marley stood up and rose her hand after President Gabrielle asked our sorors if there were any announcements or closing remarks.

Always looking painfully nervous whenever the chapter gave her their undivided attention, she fumbled with her fingers and swayed in her pleated brown dress before Gabrielle handed the mic to her. She looked at me, then shrugged her shoulders and flashed a slanted smile. I knew exactly what that exchange meant, my heart pounded with anxiety. Yet, I smiled sweetly with bright eyes, disguising the ranting that took place in my head. *She better not. If she mentions my situation, I'm gonna hurt her! If she wants to live to see tomorrow, she better not dare mention me. Don't do it! Do not do it!*

Marley cleared her throat, "Actually… Nola, may kill me for bringing this to your attention…" *You're already dead*!

Despite my icy glare and forced smile, she continued, "…but I couldn't bear to hold it to myself. She's an amazing woman to us. When a soror faces hardships, I don't care if they say they have it under control, it's our duty as a sisterhood to uplift one another. We must be a blessing to each other whether it's through encouraging prayer or words, or through gifts of monetary value. It's our duty to be there."

Some of our sorors were nodding in agreement, while some where sliding me facial expressions of confusion and concern. I sat stone still with the same phony smile, cringing on the inside as I prepared to redeem myself from looking like the charity case that Marley was about to make me into.

She continued, "With that being said, I sadly announce that Nola's condo caught fire last month. Although she was able to recover all of her belongings, she and her fiancé have no choice but to live in a hotel until they get something permanent."

Our sorors gasped, and I burned with aggravation. The ones at my table patted my hands and shoulders with empathy. Marley looked choked up with emotion as she gestured towards me.

"She plays such a pivotal role within our chapter. She was so gracious enough to fund our retreat while she's getting married next year. The least we could do is lift our soror up in prayer and bless her with an abundance of donations."

By this time, sorors began to stand and gather around my chair. The pity party had officially begun, and I wasn't at all about to be the celebrated host. So I rose, walked towards Marley, snatched the mic with a smile of course, and shut it all down.

"Sorors, please. The absolute worst thing you could do is send me donations." It took me six years to build my notable reputation within the chapter. I wasn't about to have that transformed into "the soror in need," especially for something that didn't happen anyway.

I continued, "Yes it's been a crazy month for me, but believe me, it's all taken care of and under control."

I patted Marley's shoulder. "Marley, sweetie, you can sit down now."

President Gabrielle, who completely disregarded my pitch, stood and took the floor.

"Sorors, Marley has made a great point. Let's all organize donations and care packages for Soror Nola and her fiancé." She turned to me, "Could you let the chapter know in which hotel you're currently residing?"

My mind scrambled. Part of me wanted to tell the truth and reveal that I'm pretty close to being broke, I had no job, and that I was living with my parents. A bigger part of me wanted to cover it all up. They didn't need to know the truth. The truth distorts perception.

I exhaled, "I'm actually staying at my parents' house in Delaware in the northern section of Wilmington."

I scanned the room for reactions. Although some of my sorors looked as if they were confused, most of them had stains of pity left on their faces, and that bothered me to the core. I couldn't have that. No. Hell no. I'd much rather have the entire chapter talk crap behind by back, than to have them look at me with sorry eyes, offering cheap advice on how to get my life together! As far as they were concerned, I have my life together, and I needed that conception to remain. So, the lies flowed and flowed like the Mississippi River. I told them that my parents needed help with my baby brother, Dominic, and that I decided it was the perfect time to step down from my career to further my education. I added that I was starting an internship with one of the top Real Estate agencies in the state. They looked intrigued, so I continued. "This is why I don't need your donations. Everything happens for a reason. If anything, what I need from you all is support."

I placed my hand on my chest and mimicked the same choked-up expression that Marley used earlier. "Trav... Travis Beaumont didn't lend his support... So... we broke up... The wedding is off, but what doesn't kill me makes me stronger! I'm not at all affected by losing my condo or my fiancé. Sometimes in life, you have to make an ass out of adversity, before adversity makes an ass out of you!"

Pity left the building, and admiration filled the air. There were smiles on my sorors' faces - warm, genuine smiles. There were compliments and encouraging words. At the end of the meeting, Marley mentioned to the chapter that she felt lucky to be my mentee. I soaked it all in like it was a lavender infused bubble bath.

CHAPTER 6

One year two months later…

"I'm outside," Marley said when I answered my ringing phone that added to the pain in my head.

"Why?" I grumbled.

"Church! Remember?"

"Go home," I moaned.

"Nola!"

I disconnected the call.

The doorbell chimed. I rolled over, smothering my face into the pillow. I had a few drinks the night before, and remnants of pomegranate martinis clung to my taste buds and seeped through my pores. I was a wrinkled mess, clothed in yesterday's taupe midi-dress, suffused in yesterday's glittery make-up. The big, poufy, grease-mop on my head sopped up all of the cigar fumes from yesterday's lounge. I couldn't go to church for the first time in over ten years feeling like a brothel escapee!

"Marley is downstairs!" my baby brother, Dominic, cheered at my bedroom entryway.

He smiled wide enough to expose all thirty-two of his teeth. His eyes glowed like two full moons.

"I love her!"

"I know, but remind me to never respond to her text messages while I have a drink in my hand."

Dominic nodded in all seriousness, "I will."

I dragged myself out of bed and stood on the tips of my toes to kiss his forehead. While he happily bolted back downstairs to join his crush, I straggled down the hall to shower. Yesterday, I would have become Mrs. Gonorrhea, and only a small part of me yearned to be in relationship again, which was great considering my history. My line sister, Bailey, and I caustically celebrated the nearly $150,000 dollars that my parents wasted on a wedding that never happened and the $8,000 that they were able to recover from a returned wedding dress. I danced on our booth, puffed a cigar, and stuffed my face with German chocolate cake as I officially tore out the pages to a chapter in my life that never finished.

I scrubbed off yesterday, skipped make-up, slipped into a floral maxi dress and strappy heart shaped Louboutin heels, and brushed my mane into a sleek and low ponytail. It was the best I could do considering I didn't look or feel like myself anyway. It was just church. I just had to sit pretty for about two hours, then go home to my bed!

Marley didn't look like her usual self either. She was dressed in a chrysanthemum pink skirt suit with an olive green blouse—our sorority colors. Her hair was freshly spiraled, and her face was glammed to the gods with a hot pink lip glass I spotted from the top of the stairwell. In the nearly two years I've known her, she had never worn hot pink lip glass. *Hell, she barely wore lip glass at all.*

The last time I'd seen Marley was at last month's chapter meeting. Today she glowed. She sat patiently, looking as if she was sitting at the end of a rainbow with a pot of gold. Dominic had his head resting on her shoulders, while her manicured hands held tightly onto one of his train figurines. Across from them was Dominic's manny (male nanny), assembling a brand new train track model. My father, I imagined, was upstairs in his office researching for another criminal case he'd predictably win, and my mother was more than likely at the hospital assisting a surgery.

"Nola, you don't look very good," Dominic said with concern. I knew Dominic meant "well."

"I know baby. I partied last night," I replied. I cut my eyes to Marley. "You owe me coffee or tea from FeliciTEAs and brunch, and whatever else I demand."

"I got you on the coffee, and I have you covered for brunch. I know an amazing cook."

"I'm holding you to it, Shirley Temple."

She smiled and cheerfully. "I used the flexi rods you got me months ago!"

"… And, you're rocking a bold lip that Stevie Wonder could see."

"I got it from that place you told me about… MAC!"

Suddenly, I wanted to divorce my favorite beauty supplier.

***

Marley zipped down the highway blasting gospel music. She was tapping her stirring wheel to the beat and swinging her head side-to-side, while late March's spring breeze blew through her curls. When she exited and reached a stoplight, she turned the volume low.

"Okay. So, I went to dinner with Greg last night and—"

"Greg?" I asked as my eyebrows curled with confusion.

"Nola, you met him at the playground build in September."

"Oh, the young shy guy with the glasses? You're dating *him*?"

"Yes! Since September."

"I don't know about that, Marley. He seems timid. And *you're* timid. It will never work. I'm sorry. It never does. You need someone outgoing and outspoken to yank some spunk outta you… Light is green."

Marley made an exaggerated pouting face and pressed the pedal. "I happen to love that he's timid."

"Love?" I playfully slapped her arm. "You got some last night! *That's* why you're so dolled up."

"Last night, he proposed!"

I glanced down at Marley's bare finger and asked, "Proposed what?"

"Marriage, silly!"

I laughed.

"My father approves. My friends love him. He treats me amazingly. He grew up in church, he has a wonderful job, and he's everything that I have asked God for."

"Congrats… I guess. But, if he has a wonderful job, then why is your hand naked?"

"He's saving for something marvelous."

I was once told that if a man proposed without a ring, then the only thing engaged is pathetic conversation. However, I kept my mouth shut on that. I dug in my make-up bag for lipstick.

"We're getting married in August."

Found it! Passionate Plum. I puckered my lips at the visor mirror.

"I want you to be a bridesmaid," she gladly announced.

"Absolutely not!" I fired back. *The nerve of her.*

"Maid of Honor?"

"The answer remains, No."

She batted her hopeful eyes the same exact way she did when she visited our chapter meeting for the first time. With the back of her pants gathered in her behind, she anxiously stood in front of ninety other sorors and introduced herself as "a neophyte fresh out of college, eager to find a warm and welcoming chapter she could transfer into to, to begin an exciting life as a grad-level soror.*" Child there is nothing exciting about grad-level*, I wanted to tell her at the time. Just as I wanted to tell her that it was nothing exciting about being engaged to a man she had just met. Nine months isn't even enough time to figure out if he's a cock-burning nymph like Trav.

Marley parked in the PASTOR'S FAMILY spot at her church and turned off the car. "I think you will make a perfect Maid of Honor or bridesmaid." She counted on her fingers as she listed the reasons for her choice. "I love you like a big sis, I value your opinions, and… it would mean a lot to me."

"It would mean a lot *to me* if you didn't talk to me about your wedding the day *after* I was supposed to have mine," I retorted.

Marley lowered her head in deference and spoke wobbly. "Nola. I am so sorry…. I forgot... I...-I wasn't thinking."

The both of us sat in silence moments before I caved. "Fine. I'll be your *advisor*. I'm not ready to be anybody's Maid *anything* for *anybody's* wedding."

Marley pressed her hands together. "Oh thank you, Jesus!" She then threw up her hands, "Fine. Perfectly fine. I'll take that!"

She led us through the church doors of Worship Way Baptist Church, and we maneuvered through a maze of smiling and extremely affectionate people. In the lobby area, there were flat screens mounted on the wall and plenty of chairs for overflow. I motioned to sit there but Marley mentioned that her father wanted her to sit front and center every service.

I was amazed at how modern even medium-sized churches have become since I'd last attended a service. The announcements were done via slideshow on two large screens—not delivered by an old lady wearing a ginormous hat. The choir didn't hold those rigidity red Hymn books either. Instead, lyrics to the songs appeared on the screen as well. Her church partied how Marley partied all the way there, just ten notches higher. Even children stood and jumped and clapped their hands. I didn't want to be the only unstirred soul in the building, so when Marley clapped, I clapped. And, when Marley stood, I stood—even when I had no idea why I clapping or standing.

After the choir sung, a tasteful bald pastor who looked to be about my age, if not older, rose and approached the podium. He was sitting next to another pastor who had to have been Marley's father, with his hoary beard and pudgy physique.

As the pastor at the podium delivered the sermon, I zoned completely out, burning with fervor. Who knew pastors were even capable of possessing that much pulchritude and swag? The way he strolled across the altar while he preached with one hand in his pocket, but not enough to hide his Movado wrist bling, had my full attention. The other hand was waving and pointing with each passionate

39

emphasis. There was something about the way his natty suit laid perfectly tailored, disregarding a corny church robe. The grey opened jacket. Pure white shirt—free of a bulging belly, unlike his colleagues—adorned with a soft yellow, skinny tie which gave his attire the perfect finishing touch.

While he preached, flashes of romantic dinners, spicy nights, and all kinds licentious thoughts took over. It was then that two things occurred to me. One, I was sexually deprived and the so called "small part of me" that needed to be with a man, was actually large… way large. Two, *he* was the reason Marley dragged me here! I grabbed her arm and rested my head on her shoulder. I smiled, giving her a tacit approval, and she patted my hand.

After the service, Marley and I waited in the lobby for her father. I stood casually, but deep inside, I wanted to nudge her and send her off to find the pastor who preached.

"I take it you enjoyed the sermon?" Marley smiled.

"Of course! I just wish my hair was on point," I said as I flipped out my pocket mirror to ensure my ponytail was still intact.

Marley giggled, "Seriously, Nola. What did you think about the message?"

The look on her face made it clear that she didn't bring me there for a hook-up after all. The girl really wanted me to hear the message, and instead, I was busy lusting over one of her pastors. I felt like the wanton of Worship Way. I grabbed her hand, and lied.

"Powerful. I loved it."

She clapped, and cheered, "Yay! So that means we will see you again?"

"I don't know about that."

"Oh, come on."

"I'm not a church girl. You know that." I had my eyes fixed on the throng of worshipers either chatting or exiting. I was hoping I would spot the pastor of the hour. He was nowhere in sight.

"Well, I think you should become a church girl," Marley pressed. "You even said at the meeting that your classes and internship were getting tough for you. God could help you. Allow Him to guide you. God is…"

"Alright! You're right. I will visit once more," I finally agreed.

Marley bounced, "Hallelujah!"

"Just once… so you can quit preaching."

"All God needs is once, Nola," Marley beamed.

The lobby began to clear and my stomach grumbled for breakfast food.

"Where. Is. Your. Father? He better hurry before I change my mind about ever coming back."

"I should probably get him. Sometimes it takes him a while."

"And, maybe next time I visit, he'll actually preach."

Marley raised her eyebrow and replied with a slight chuckle, "Wait, I can't tell if you're joking or serious."

"Joking about what?"

She laughed, "Wow! You really are serious."

"Serious about what?" I asked, agitated.

"Nola that *was* my father preaching."

"Wait, what?" I shot Marley a suspicious side-eye. "The man with the yellow tie?"

"That's my father," she said assuredly.

I wanted to be clear, so I said asked, "The one who preached just now?"

"Yes, Pastor of the church. I told you that. That is my dad."

"How?"

Marley was amused. "He gets that a lot. I'll be sure to tell him the compliment… Oh! There's someone I wanted you to meet… Silas!" Marley shouted past me and flagged her arms. A tall, lanky man in a golden suit with red hair approached us. "Silas, this is my soror I was telling you about. Nola, this is Silas."

41

"Wow, it's true what they say about the poised ladies of A.K.L," Silas said as he extended his hand. "How are you, Nola?"

After I bullied my mouth to smile, I gave him my finger tips and quickly snatched them back. I once dated this guy who had a knot on his neck that was the size of a golf ball. His style won me over. Then, there was this Caucasian Jamaican. He was five years younger than I was, and the only thing he had to offer was sex. Just sex. Great sex nonetheless. Then, of course, there was my darker than darkness ex-fiancé. Even the palms of his hands were dark, and that's no exaggeration. I've always had strange love, but never have I ever dated exact replica of a No. 2 pencil kind of strange. I wanted to kill Marley. I wasn't at all impressed… especially after seeing her father.

Her father… I couldn't believe—didn't want to believe—that the sexy holy beast on the pulpit was her father! How? I asked myself again.

"I'll let the two of you get acquainted while I find my dad."

Marley disappeared down a hall, while Mister Pencil-Body burned a hole into my head with his cloying smile.

"You're beautiful."

I replied flatly, "Thank you." *Now walk away.*

"You know, for some reason you look familiar."

"I don't see how. This is my first time visiting."

He stroked his chin as he tried to call which of his whimsical dreams I visited. "Marley told me you're in real estate."

"I am…"

"I'm in advertising. Maybe we crossed paths there."

I nodded phlegmatically and threw a thumbs-up. "Nice… and maybe," I replied, hoping he would disappear.

Aside from his ridiculous fashion sense, Silas wasn't all that bad looking. I found his above average height and freckled nose kind of attractive. I just had my sights already set on his pastor, who also happened to be my soror's father. *Whyyyyy?*

"Look, I'm not great with initial introductions. How about you take my number, and we could start fresh over dinner?" Silas said.

I happily replied, "I left my phone in the car."

"That's cool. I'll just take yours."

Before I could give Silas ten random digits, Marley popped up with her arm interlocked with her father's.

"I literally had to drag this man from his desk!" she sighed as if she had been in a real struggle.

Pastor Robinson flashed a charming smile, and I melted. "Silas, what's going on, son?" He took Silas in for a bro-hug. The pastor was tall as well but a few inches shorter than Silas.

"I'm good, I'm blessed. Aye, great sermon today."

"Thanks, Brother."

"Daddy," Marley gestured towards me. "This is Nola."

My body stiffened. I could barely lift a finger to wave. Every inch of me was frozen, except for the big asinine grin plastered on my face.

"Nice to finally meet you, Nola." Pastor Robinson opened his arms and welcomed a hug. As I floated into his embrace, the sweet and enticing scent of his cologne met me half way.

"Mice to neet you, too... I mean…" I slapped my forehead, abashed. Everyone laughed. This man, unlike any man ever, had me behaving disgustingly sappy. I had to step back to regain my cool, especially around Marley. I didn't want her feeling too awkward to bring him around me. I laughed with them. "I guess missing coffee and brunch is getting to me."

"Oh trust me, I understand!" Silas co-signed, looking even more turned on by my folly.

Marley patted her father, "I promised Nola I'd get her some coffee."

I added, "Or FeliciTEA's."

Silas perked up. "*THAT'S* why you look familiar… you're the one who snapped on me in FeliciTEA's a little while back. You told me to go study my bible in church!"

Embarrassed and flushed, I looked at the Pastor. "I didn't say it exactly like that. I'm sure it was, a lot… way sweeter."

Marley laughed. "Don't take it personal, Silas. And, if it's the night I'm thinking it was, she was under a lot of stress. Her condo caught fire."

Silas nodded. "Nah it's cool." He kept his focus on me. His eyes fixed down on the crown of my head, bright like a lighthouse. "Let's catch up at FeliciTEA's? Start fresh."

"I don't know. All I can think about is food."

Marley smiled, nudged me with her shoulder. "Then, I better feed you before you pass on a date." Marley used her thumb to point to her father. "Nola, meet the amazing cook I told you about."

My insides leaped.

CHAPTER 7

Before Marley and I got out of her car, I applied some make-up and smoothed down my hair while she flirted on the phone with her new fiancé. She wanted to wait for Silas to arrive before we headed inside. Silas wasn't coming, but so far, I was the only one who knew:

"Is it okay if we head to Jersey for brunch at my dad's?"

Yes! Hell, yes! "I don't have a problem with that," I replied casually.

"Silas, why don't you come too, brother."

"Yeah I'm down." Silas accepted Pastor Robinson's invitation and I almost huffed aloud.

"I'll send you my address," the Pastor said.

"I'll send it!" I interjected. I pulled out my phone that miraculously appeared in my purse. "Marley can give it to me, and that way you'll have my number, Silas."

On the way to the pastor's house, I texted Silas an address that would send him twenty minutes out of the way, and then I turned off my phone. I needed him to get lost... and, I needed him to get lost literally.

Pastor Robinson lived in a large and gorgeous house in Medford, NJ. It was a single home surrounded by beautiful landscaping. His driveway was a cobblestone semi-circle. As we sat and waited for Silas to never show up, I imagined my Range being parked right where we were. Every single day.

About ten minutes later, and after her phone conversation ended, patient Marley grew impatient, and we finally went inside. It was just as immaculate as the outside. He had high ceilings and modern yet masculine home décor. His living room was suited for a single and widowed man—equipped with dark leather reclining sofas, surround sound, and an obnoxiously large flat screen.

We met Pastor Robinson in his kitchen. He had already thrown off his suit jacket and loosened his tie. He sat the breakfast ingredients on his granite countertop, then excused himself so he could change. Marley began prepping breakfast, and I hopped in a pub-styled chair by the window. I gazed out at his massive backyard. I imagined the two of us lounging poolside while I paged through my favorite e-magazine, and as he barbecued on the grill, shirtless.

"Ever since my mom passed…," Marley popped the dream-bubble above my head. "He's been so big on cooking that it became his outlet. Now that he's gotten so good at it, it's like his favorite pastime. God forbid I miss one of his meals."

"Cooking is his pastime? Doesn't the man date?" I pried, trying to measure the size of my challenge.

Hmm. Not that I'm aware of. So many women at the church throw themselves on him. He's a catch! You know? He's great looking for a 50 year-old, and I'm not just saying that because he's my father. But, he's not impressed by pushy women. That turns him off. I think what he needs is a woman who is relaxed and Godly *–especially* Godly. He needs someone who isn't thirsty for his looks or success… someone who would allow him to chase her and not the other way around. He absolutely needs someone who will love him for him."

I nodded, taking mental notes. Then, I maneuvered to his pantry and found his generous alcohol stash. "Girl, your father gets down. Looks like he needs a woman who can throw a couple back, too!" I teased.

"He drinks socially," she said defensively.

I waved a bottle of Moët. "Let's make mimosas!"

"Let's not. I can't drink it."

I rolled my eyes. "Child. You will be twenty-one in September."

"October 5th."

I rolled my eyes again, "Same difference... You need to loosen up." I placed the bottle back on the self, but kept it in the front just in case he and I needed it when I came back to visit.

Pastor Robinson returned wearing a black button down, dark jeans, and Vans canvas sneakers. He looked sexy even when he wasn't trying. Although Marley felt uncertain that her father wasn't seeing or at least sleeping with anyone on the regular, I wasn't about to be convinced that he. He had way too much sex appeal not to be.

The way his lips curled upwards when he smiled. The way his right eyebrow would rise and then fall when he made a point. The scowl in his eyes, and the way he rubs his chin as he listens to us speak were all the reasons I needed to be more acquainted with him. Through it all, I managed to keep my cool while I watched him work the kitchen. I made sure not to laugh too hard at his jokes. I kept my questions to a minimum. Plus, I only gawked at him when I was sure that neither he nor Marley was watching.

I volunteered to set the table. After we sat down and said grace to dig into the pastor's culinary masterpiece, I told the both of them that Silas sent me a text message stating that he changed his mind about coming. I only did this because I grew tired of them questioning his whereabouts. Marley served me a pity pout as she passed me a tray of crème brulee French toast.

"I'm sorry Silas belled, Nola. I could tell you really liked him."

I couldn't keep my face from scrunching. "How?"

"I saw how stiff you were," she revealed while drizzling syrup over her short stack. She even managed to spill some of it onto the marble top dining table. I cringed for the pastor. She continued, "And then, how you stumbled over your words!"

Girl, you have no clue. "Please. Stop," I said.

"Daddy, Nola never stumbles over her words," Marley teased. "She's never nervous. Silas had her like putty. I saw it!"

I wanted to kick Marley from under the table when her father laughed. "Actually, Marley, I don't know what you saw, because I'm not at all interested in Silas."

"Why not?" Pastor Robinson asked, looking directly at me and shooting a thrust of tingles throughout my entire body. It was the first time that I noticed how wizened the corner of his eyes were. The only evidence, besides the few specks of salt in his pepper colored goatee, that he was about twenty years my senior.

"I don't think he could handle a woman like me," I replied.

The pastor's eyes widened before he directed his attention to his plate. I smirked as I imagined the thoughts that probably flew into his head.

"Nola is bold. She's opinionated and outspoken," Marley said with her mouth full. "That's why I look up to her. She's the complete opposite of me."

I nodded at my spokesperson.

"Well," the pastor began as I watched, in what seemed like slow motion, while he licked a crumb from the corner of his mouth. "A lot of men need a bold woman. Don't count him out. He's a cool dude."

I smiled coyly, "Thanks, Pastor."

"You're in my house. You can call me Ronnie."

"Ronnie…" I practiced rolling it off of my tongue. "Nice name."

"He makes everyone call him that, even Greg." Marley was in between bites. It was then that I noticed she looked nothing like her father, especially the way her nose flared while she chewed. I redirected my attention to Ronnie.

"I love the French toast. You have to give me the recipe."

"Oh, do you cook?" Ronnie asked.

"Occasionally," I answered with a flirtatious smile.

"That's a 'no.' There are no occasional cooks. When you cook, you always cook," he said confidently.

I laughed, "Maybe you never met an occasional cook. Allow me to introduce myself."

Marley chimed in, "Daddy, Nola does make a good box cake."

Ronnie belted out a laugh that echoed in the dining room. His smile was adorable and youthful.

"Don't listen to Marley. I mean, *I do* bake a mean box cake, but I can get down on the stove as well. I'll prove it to you some day."

Ronnie rubbed his shaven yet scruffy beard. "Hmm… I'll take you up on that."

"Be careful, Nola" Marley added. "If you're any good, he'll make you work in his restaurant."

"You have a restaurant?" I was intrigued.

"Continue to speak it into the atmosphere and I will by next year."

I was impressed. "Wow. So cooking really is your passion."

"What is yours?" he asked in return.

"Huh?" I heard him the first time. Just, his question was unexpected. He looked into my eyes and repeated the question.

"I asked, 'what is your passion?'"

This time I held his gaze, pausing the connection that I felt between us. I was soaking in the haze that filled the place, veiling Marley's presence.

"Good question, Ronnie. I'm in real estate, but I'm not even sure if it's actually my passion. I have to figure it out."

His eyes smiled as he stated, "Don't take too long."

I melted.

"You're a leader," Marley blurted, breaking through our fog. "When you discover your passion, you will be a boss at it. Mark my words!"

"Of course! I'm a boss at everything I touch," I boasted.

Ronnie laughed with his eyebrow raised and asked, "Are you, now?" Rather than verbally answer, I gave a sly wink and a smile.

CHAPTER 8

Later that evening, Dominic helped me carry my shopping bags to my bedroom. After Marley dropped me off home from hanging out at her father's house, I immediately hopped in the Range and dashed to the mall. I hit Nordstrom, Bloomingdales, and a few other stores. If I was going to attended church every Sunday, I needed more suits…with matching hats… fabulous ones that a first lady would wear… I needed matching shoes too! And, a purse for my bible…. and a bible.

"All this stuff, Nola?" Dominic tossed my bags into my walk-in closet.

"Careful, Dom. Look, boo, I got you something, too."

I tossed him a small bag and watched as he pulled out two Armani Exchange T-shirts. I loved how Dominic looked in A|X shirts, because they helped him look more his age. Although Dominic could care less about apparel, he appreciated A|X t-shirts, because they didn't have the scratchy, flapping tags on the back which drove him absolutely insane.

"Thank you, Nola. I love red shirts," he stuffed them back into the bag. Then he suddenly grinned big and pointed his finger at me. "What is the name of the source of electric power for a subway car?" he asked.

"Aw, man. Another pop quiz?"

Dominic smiled, anxiously awaiting my answer. It was a warming smile - a smile that had enough power to brighten any of my worst days… a smile that I've often needed growing up.

Dominic was born on my tenth birthday, and he was the best gift my parents have ever given me. He came at a time in my life when it was difficult to make friends, and when I often felt isolated from my family.

"I don't know. Electric train?" I answered from inside of my closet.

Dominic burst into a roar of laughter. At his age, most guys were interested in bagging women, enrolling in maybe their second semester of college, pledging a fraternity, or deciding which house party to crash next. Dominic's preoccupations were trains. In fact, he was the walking and talking Wikipedia on the subject. When he wasn't educating us all on trains, he was showing a rare but genuine interest in people's thoughts and emotions. He housed many of my secrets and deepest thoughts, because I trusted Dominic more than anybody I've ever known. I trusted his advice, his criticism, and his opinions. Where most people see a socially and behaviorally impaired young man, I saw a genius life coach, and I sometimes imagined he was one.

When he finally stopped laughing at my incorrect answer, he answered, "Third rail, Nola!"

I snapped my finger as if the answer was on the tip of my tongue and said, "Aw, man. I should have known."

"Next time you get it right like Derrick did. Derrick is smart."

I poked my head out of my closet.

"Derrick was here?"

Dominic nodded enthusiastically.

"Why was he here?" I pried.

"Derrick took Manny to eat."

I smirked. "Those fools are at it again. What an idiot!"

"Nola, you hate Derrick."

"No, Dominic. I don't. Hate is a very, very strong word."

"You do," Dominic insisted.

I hung one of my suits on the rod and cupped Dominic's face in my hands to get him to look directly at me. "I do not hate our older brother. Hate is a strong word. I hate my natural hair color. I hate when I overdraft my checking account and I have to tap into my trust fund. I told you before, I do not hate Derrick... I just don't love him the way that I love you."

"Why don't you love Derrick?" Dominic asked innocently.

I released Dominic's face, closed my eyes, and bit my bottom lip. "I love our brother, Dominic… just not how I love you."

I tried to explain, but I couldn't find the words, only vivid memories. I especially recalled one memory in particular. Before my parents moved here to Delaware, two years before Dominic was born, we lived in Bowie, Maryland in a big house located in a small development. I was walking home from my bus stop on the last day of the school year, and a group of girls from our development were following me.

They were chanting, "Witch of Bowie, why is your hair so big? Witch of Bowie, we wish you were dead!"

They chanted this every school day, as a matter of fact. They chanted that awful song so much that it sometimes still haunts me at unexpected times. Each day, I would speed walk ahead of them all the way up the hill to our home, never looking back. This particular day, I guess I didn't walk fast enough, because after they chanted, 'Witch of Bowie, we wish you were dead,' the unexpected happened.

SMACK! I was shoved to the ground, and my face slapped the concrete pavement. I remember tasting a blend of blood and saliva in my mouth. The four girls rolled me on my back, and it felt like a piece of the sidewalk was attached to my face. That's how bad my face stung.

"Eww. She's all bloody."

"Ain't witches' blood supposed to be green?"

"Maybe she's not a witch."

"Shut up, you three. She is a witch! She's the only person in the world her skin color with that wild and ugly hair!" the leader of the evil crew demanded.

They tied twigs to my sandy brown and blonde hair and dragged me half a mile to our front lawn, using the sticks as handles. When they left my bruised body on my front lawn, I ran across our yard and busted through the door with a swollen and oozing lip, a bloody shirt, and dingy jeans.

I ran straight to my mother and cried, "They me beat up!"

My mother grabbed "Nola! You're such a tomboy."

With twigs still knotted in my hair, my father led me to the kitchen and tossed me an ice pack. "Daddy, it was four of them! The ones that always tease me. *I hate it here!"*

He lifted me onto the bar stool and roared, "Shut up! You're a Victor not a victim. If you're gonna play rough, then you better be tough!"

I lowered my head, and my fallen tears met my bloody lip and converged on the icepack.

"Stop it! You're being a wimp!" he scolded through clenched teeth. "Stop crying!"

I tried so hard to make the tears stop, but I couldn't. I had enough of it all. The bullying from the kids at school, the pressure, confusion, and constant name calling from my father, mom's passive aggressive reaction to almost absolutely everything, and even perfect Derrick.

I remember he smashed through the door while I was being chastised for being bullied. He was waving his report card like it was Willy Wonka's golden ticket.

"I'm being skipped! I'm being skipped!" he cheered.

As he always, my father reached into his pocket and pulled out a wad of cash. "I don't know what to do with you, Nola. I never knew what to do with you."

He tucked the money into my hand and went off to join Derrick and my mom in the living room. From the barstool I was sitting on in the kitchen with sticks in my hair, an iccpack in one hand, $150 in the other. I watched as Derrick was praised. My parents gave him proud smiles, benevolent eyes, and exuberant pats on the back, shoulders, and head. I watched as our father morphed into butter right before my eyes. If I had ever wondered before, that day it was confirmed that my feelings meant nothing to them. If time had been frozen and placed in their hands to control, our parents still wouldn't have used that time to be there for me, because my father didn't like me. Even though my eight year-old body had been tortured by the town's worst bullies, they chose to shower Derrick.

That day in particular, summed up how it always had been for me growing up. Derrick was exalted and shown off to family and friends, while I was merely paid to stay out of trouble, be happy, and forget it all. Derrick always had our parents' attention, and I was left having to prove that I was worthy of that same attention, acceptance, and recognition, too. I carried that weight with me into my teenage years and adulthood. I spent my life constantly vying for attention, even if it meant breaking some rules. I was vying for recognition, even if it meant starting fights just so I could play the hero. I was vying for acceptance, even if it meant putting on a façade from time to time or falling for all kinds of guys—the goods, the bads, and the uglies.

Dominic stretched his 6'1', 206 lbs. body and headed for the door. Just before he exited, he said, "I'm proud of you, Nola."

I smiled at his random but regular compliment.

He chanted, "Push hard. Pull hard. Chug hard like—"

"Like a train," we said his favorite advice to me in unison.

He high-fived me and gave me a warm smile. As he left, I thought about how Dominic would never fully understand my animosity towards our brother, Boy-Perfect. He wasn't there during my terrible childhood nor was he aware of the isolation I felt for the first ten years of my life. I didn't actually hate Derrick. I despised our disparity. While I struggled with never feeling good enough, Derrick was celebrated daily. He was the perfect blend of our parents characteristically and physically. He was perfectly intelligent and spoke with perfect diction. Then, he grew up and graduated college with perfect grades and wound up working for a perfect Fortune 500 company. He was married to the perfect wife, and together they created a perfect baby girl. He lived in a perfect home in the most perfect section of Philadelphia… and, the man even had the perfect secret.

After I finished putting away my clothes, I finally turned my phone back on. There were two voicemails from Silas. The first one was energetic: *Hey it's Silas. The address you gave me sent me to some farm. Call me back!* The second one was low and flustered: *Yo, it's Silas. I guess you aren't getting service. Every time I call, I get your voicemail. Anyway, I've been driving around for ten minutes, and I don't see anything residential…. Uh… uh, I guess I'll wait another five minutes for you to call back. Call me back!*

I giggled while I deleted both messages. Moments later, I received the phone call I was anticipating all evening.

"Hey, what's up with your phone? I have been trying to reach you since I dropped you off," Marley said.

"It died without me even realizing it. I'm sorry. What's up?"

"My dad said you left your wallet at his house."

"Oh no!" I said dramatically, trying my best to sound surprised. Before I pocketed my driver's license and a credit card, I strategically wedged my Givenchy wallet between Ronnie's sofa cushions right next to his remote.

"Don't worry, I'll pick it up for you tomorrow after work. But, it'll have to be right after I leave this boutique, if that's okay with you. I'm bridesmaid's dress hunting tomorrow." I could hear Marley smiling through the phone.

"That's exciting. You know what, Marley. Don't even think about going out of your way for my wallet. I have Ronnie's address. I'll just get it myself." Marley sighed in relief. I smiled mischievously as I continued to erase any chances of her ruining my plan. "Your focus should only be on finding a dress for your bridesmaids. That's very important. Plus, it can get pretty challenging. *You know that I know.*"

"Awwwwww. Thanks, Nola. You are so thoughtful," Marley fawned. "Are you sure?"

"I'm sure about everything I say."

Marley asked, "What time should I tell him to expect you?"

"I don't know. My hair appointment is in the morning. Just text me his number. I'll let him know," I said cautiously, trying not sound like I was up to something.

The naïve Marley replied, "Okay. I'm texting it now."

I blew imaginary smoke from my imaginary gun. Two birds. One bullet.

CHAPTER 9

Delilah, my stylist, gave me the works that Monday morning. She dyed my hair chestnut brown with honey highlights and tossed it with loose and bouncy s-curls that laid gracefully about my mid-back. It was layered to perfection. I flipped the front of it to the side just enough to expose my neck. My diamond studded cross necklace and matching earrings winked at the sun as I sat at the table by the large window that faced my old condominium building. Its view slapped me with nostalgic memories of strutting across Market Street in my Giuseppe heels with my hair dancing against the wind.

An empty chair and an empty tea cup were placed across from me while I sat patiently yet anxiously waiting for Ronnie to show up. Five minutes prior, he texted that he was wrestling through the Center City traffic for parking. Since I looked a mess on Sunday, I reached for redemption by wearing a navy high-waist skirt that kissed my kneecaps and a tan cropped blouse that gave my abdomen a peek... just little peek. I tapped my red bottom nude gladiator sandals on the floor rapidly. I wasn't nervous. I was just excited to see the man that I wanted badly. When I texted him the night before, he told me it would better to meet somewhere in the Philly area since he'd be out and about. Immediately I picked FeliciTEAs.

I felt my body heat rise when he walked through the glass doors. He looked so damn good in his light denim jeans, dark blue t-shirt, and knit grey slouchy hat. He looked absolutely nothing like a pastor, but everything like a Diesel model, except sexier. He flashed his dimple and smiled when he spotted me. I wanted to leap into his arms. Instead, I slowly rose and met him a quarter of the way so that he could check out the silhouette of my petite yet curvy shape. I led him to our table and made sure to flip my hair as I sat back down— men love that stuff.

I smile and chirped, "Good to see you!"

Ronnie dug into his pocket and pulled out my wallet. When he placed it on the table, I noticed his toned arms which were not too bulky and not at all scrawny. They were just perfect for his slender yet athletic body. Physically, we looked like the perfect couple.

"Sorry to keep you waiting. Traffic is a challenge in the city."

"I know. I used to live there," I said as I pointed out of the window toward my old place.

"Did you? Living large, huh?" he teased.

I chuckled, "Of course." I gestured at his tea cup. "Have a seat. You have to try their tea before you leave."

Ronnie adjusted his hat, then he hesitated before he sat. I motioned for our barista.

"I'll have another mango green tea. Could you get him the black cherry special?"

"Actually," Ronnie spoke up. "Could you make that for two, and can we grab an extra chair?"

The barista nodded and went off for our drinks. I sat confused while Ronnie grabbed a chair from another table and brought it to ours. Before I could part my lips to ask who the other chair was for, he was waving to a woman who had just entered the store, dangling car keys. She had big round eyes, a tapered haircut with dark roots and blonde tips, and she wore a khaki colored button-downed flare dress with those disgusting $2 flip flops from Old Navy.

"I finally found a good spot," she said as she approached us. She handed Ronnie the car keys and then looked at me and smiled big. "Hi!"

Ronnie quickly introduced us. "Nola, this is my lady, Carmen. Carmen, this is Nola."

Carmen sat down, "Nice to meet you."

I looked at Ronnie, "Oh I'm sorry. Lady what? Lady of the usher board? Lady of the deacons?" *She couldn't have been his lady-friend.*

Carmen giggled and patted my hand. "No, Sweetie. There's no such thing."

I snatched my hand away. I wanted so badly to say, "Wench don't touch me. You don't know me." However, I bit my tongue.

Ronnie nodded slowly. "She's my lady—my girl."

My heart sunk, but my exterior didn't let it show. I dryly said, "Oh. How nice."

Carmen smiled. "Ronnie told me that you're his daughter's sorority sister."

The barista placed our tea on the table, and I quickly sipped some to keep my mouth from blurting out something that could hurt her feelings.

Carmen continued, "I always wanted to be an A.K.L."

I swallowed my tea. "We don't pick any ole-bodies. We're very selective. I'm sorry you were rejected."

"Oh! I wasn't rejected. I just never… You know what? Never mind that," she said, rolling her eyes.

I rolled my eyes. "Thank you."

There was an awkward pause before I looked at Ronnie and smiled. "How come Marley doesn't know about, Camilla?"

Carmen retorted, "It's not Camilla, it's Carmen. Ms. Carmen"

My eyes never left Ronnie as I continued, "Marley thinks you're single."

Ronnie stroked his chin, and glanced at Carmen. "We're taking it day by day."

I chuckled, "We all know what *that's* code for."

He said, "Code?"

I gladly explained, "Listen, when a man is really into a woman, he can't wait to introduce her to his family and friends."

Carmen wrapped herself around Ronnie's arm and rested her head on his shoulder. "I have no doubts that my baby is into me."

Although I felt my blood boil, I hid my hostility and changed the subject. "Try your tea," I said to Ronnie. "…before it gets cold."

Ronnie sipped and nodded. Carmen continued to cling to his arm. "Nice," he said. "And by the way, I like it here."

I beamed. "Really? This is my favorite spot along with this Moroccan Restaurant not too far from here."

"I love Moroccan," he said with a smile.

"Seriously? I'll have to take you some day."

Ronnie looked at Carmen whose smile had long disappeared. "Cool. That shouldn't be a problem. It's not often I get to hang out in this city. Why not?"

Carmen unlocked her hold and glared at her wrist watch. "Bae, we should get going. We don't wanna miss lunch."

Ronnie rose and pulled his wallet from his back pocket. "I'll take care of everything. Where do I pay?"

While Ronnie scurried off in the direction that I pointed, Carmen sat across from me with her arms folded, burning a whole into my forehead with her gigantic eyeballs. I smirked. "I'm sorry but I gotta ask. What's the age difference between you two?"

"Ten years. Why?" Carmen asked defensively.

"Hard to tell," I said. "You look so *old*."

She flexed her jaw and rocked side-to-side like she was hoping I'd say the right thing to set her off. Since I've never responded well to intimidation tactics. I gave her exactly what she wanted.

"You seem threatened by me," I gave her an affected grin.

Her response was quick. "Believe me baby girl, I have *NO* reason to feel threatened."

With my elbows resting on the table, I took a sip from my tea cup. Smiled. Took another sip, and then smiled again. Before I sat my cup back down, I looked directly at Carmen and raised my eyebrow. "Better watch your dress before you get tea all over it."

This set Ms. Carmen off. She jumped out of her chair and wagged her finger in my face. "I wish you would," she begged. "I wish... you would."

Before I knew it, Ronnie was behind her tugging on her arm. He was trying to calm his woman down.

"Ronnie, this is embarrassing," I said standing up and waving my hands, "I can't deal with trashy behavior. Thanks for bringing my wallet, but goodbye!"

As I walked towards the door, I could hear Carmen yelling, "She said she'd throw tea on me! She said she'd throw tea on me!"

I laughed all the way back to my car. Moments later, my phone buzzed through my purse. My heart skipped several beats and did a cartwheel when I saw Ronnie's name flash across the screen. It was a text message:

"Sorry for what happened just now."

I responded: *"It's okay. Although, the altercation was random."*

I sat in my Range while I waited for his response. When his name flashed across the screen, my heart skipped a beat again.

"It was nice speaking to you today."

I replied with: *"Let's do it again. ☺"*

Less than a minute later, my phone buzzed again. However, this time it was a text from Silas, the guy from church.

He sent: *"Hello, Beautiful."*...That one was ignore.

CHAPTER 10

"She's my girlfriend." Dominic blushed and smiled. "We kissed in the stock closet. We always kiss in the stock closet."

"Dominic…"

"It's alright, Nola. She likes it."

I couldn't help but to laugh. He was happy, and I loved it. It was the first time I'd seen Dominic infatuated by a girl. Wasn't too long ago that I wondered if he'd ever experience romantic love like Derrick and I got to. And now, just an hour after the Carmen chaos, and over hoagies and BBQ potato chips, he was dishing details of how he made-out with his co-worker, Angel—a girl who also went to his school.

"You were supposed be working not sneaking around smooching."

Dominic lowered his head, smiled, and fumbled with his name badge which had train strikers all over it. Since I moved back home with my parents, I made it my obligation to stop by Dominic's job to have lunch with him at the same time every day. He worked at a book store as a stocker in downtown Wilmington, DE. It was the perfect place for him. It was quiet, and his duties were consistent. What's even better, is that he got to work with Angel. We learned the hard way that Dominic couldn't handle working at bigger stores. His first job was at a Target, and that ended in a disaster.

He gushed, "She likes learning about my trains, Nola. Her favorite is the diesel locomotives, because diesel locomotives are less likely to start fires. We always talk about trains, and she likes it."

I smiled. "Dominic, you smile like I do when I think about my crush."

"Good, that your crush makes you smile." Then, Dominic snarled, "I hope your crush not Travis. I hate Travis."

From the moment I told my younger brother absolutely everything that went down between Trav and me, the thought of him infuriated Dominic. He was super protective of his big sis, and I loved that about him. I popped a chip in my mouth. "Don't say hate. And don't be pissed about it. I'm over it. On to the next..."

"Who's next?"

"Marley's father."

Dominic stared at me blankly, probably waiting for me to say that it was a joke. When he realized there wasn't a punchline, he shook his head.

I giggled, devilishly.

Dominic said, "No."

"But, he makes me smile," I defended.

Dominic looked as if he paused to think, and then he sighed, "Marley will be mad with you, Nola. Marley wouldn't visit no more."

I doubted Marley would even notice. She would be too preoccupied planning her 1-2-3 step, thrown together wedding to be worried about me pursing her father.

Our lunch was cut short when a customer started rapidly pressing the bell at the register. Dominic and I poked our heads from the office and saw that the sales rep wasn't out there. She was a 70-year-old retiree who only worked to stay busy. She must have taken a lunch break herself and forgot to lock the door. The customer flagged his newspaper when he spotted us.

"Hellllllooo. Can I get some assistance? Please!" He was a tall muscular guy with olive-colored skin. His pant suit was so tight that it looked like all he needed was to sneeze and he'd bust right through it. "Doesn't either one of you work here? I need this rung-up. I'll miss my train!"

Dominic made his way to the front. "I work here!"

I followed behind, "Dominic, you sure you can work the register?"

"I'm gonna help this man get the train, Nola."

The customer slapped a five dollar bill on the counter. Dominic pressed the correct button to get the drawer to pop open, but he didn't know how to ring up the amounts or receipt. He simply picked up the $5 bill, placed it in the drawer, closed it, and then he grinned.

"Thank you for shopping at Market Street Book Store!"

The pissed man grunted and held out his hand, "I want my change!"

Dominic was confused and frowned. I stepped up. "I'm sorry about that sir."

The man turned red and raised his voice. "It's just a $5 bill! How do you screw up five dollars?" Then, he looked me up and down. "Do you even work here? Who wears an outfit like that to run a book store?"

I blew air from my cheeks and covered my peeking abdomen with my arm. His attitude reminded me of why I could never keep a job in retail when I was a teenager.

"Sir," I said calmly. "Can you tell me how much the newspaper is? I'll just ring it up for you so you can get your change."

The customer huffed, "He should have already known! It's not rocket science! What kind of idiots do they have working here?"

It was all I needed to hear for time to suddenly pause, for the heat to suddenly rise, and for my hand to suddenly fall upon a hardback book to sling it. The spine of it clocked the customer between his eyes. While he screamed in agony, I grabbed Dominic's hand and walked into the office. I locked the door behind us and dialed 9-1-1.

See, the thing is, when you're the daughter to one of Delaware's top three and most famous criminal defense attorneys, you get away with assault. So much so, that the person you assaulted *always* ends up apologizing to you. *Always*. Most of the police officers in Wilmington, especially the crooked ones who don't even deserve a badge, are sitting by the phone waiting for the opportunity to personally repay *thee* Walter Victor for the mess that he has dug them out off. Mess that money, although we're grateful, could never buy.

As expected, this little incident was swept under the rug. No police reports, no witnesses, the man got a couple dollars and a ride to wherever he needed to go, the old store owner lady was briefed on how the *customer* attacked us, and my father didn't even have to be notified.

***

Later that evening, I found Walter Victor sitting on the patio smoking a Cuban cigar and sipping on Johnnie Walker Scotch whiskey, not to be disturbed—his little ritual the day before a case. I watched from the kitchen as he ran his fingers through his thick white hair and reclined with his feet up, watching the ducks swim in the pond that glistened across from the backyard. I smirked as I thought about how he probably didn't have a clue that I liked smoking cigars occasionally, too. If we had that kind of relationship, I would have joined him. Would've sat on the chair adjacent to his with my legs curled beneath me, telling him all about the shit that went down in the coffee shop and book store. Then, I'd listen to his unsolicited advice on how I need to stop taking advantage of the law, and how I shouldn't steal another woman's man.

"Nola, these came for you today." My mother, dressed in her sky blue scrubs, walked in carrying a huge arrangement of orange and pink tiger lilies that were so tall they blocked her face. She sat them on the counter.

There wasn't a name on the card. Just a message: NOLA, I NEED TO SEE YOU AGAIN. MEET ME AT LACROIX IN CENTER CITY, PHILADELPHIA. OUR RESERVATIONS ARE AT 7.

My mom leaned against the counter. "Who are they from?"

"It doesn't say, but I have an idea."

My mother pulled out one of the lilies and played with the petals. "How's the job hunt going?"

"It's going,"

"Nola, you always say that."

I turned my attention to my father who could be heard coughing a little on smoke. He took another drag and that time puffed successfully.

"He wants you in your own place," my mom said, handing me the lily before making her way to the refrigerator.

"Of course he does. He never wanted me here," I responded.

My mom defended my father as usual. "He just wants you to do better… make something of yourself."

"I'll tell you what, when I get a good paying job, I'll move out and take Dominic with me. That way neither of us will be in your way."

My mother spoke from behind the refrigerator door. "It won't be that simple. Your father thinks that your lifestyle needs to change first."

"My father is the one who taught me this lifestyle," I fired back.

She closed the refrigerator door and sighed. "You told us your therapist helped you to realize that you can't blame anyone but yourself."

"I haven't spoken to my therapist in five years" I grew agitated "Why are you bringing her up?"

"You need to see her again. You haven't saved a penny since you started staying here. Every day you're walking in carrying shopping bags."

I glanced at the stove's clock.

"You can't let your habits spiral out of control again—"

"I better get ready."

"You don't have a cushion, Nola… He wants to cut you off on your 30th birthday, so you have until December."

My mother pouted her pretty little face and tucked her hair
behind her pretty little ears. I stood there with my arms folded. I was
disappointed… disappointed by how skillful she was at narrating my
father's thoughts and opinions but never bold enough to speak her
own.

"Mom, why do you act like you don't understand that I need
time?"

"Derrick hasn't lived here since he left for college…" she
started.

"You're a moron," I interjected.

"Excuse me?"

I pointed at her with the lily. "I don't need to see my therapist,
you do," I said. "And, you need to ask her to help you figure out what
you did to your spine… Or did *he* knock it out of you?"

***

I had two hours to meet Ronnie at the restaurant. In that two
hours, I was able to wax, shower, try on five different dresses before
choosing a Vera LBD, and speed and dodge through traffic. I was only
ten minutes behind, which was great timing for a first date. The
restaurant was dimly lit, and there was even a live band performing
soft music. It was a romantic atmosphere, and I couldn't wait for the
hostess to seat me so that I could tell Ronnie how much I approved.

Unfortunately, it wasn't Ronnie waiting for me at the table.

Trav sat there at the booth slouched, eyes slanted, and grinning.
He had two cognac glasses in front of him. Both of them pretty empty
with a little bit of ice left. He was predictably dressed in a navy Boggi
suit, and he had his grey tie dropped around his neck. He was
obviously feeling his drinks heavily, and I remembered how I once
upon a time found this sexy. He handed me the drink menu, and
without bothering to open it, I ordered a bottle of Riesling and a
double shot of Patron.

Trav bit his bottom lip. "Yeah… drink up, baby girl."

I cut my eyes at him. "Why are we here?"

"To celebrate," he slurred while raising his empty glass. "You would have been my wife last night."

"That was two days ago. Why are we here?"

Trav slapped the table. "Alright, Alright, Alright. You wanna know why we're here? I'll tell you why we're here."

I folded my arms and rolled my eyes. Had I known that it was Trav who had sent the flowers and invited me to dinner, I would have trashed them and left his drunk behind waiting.

He chuckled and teased.   "You wanna know? You don't wanna know."

The waitress returned with my drinks and after she poured my glass, I threw the shot back and chased it with the Riesling. Trav ordered us both a plate of fried calamari and sent the waitress away.

I looked him directly in the face and demanded, "You have exactly two seconds to tell me what you need to tell me, or I'm walking up outta here. 1…"

Trav straightened his body and lifted his hands. "Whoa, whoa. Chill out. Chill out."

I grabbed my clutch. "Two."

I rose and Trav reached over the table and grabbed my wrist. Then, he quickly released it as if he had a flashback of when I spit in his face a little over a year ago.

"Nola. Nola, just… just sit down."

I snapped, "Why are we here??"

Trav slammed his elbows onto the table and threw his face into the palms of his hands. He spoke low but coherently, "I saw my doctor today. He told me that I have Gonorrhea. I'm being a man and letting you know that you have to get tested."

I sat down slowly, sipped my Riesling, and swirled it in my mouth. He took his hands down and lifted his head as if he was checking for my reaction.

I casually asked, "Are they absolutely sure that's *all* you have? Nothing *else*?"

Trav looked offended. "What?"

I sipped again. "I treated mine a long time ago, boo. I'm just saying that you... You're dirty. There's homeless heroin addicts safer to screw."

Trav threw his head back and laughed. Then, he spoke, sounding as if he suddenly sobered up. "So you didn't bother to tell me you had the disease?"

"You gave it to *me*. What the heck was there to tell? Didn't your penis drip? Sting? Smell? Matter of fact, if you weren't such a hoe, there wouldn't have been anything to tell you."

Trav poured some Riesling into his glass. He nodded, then chuckled. And then he shook his head, having the nerve to be in utter disbelief. "Nola, you ain't shit. You weren't shit before I met you and took care of you, and you aren't shit now. I hear you're out here telling people that you're in school and interning, you lying bitch."

I snatched my clutch and stood up, making sure to bump the table hard enough.

The bottle of Riesling toppled over. Trav jumped to his feet. "You're the brokest rich bitch I know," he shouted to my back. "You will NEVER make it in the real estate industry. And, I'll make sure of that!"

CHAPTER 11

Nothing, I'm fine. I just hate waiting." Marley looked pissed, but I just didn't care

That Friday evening, I met with Marley and Bailey at FeliciTEA's to tighten up last minute details for our annual retreat that was taking place in just two weekends. We were already three days into April. Our final Chapter meeting before summer break was the next day, and we needed to report all of our retreat details there. Everyone was on edge and stressed about it, and Marley was in a funk because I was twenty minutes late. First of all, I've *always* been late to our meetings. It has never been a big deal. Usually, they were too busy sipping tea and choking down tea biscuits to even notice. For some reason, today Marley wanted to show attitude, but I wasn't here for it. I had much rather been at home lounging on the couch and watching reality shows, and my look showed it. I had my hair pulled up into a sloppy high bun, and I wore a long cardigan with denim cut-off shorts and pink cowgirl boots. I didn't even bother to apply any make-up, just lip-gloss. And rocked no jewelry besides my diamond studs.

I huffed. "Marley get over it. You're not the only one with a life."

Bailey immediately took on the role as peacemaker and tried to expunge the tension. "No, no, no! Sorors," she waved her hands and shook her head. Her natural curls swayed and swept her shoulder blades. "We did not come here to be catty with each other. Let's squash this right now."

Marley looked down at her fingernails and pretended to look unbothered. "Let's just get started," she said in almost a whisper.

I gave Bailey the okay to start updating us on the details of the retreat.

"Okay. Well I actually have good news and bad news. The good news is that we have all of the facilitators in place. Sorors were ready to volunteer, I didn't have to pull teeth like last year."

I scrunched my eyebrows when I asked Bailey what the bad news was. Marley even lifted her head for the answer.

Bailey exhaled, "Well... the vineyard. They can't host us anymore. There was overbooking."

Marley's eyes widened.

I asked, "How long have you known this?"

"Two weeks ago."

I snapped on her. "Why am I just finding this out two weeks later?!"

Bailey tried to speak, but I didn't give her the chance.

"As Chair of this Committee, I need to be notified of any changes. My name is on the line!"

Marley looked at me. "All of our names are on the line, actually."

I put my hand to Marley but looked at Bailey as I continued, "I don't mean to snap on you or anything, but you should know protocol."

Bailey nodded. "It slipped my mind. I understand your stress, Nola. We all have something going on with us. You have your career and taking care of your brother. Marley is planning her wedding that's in a few months. I'm dealing with my boyfriend's baby-momma drama. A lot is going on. Let's just all relax, and brainstorm a location right now."

I folded my arms. "We don't have to brainstorm. I say we do Marley's father house."

Marley looked caught off guard. "Why do you suggest my father's house?"

"Because his house is beautiful..."

"Nola, your parents' home is just as beautiful."

"Let me finish--It' beautiful and the backyard is huge. It has to be about two acres. Bailey, you have to see it. The landscaping is immaculate. We could host it out there, Marley your father could cater it since he loves to cook, AND if I recall, I saw a sign for a farm close by there. We could go horseback riding afterwards!"

Bailey beamed, "See Nola, I knew you would come up with something. You're always on point with it!"

I nodded and looked at Marley.

Marley shrugged. "I don't know about this. I would have to ask him and get back to you."

I asked, "Why don't you just ask him now?"

"Because, it's Good Friday, Nola. He's probably busy."

"Ask him now," I pushed. "You have to do it now. This is crunch time. Call him now."

Marley hesitated briefly, and then she pulled out her phone.

I said, "Put it on speaker."

Marley pressed the speaker button and sat her phone on the table. When Ronnie answered, the sound of his voice was music to my ears. It made me wish that I could be beside him while he did whatever it was that pastors do on Good Friday.

"Hey, Daddy," Marley spoke with a childlike tone. "I hope I'm not bothering you. Ummmmm, I'm sitting here with my sorors. We kind of ran into an emergency, and we need your help."

I took over. "Hey, Ronnie, it's Nola."

Ronnie's voice sounded as if it perked up when he said, "Hey, Nola. What's up?"

"Well, it's short notice, but we were wondering if we could use you and your home for our retreat."

I explained the situation to Ronnie, and with only a little bit of hesitation, he said we could do it. Bailey and I cheered and high-fived.

"I'm so excited, Ronnie. Marley or Bailey will contact you within the next few days to go over details." I looked at the both of them for confirmation and they both nodded in unison.

After our meeting was over, Marley asked me to hang for a bit, so she and I could talk. Her face still wore a funky expression. Today was the longest that I've ever seen the girl go without a smile. That was a shame, because other than the ugly look on her face, she was dressed really pretty and neat again. Her hair was swept back into a neat, low ponytail, and she wore green skinny pants and a white fitted top. The outfit almost looked like something I would wear, except those pants would have looked better with a low-scooped top and a pair of nude heels. She wore corny grey flats, and the style of her shirt was basic.

I said, "So what's up with you?"

Marley sighed, "I met my father's girlfriend."

I felt my heart stop. I was disappointed, but I played it cool. "Then why are you acting sad. Are you not happy for him?"

"I'm happy for him. I'm just upset that you didn't bother telling me that you met her. My father told me that y'all met when he brought you the wallet."

I snapped my head back, "Marley that's not my place. That's between you and your father. "

"But you are my soror. You are supposed to let me know these things. No secrets."

"Girl, it wasn't a secret." Suddenly it felt like I was talking to a fourteen year-old girl. "Is that why you had an attitude?"

Marley lowered her head. "I thought we were close enough that you would tell me these things."

"Marley, you have to grow up. It wasn't my place, and I am not obligated to tell you everything just because we're sorors."

I was irritated and ready to go. But, because I saw an opportunity to influence my opinions of Carmen onto Marley, I lingered. I apologized for not saying anything, ordered Marley a sandwich, and I began to plant my seed. If I got Marley to dislike Carmen, Marley would most likely express her feelings to her father.

Since Ronnie and Marley shared a tight bond, Carmen would be kicked to the curb in no time.

"Well if you must know, I didn't like her at all," I said to Marley. "She was nasty to your father. She spoke down to him as if he was a child. I don't even think your father notices."

Marley spoke between bites of her Panini. "Really? She didn't come off that way."

"You have to pay attention closely. She's ratchet, too. She snapped on me while your father was at the cashier. Accused me of threatening to throw tea on her. Do I look like I would throw tea on someone? *That's ratchet*! That's why I haven't told you anything. We had a horrible encounter."

Marley's mouth was hanging open. "Are serious? Wow! Nola, you should have told me."

"You should develop your own opinion. I just know she's nothing like how you described your fathers' ideal woman to be... Just watch her. Watch her closely."

Marley nodded. From the look on her face, I could tell that I was getting through to her.

By the end of our conversation, she seemed to be in a happier mood. Before we parted ways, she asked me to meet her at the bridal shop tomorrow afternoon—after the chapter meeting—to meet her bridesmaids and help her choose their dresses. I wanted to get in her ear some more about Carmen, so not only did I agree to come, I also told her we could even do lunch afterwards.

CHAPTER 12

"Why is she here?"

"Trisherica, be nice. She's our soror. She's here to help."

"Is she a bridesmaid?"

"No…"

"Well, we already chose our dresses. So why is she here?"

We gathered in the back of some tiny boutique in New Castle, Delaware. As soon as I pulled up in the range blasting, "Ego" by Beyoncé', all of their eyes were on me, and I felt their stares as the owner led us to the back. I kindly plopped my booty on one of the two white cushiony chairs. Marley sat in the other, and the bridesmaids were left standing. I don't think the Maid of Honor liked that. And I also didn't think any of them liked my white t-shirt with the black, bold, and tall lettering that read: **I DON'T GIVE A F*CK**, because usually when you meet a mutual friend, *ESPECIALLY A SOROR*, you greet them with a big smile, a friendly hug, or maybe a kiss on the cheek. These chicks flashed phony smirks and stood several steps away from me as if I had the Ebola virus.

The Maid of Honor, Marley's line sister, kept it up, and this time turned to me. "No offense or disrespect to you or anything, but I'm just trying to figure out your place."

The big mouth wore a fluorescent orange tunic dress, her hair was in a thirty-inch Brazilian wig, she wore false eyelashes that looked like two hairy caterpillars took up residency on her face, and the liquid leggings I wore looked more moisturized than her lips. Her place was the Cirque De Olay, but I kept quiet that time… for Marley's sake.

Marley spoke up, "Nola's been there, done that with weddings, so she's assisting me every step of the way. Plus, she has great taste in fashion." She looked at me, smiled, and patted my knee. "I value her opinion."

Another bridesmaid --Marley's other line sister—belted out a sarcastic chuckle. "And, we don't?"

This time I'd had enough. "Listen, I'm here because I'm *clearly* the only of Marley's friends who knows how to dress. She needs my expertise. If you have a problem with it, you can be replaced."

Marley quickly popped to her feet. "Nola, no... Nobody is being replaced. We're not about to take it there."

Marley pressed her hands together, and faced her crew, "I need you all for individual purposes. Y'all are my childhood friends. Y'all are my girls. You are my line sisters. And my sisters in Christ. I'm not dropping anyone from the wedding."

The Maid of Honor folded her arms and cut her eyes to me. "Which chapter are you from anyway?"

I crossed my legs and scanned her from toe to head. "The Omega Tri-state Chapter--Marley's chapter."

She replied, "Yeah, but Marley didn't pledge that chapter."

"That's a grad chapter." Trisherica backed her up. "So you became an Alpha Kappa Lady *after* college?"

I sarcastically asked, "isn't there' only two different ways?"

She got a kick out of this. "So you ain't even pledge! You didn't have the real, real Greek experience."

I nodded, appearing unfazed. "Sure… just about as real as that Chanel bag."

The Bridesmaids laughed. Only a few hung their mouths opens. Marley had her face buried in her hands.

The Maid of Honor adjusted the straps of the bag that hung on her arm. "I don't know about your process, but my bag is definitely real."

"Show me your numbers," I said.

"My numbers?" she snapped her head back, confused.

"My point exactly..." She probably had no clue that all authentic Chanel bags have seven-digit serial numbers in the inside.

Anyway, the bag she carried was supposed to be the replica of a $2500 tote. There was no way she was rocking a bag that probably cost more than her monthly rent for five months. I flagged my hand. "That bag is about as real as that ugly lace wig."

My last insult obviously hit a soft spot. The Maid of Honor charged for me.

"Trisherica, no!" Marley screamed.

She was probably one-fourth of a centimeter from pulling me from my seat before Marley and the other line sister pulled her away and dragged her out. I was still sitting comfortably. The other ladies looked appalled. One of them had her hand on her chest with her mouth hanging open.

"I apologize on behalf of my sorority," I said. "We aren't all like that. All organizations have a couple of hoodrats. I'm sure you've experienced a few in church."

A bridesmaid laughed. "I can't even deny that… as much as I want to!"

Moments later, Marley and her line sisters returned. The one who tried to hit me was much calmer and avoided eye contact with me. In my opinion, Marley's bridesmaids were ugly inside and out, with their stank attitudes. They were nothing like Marley, and I couldn't imagine them growing up with her. Except for the one slim and short girl. She was pretty, tiny, and quiet, but at the same time, she avoided eye contact with me as well, so I couldn't tell.

The Maid of Honor sucked her teeth and mumbled something underneath her breath, which made the other five girls laugh. Their whispers, side chatter, and giggles made my blood boil a little. Luckily, I learned a long time ago how to fight snide women without even balling a fist or breaking a fingernail. I sat back, crossed my legs, and breathed.

While a few of the bridesmaids went into the dressing rooms to change, Marley sat beside me looking like the ray of happiness that most brides are. It seemed like every time we got together her appearance got better and better. This time she wore a yellow floral printed dress, and her hair was pressed bone straight. I mean, she could have used a few extensions to fill it out, but other than that, she was exceptional. She looked exactly how I've been trying to get her to look since we first met. I guess a little bit of Greg was all she needed to keep it consistent.

One of the bridesmaids, the short slim one, stood off to the side waiting for a room. Marley pointed at her.

"Does she look familiar?"

The little woman had baby doll eyes and neat medium-length hair. She had full red pouty lips, and her skin was like milk. She wore black and pink Jordan's with black leggings and a plain white t-shirt. I found nothing about her familiar.

"She has an identical twin. I'm not close with the twin, but I thought you might know her. She works for Trav. She said she knows him personally."

I rolled my eyes. "Marley, anybody with a vagina knew Trav personally."

"I'm sorry Nola. I thought he was great - the ideal man."

"Yeah a great hoe - the ideal asshole."

Marley covered her mouth to stifle her laugh. When she got it together, she asked "Why didn't you tell me?"

"Not this again."

She threw up her hand. Ok, ok. I won't take it there, but there is more."

"What?"

"The twin said that you spit in Trav's face, and *that's* why you're fired. She says it wasn't because you left to take care of Dominic. Nor was it because you're furthering your education, and nor was it because—"

I flagged my hand, "I'm not about to sit here and entertain this bull."

"Nola, she said you're blackballed and broke."

"I didn't know Christians gossiped so much."

Marley reached over and patted my arm. In a whisper, she said, "Nola, if you need anything - money, leads for a job, anything - I got you. The chapter has you."

I snatched my arm away. "Do I look broke to you? Look at me. Look at my car. Do I look broke?"

"Nola... I just..."

"I'm disappointed in you Marley. You're the absolutely last person I'd think would listen to some rumor and then bring them back to me as if you believed it be true. You are truly a child. I'm an adult. I can't. I don't tolerate petty gossip and disgusting rumors."

Marley stared at me blankly. Then, she sat back.

We sat in awkward silence for moments until I broke it. I didn't want to lose focus of my real reason for coming out today - to sabotage Carmen. Therefore, I laughed to soften the mood.

Marley looked at me with a raised eyebrow.

"It is funny, though - the rumors... How do people come up with this stuff?" I giggled again.

Marley smiled. "Yeah, I guess I was silly for believing them. I'm sorry."

"You're good. Just don't let it happen again. I can't have the negativity in my aura!"

Marley laughed, "Me neither, girl!"

"Exactly... Focus on you, Greg, the wedding... and your father."

Marley looked puzzled. "My father?"

"It's something about Carmen. Something isn't right with her. She has a loose screw or something."

"Well, I'm supposed to see her again tomorrow evening. For Easter dinner after I worship at Greg's church. I hope she isn't as bad as you—"

Our conversation was cut short once the bridesmaids started emerging from the rooms. The girls stood side by side while Marley stood up to gaze at them all.

I choked on laughter and nearly cried when I saw them in their gowns. The gowns were gorgeous… but their faces… let me just say that they ALL (except for the short one) looked like pugs stuffed in chiffon. I wanted to check behind them to see if they had tails.

The Maid of Honor barked, "What is so funny?"

Another bridesmaid who wore a shiny synthetic wig, snapped, "You better get your soror, Marley. I'm about tired of this chick. I can understand if she's here to give you feedback, but that laughing will get her smacked!"

"Oh, *really*?" With that I kindly grabbed my purse, stood up, and walked right out of the boutique.

As I calculated, Marley was trotting behind me just as I hopped back in the Range. "Nola, please don't leave."

Marley hung onto my car door.

I slid my sunglasses on and started up the car. "I'm not with the ratchetness, Marley. Fighting? In a boutique? You know that's not even of my caliber."

Marley pouted. "I know. They're just protective. They…"

"Protective? That's ratchetness! I need you know the difference."

Marley begged, "I'm sorry that they upset you. I really need you here with me… I want you apart of this."

I began checking my lipstick in the side view mirror. "Then those chicks need to go."

"Who?"

"Your line sisters. And the one with the shiny wig."

"I can't dump Trisherica, Amber, and LeTonya!"

I put my car in drive. "Bye, Marley."

"Nola, please don't make me choose."

"Marley, as soon as I pulled up those women had a problem with me," I said removing my glasses and looking directly at her. "You missed the stares and nasty comments while we walked through the store, but that's fine. I'm used to women hating me for no reason. They always have. But what I can't stand is that you're too naïve to realize that Amber, LeToya, or whatever her name is, and your frumpy Maid of Honor with her ugly K-Mart dress, they don't even like you!"

Marley looked at me as if I just told her that a cat got pregnant by a dog and together they created a duck.

"They don't like you, Marley. They haven't liked since you transferred to our chapter. Which is sad, because we're supposed to be one. Hell, they probably haven't liked you before then. You're not the person you used to be - the one they knew. You're completely different from them with my help! *That makes them jealous*. They're goal is to sabotage! Why do you think they are snapping and picking on me? Come on, who gets fired up over laughter. *Laughter*? They want me out! They want your entire wedding out, and you're being too stupid to realize it!"

Marley released her hands from my car door and bit her bottom lip. I could tell that her mind was going a million miles per minute.

Before I put my shades back on I said, "Watch them Marley. Watch them and watch that Carmen. If there's one thing I have, it's a great judgment of character, and those women are up to no good. Listen to what I'm telling you! I haven't stirred you wrong since I've met you, and I wouldn't stir you wrong today. Get rid of them!"

And with that, I sped off.

CHAPTER 13

When I got home from shopping at Neiman Marcus that evening, the smell of dark roast coffee greeted my nostrils as soon as I walked through the door. Right away, I knew that Derrick was there.

The manny was in the living room wearing his signature outfit—Bermuda shorts and an American Eagle tank. He was holding a mug to his mouth, and with his legs crossed, he shook his dangling foot and bobbed his head to the tunes of the hit show GLEE. He was happily enjoying his downtime now that Dominic was asleep. He was so into his show that he didn't even glance at the shopping bag that I dropped onto the couch, right next to him. And usually, he digs right in hoping to find something that I was willing to give.

I plopped my Givenchy tote on the kitchen counter, nearly startling my older brother who was just powering off the Keurig.

"I thought y'all broke up."

"Alicia and I are happily married. You've seen Facebook. Why would you think we're broken up?" Derrick's diamond cufflinks sparkled as he buried his nose in his coffee mug and took a hefty gulp.

He was a social media celebrity just because he was so freaking perfect and the world adored him. He had that type of perfection that would make you barf. In fact, he was like the male Beyoncé—there wasn't anything he couldn't master. His Instagram account was loaded with pictures of the perfect two-week international vacations that he and his wife haven taken, the perfect gifts that he showers his parents with, and his perfect hobbies like mountain climbing and feeding the hungry in Peru.

I snatched his mug and sat it on the counter. "You know who I'm talking about. You didn't drive all the way here from Philly, *two* nights in row, for Keurig coffee out of mom's and dad's kitchen."

"Remember, just because you know, doesn't mean I have to answer to you. How many times do I have to reiterate?"

I snarled, "You're every wife's worst nightmare."

"And, you'll probably never know what it's like to be a wife."

I slid Derrick his mug and flipped him the finger.

"Where are you coming from?"

I ignored him and hopped on the counter. I pulled out my phone and began re-reading Ronnie's text messages. I wondered why he hadn't shot me a *"Hey, I've been thinking about you"* text yet, or did I need to be the one who reaches out? *Hmmm I bet a selfie with cleavage would be a good conversation starter.*

"Why are you smiling like that?"

"Like what?" I switched my phone to the camera and checked my reflection.

Derrick sipped then point at me. "We may not speak as much as we should, so you can play dumb all you want. But I know you, Nola. I know that look really well. So tell me, who are you screwing?"

"Stay outta my panties and get your own, Derrick. Besides, if I told you, you'd probably find him and screw him, too."

"Like the couple of times I bent over Trav?"   Derrick burst into laughter when I shot my head up from my phone. "Calm down. I'm kidding."

I punched his arm. "You're so disgusting!"

"Who are you screwing?" he pushed again.

"Who are you screwing in Delaware?"

"Don't be childish."

I smirked. "Alicia is gonna find out one day. What's done in the dark, always come to light."

Derrick snickered and ran his hand through his curly hair—jet black, silky curls that the girls from our neighborhood used to fall for. "We never do it in the dark."

"You're disgusting."

"So you're not gonna tell me?"

I hopped off the counter and grabbed my tote. "His name is Ronnie… and he's Marley's father" I tossed my phone back into my purse. "Goodnight."

"Wait, say that again?"

"You heard me."

"And you're calling *me* disgusting?" Derrick threw his head back and laughed almost uncontrollably. "So Marley is fine with you sleeping with her father?"

"We aren't sleeping together…yet. And, we aren't seeing each other…yet. But, if we do, when we do start seeing each other, she'll be just as fine with it as Alicia is fine with your cheating."

"Don't date the woman's father. She's supposed to be your friend."

"And Alicia's supposed to be your wife."

"When Marley kills you, just know I'll be at your funeral laughing."

"You'll already be dead. I'm so sure your wife will get to you first." I glanced over to the living room area. The manny was deep into the television. "Seriously, you need to stop before it gets ugly."

Derrick rubbed his forehead and yawned. "Don't go there with me tonight, Nola. I'm too tired."

After he grabbed his mug and walked away, his phone vibrated next to me on the counter. The word "WIFEY" flashed across the screen, as if we had spoken her up. I flipped the phone over, grabbed my bag, and left it to buzz.

CHAPTER 14

"No, thank you. I'm gonna sit in the front."

The usher in her white gloves pointed to the pew furthest in the back and way to the left. She nodded her head as if she didn't hear me.

I said it again. "No. I'm going to sit in the front."

She shook her head and pointed once more. This time, I tried to slide by her, but she bumped and blocked me like she was a nightclub bouncer!

"Dang. Is it that serious??" I snapped.

She didn't budge. Standing there with her arms folded and her lips tight. She was looking directly in my face like "*try me if you want to.*" But she continued tapping her foot to the rhythm of the booming drums, horns, keyboard, and the boisterous choir. To save myself from any more embarrassment, I kindly tilted my gigantic floppy hat and maneuvered my way to a pew in the pack.

I came to church alone since Marley wanted to spend Easter with her fiancé and his family. I thought about bringing Dominic, but as I practically climbed over kneecaps to sit elbow to elbow between an elderly man and a teenager, I felt glad that I didn't. Crowds overwhelm him, and this time it seemed like it was way more people there than the last week.

I could barely see Ronnie, so I was sure he couldn't see me even in my oversized floppy hat. That was disappointing, because I wore my dress for him. A black A-line Marc Jacobs with embroidery along the sides. It was sexy yet conservative, falling just below my kneecaps. People have always said that you should dress for the position you want. Well, I felt like the First Lady of Worship Way. All I needed was Ronnie to capture the visual. ...Unfortunately, he never got the chance to do so.

After service, the lobby was packed tight like the ATL Greek Picnic. And it was hot, too. On top of that, anybody I made eye contact with wanted to give me a hug, a kiss on the cheek, and a "Happy Resurrection Sunday" in response to my "Happy Easter". When a woman managed to smear her caked up foundation onto my dress, I got tired of waiting for Ronnie and kicked off my sandals, jetting to the parking lot.

"Nola!"

My heart leaped as I swung in the direction of a man's familiar voice... but it was just Silas. Disappointed, I turned back around and continued pacing to my car.

"Nola! I know you hear me."

I heard his footsteps picking up behind me, and seconds later, he was tapping me on my shoulder.

"You have no dignity at all." I said, tossing my hat and shoes in the back.

"Why you so mean?" Silas took my wrist. "Nice bracelet. You iced out, huh?"

I snatched my arm back. "I'm not interested in you. Quit stalking me."

Silas grinned, "I want what I want. Don't confuse persistence with stalking, little lady."

"*Little?*--Don't confuse persistence with desperateness."

"Whatever. Let's go."

"What?"

Silas reached into my car, grabbed my sandals, and handed them to me. "I said, let's go. I'm taking you out." He motioned with his head. "My car is right there."

I looked at his black Infinity and then back at him. "Wow. You take desperate to another level. Now you're abducting me?"

"Don't be a stubborn mule. Follow me."

He took my hand and wedged each of his fingers in between mine. Then he gently kissed them and winked at me. His lips were soft and warm yet as powerful as a wrecking ball, almost—only almost—knocking down my wall of defense.

I smirked. "What are you doing? Trying to seduce me in the church parking lot?"

"It depends how you feel about it."

I shook my head. "You are so freaking corny!" *You're lucky you're somewhat cute.*

***

Silas sped down I-95 blasting a gospel hip-hop artist whose name he said was Lecrae.

I shouted over the music, "What if I had plans?"

"You don't."

Thirty minutes ago, I asked him where we were going. He shrugged his shoulders and told me that he was just winging it. After that kind of response, any normal person probably would have had their phone in their hand, and their thumb resting over the EMERGENCY button just in case. But I wasn't getting any alarming vibes from Silas. If anything, something about the mysterious glare in his eyes peaked my curiosity. I wanted to know more about this man... just a little bit. However, if he did turn out to be a predator, I definitely had my pocketknife and stun gun resting at the bottom of my Chanel tote.

I asked him again, "Where are we going?"

He put his finger to his lips and Shhhh'd me.

I ignored him. "How are you even sure that you wanna take me? I could be crazy, you know."

Silas smirked and glanced at me, "Could be? No, there's no 'could be.' You definitely got some screws loose up there, I can tell."

I smacked his arm. "It's too soon for you to jump from corn-ball to jackass."

He laughed, and when he smiled big, his eyes got chinky and adorable. Aside from his suits being too short for his height, Silas was pretty fly for a church boy. He had a cool, laid back, yet rebellious flare to him that made him intriguing, and I wondered how I didn't pick it up the first time we met. Maybe it was the corny, shrunken yellow suit that he wore that day. Maybe Ronnie gave me tunnel vision. Whatever it was, his overall swag was on point today, again, aside from the suit. He wore grey slacks and a checkered pink and grey button up that he loosened at the collar. It was a nice combination but the shirtsleeves stopped below his wrist. He matched his outfit with tan shoes, which were actually shoe-boots. No one would have known this had his pants legs fallen where they were supposed to. Even his thick, curly red hair looked more attractive with the way it looked blonde against the beaming sun. I was even attracted to how he drove with a lean, bobbing, and weaving through traffic, doing twenty above the speed limit, nodding his head to the beat, and humming - sometimes singing - to the hooks of the Lecrae songs. Nevertheless, I tried hard not to gape or show that I might be remotely attracted to him.

I gave him the side-eye, "Where's your family? It's Easter; shouldn't you be at a dinner?"

Silas's eyes didn't leave the road once. In fact, he stiffened as he dryly asked, "Where's yours?"

I rolled my eyes and huffed, "We're not big on holidays."

He quickly nixed the topic. "So… why you been dogging me?... I know I'm not ugly."

I couldn't help but giggle.

"I'm serious. You ignore me like I don't have a job… like I'm some untalented hood guy relying on a rap career that'll never happen. Or, are you that type who likes them bum dudes who don't have nothing going for themselves but swag?"

Humph. I wanted to tell him that I was crushing on his pastor. But then it would've been an awkward ride back to the church and most likely, it would've reached Marley. I wasn't ready to put up with her temper tantrums. Nor was I ready to listen to her spill about how she feels it in her bones that I'm NOT the step-mommy she envisioned from God. I simply told Silas that I wasn't dating right now.

He chuckled sarcastically. "Oh. I know your type. You're that woman who puts her love life on hold to establish her career."

Definitely not. Even though he was way off, I let him continue.

"You know you gonna end up forty, single, miserable and lonely? Everybody will be calling you auntie. Not mom. Not grandma. Not Mrs..... Just auntie."

I entertained his theory. "At least I'll be a filthy rich auntie! Money could buy my happiness. It damn sure does now!"

Silas shook his red-haired head and wagged his finger. "I know that you became successful at a young age and all, but trust me; you don't wanna end up like the old women at my office. They go home to Netflix every single night, psyching themselves up to believe they're satisfied with living their lives viciously through reality shows and through their daughters. Don't end up like them. You're way too beautiful for that, shorty."

***

We pulled up at a gorgeous beach house right off of the Rehoboth Beach Boardwalk. The interior was immaculate and looked like something right out of a home-furnishing magazine. It had five bedrooms, one office, and three bathrooms. There was a fully equipped kitchen, and a cozy living room area with grey furniture decorated with sea green and blue accents. There were ginormous canvas art sketches of flying seagulls, paintings of idle beach chairs, and an oil painting of the bay hung about the walls. There were large wicker blade ceiling fans in every room and an oversized patio door with an oceanic view to die for.

After touring the place, Silas tossed his keys on the kitchen counter and poured us both a glass of water in champagne flutes.

"I'm not a drinker," he said in response to my frowned up face.

"But should I suffer?"

He laughed.

"This is a beautiful home. Are you living here right now?"

"A vacation spot that I own. I come here sometimes to clear my head. To chill out--"

"I knew it. You're a loner."

" - and draw."

"Are you any good?"

"You tell me?" Silas motioned towards the hanging canvas art.

"That's your work?" I asked in disbelief. "Impressive! I assumed you spent a grand on these!"

Silas raised his eyebrows and grinned, "Chill… it's not that good."

He grabbed our glasses, and I followed him onto the deck. It was right then when I noticed that he walked with a hunch,. As if people told him, his entire like, that he was too tall.

"Pastor likes to come here for his vacation."

My eyebrows lifted, "Marley's father?"

"Yeah."

"Does he?"

"He comes every August. A preferred guest. Stays here just for the weekend, sometimes. Pastors don't actually vacation. You know what I mean?"

Immediately, I pictured myself being snuggled with Ronnie on the deck, watching the wave's crash against the sand.

Silas jerked me from my thoughts. "You hungry?"

I nudged his arm and snatched my glass. "Of course I am. You dragged me all the way down here; you could at least cook me something and get me a real drink."

Unlike Ronnie, Silas wasn't a cook. Since I haven't been over a stove since Trav, we opted for greasy boardwalk pizza, fries, and funnel cake. Silas got the food alone because I wasn't about to hit the boardwalk with my Prada's. While he was gone, I snuggled deep into the large sectional and flipped thru channels, imagining life as Ronnie's wife. We'd come here every August, parlay on this very couch. We'd be in love and in total bliss. We'd bring Dominic down with us, and maybe even get a dog, since children probably wouldn't be an option. I'd be the perfect wife for him—a housewife. I'd give him the space he needs to focus on his sermons, yet be there at his beck and call when he needed me or *needed it*. I'd be his ball of energy, keeping him young, fresh, and happy. He'd keep me happy by showering me with love, affection, and the finest gifts. He'd be the total package that he already is, and I couldn't wait to get him where he belonged.

When Silas returned, he flashed a bottle of Chardonnay and a huge grin. It was not at all my preference, but I leaped off the couch and cheered anyway. *It beats water.* We sat on the deck and stuffed our faces while I listened to long winded Silas talk about life, career, and family. I dipped in and out of the conversation to daydream about Ronnie. However, the part I did pay the most attention to was when he talked about his mother.

He spoke of how she physically abused him while he was a kid, but he loved her deeply anyhow. She was all that he had besides his crippled grandparents, and he never met his father. Then, he told me that when he was fifteen, his mother had abandoned him, marrying a man she only known for three weeks. She moved to Texas to be with her new husband and his family, and poor Silas was left in Philly to live with his grandparents.

"She said I needed to stay and finish up the school year. When that ended, she said she wanted me to do another year. By the time that ended, man, I had caught on. She had no intentions on bringing me. I stopped asking. She never brought it up. 'Til this day she hasn't brought up visiting."

My heart ached for Silas, and although I was able to relate, all I could muster was, "Damn."

I grew up with both of my parents, but I was very familiar with the feeling of being rejected by both *and* being on the other side of abuse. Mine was verbal and mental. I've only witnessed the physical abuse. My mother wasn't so lucky, having been beat up by my father up until Dominic was born.

I kept my eyes on the rolling waves—floating in deep thought, trying to decide which was worse… having your parents reject you by walking out, or having your parents reject you by acting as if you're totally invisible. I downed the last bit of wine that was in my glass, and then poured another. I tried to hand it to Silas.

He said, "Nah. And, don't pity me. I'll be thirty-five in September. I'm over it. It's in the past. I don't have resentment."

I sipped and asked, "How'd you do it?"

"Do what?"

"How'd you forgive after a childhood of abuse, rejection, and neglect?"

"God."

I rolled my eyes. "You sound like Marley."

Silas paused. Then he said, "I don't know about Marley or what she been through outside of her mom dying, but I know for me… *me*… God was necessary. He still is necessary."

I sipped some more and offered a change in subject. "Don't you have work tomorrow?"

"I'm off. Do you?"

I shook my head.

"Stay the night with me. I love talking to you."

I shook my head again. "No."

He took my glass from my hand, and then wedged his fingers in between mine like he had done in Worship Way's parking lot. "Stay with me."

"Back up. It's not gonna work this time."

"It's not?" He kissed my hand slowly. Then he reached in and kissed my cheek.

I breathed in his cologne.

He buried his face by my ear and neck. He spoke slowly and smoothly, "Stay with me."

92

"…Silas."

"Talk to me until the sun rises," he whispered. His words dripped on my ears and slid down my body, awakening sensations I hadn't felt since Trav. I looked into Silas's eyes. I wanted to ask him, *How?.. How did you do that? How did you make me melt without even touching me?*

CHAPTER 15

"Who is this wench?"

I buried my face in my hands and groaned.

Silas's offer sounded good. The scenery was right, especially with the gorgeous house, the ocean, the sand, and the sunset. Unfortunately, he was the person was wrong. If I was going to spend the night there, I wanted it to be perfect. I wanted it to be with Ronnie. But had I known I was going to be awakened to *this* after only six hours of sleep, I would have spent the night in Rehoboth with him.

"I just want to know. I just want to know!" Derrick's wife, Alicia, paced the floor frantically while she tried to solve his latest cheating mystery.

I tightened my robe, handed Alicia a cup of coffee, and sat at the kitchen table with her. She had bags under her eyes that were darker than the street. Her hair looked like it hadn't been combed in weeks. I was used to this, though. She used to come to my condo and sometimes my job, every couple of weeks to vent about Derrick and his "possible" infidelity. And, now that he was at again, so was she.

"He won't sleep with me. He won't touch me. I know it's happening again. I just wanna know who this wench is."

Like slobber, the words "He's GAY!" formed in the corners of my mouth, ready to be spat. Instead, I asked, "How do you know there's a wench, Alicia? You know Derrick. He works so hard. He's probably sleepy by end of the night. Trav used to be the same way."

Over the course of their relationship, I've found it much easier to try to avoid Alicia than to mingle in her world of incredible oblivion. Sadly, she had no family or real friends here besides her co-workers, so I was the only one she could vent to about their problems. She was from Albany, NY, she and Derrick met at Temple University. After college, they married and she never moved back. There were times when I wanted to show up at her door with movers and a truck, because *I knew*. I've always known. But my loyalty was to Dominic. He loved his manny, and ever since the manny had been in his life, Dom's darkest demons stayed away. If I would have let the secret out, it would've been a wrap! So kept my mouth sealed, not for Derrick, but for Dominic.

Alicia sobbed, "Nola, he didn't come home last night. Why wouldn't he come home? If he wasn't cheating why wouldn't he come home?"

I tapped my finger nails along my mug. No amount of tears collected on my shoulders could make me tell her what I've known since we lived in Bowie.

Besides his boyfriends, I was the only one who housed Derrick's secret. What I didn't understand was how my parents never figured it out, *especially* my father. He had a way of figuring out everything.

I remember when I was eleven and my father found out that I was kissing on this boy who lived just a few houses down. I never opened my mouth to confess it. I didn't have to. I came through the back door, and was just about to exit the kitchen when he grabbed me by my shoulders.

"She's been kissing boys," he said to my mother. "You've been kissing on boys haven't you?"

I didn't have a chance to deny nor tell the truth. Before I could open my mouth, he gripped me by my ponytail and tied me to the refrigerator door by it. Not even a week later, I caught 13-year-old Derrick kissing on that same exact boy. When he came home that evening, I waited at the top of the stairwell listening for my father's reaction… it never happened. Since that day, I never saw Derrick with a boy –only really pretty girls. I always figured maybe the kiss was a dare or phase until the night I caught him with Dominic's manny.

I whispered, "I wish I could you tell you why." I squeezed Alicia and rubbed her back. Then, I grabbed a tissue and wiped her eyes. "I tell you what. How about a spa day on me? Were you on your way to work?"

Alicia sniffled and nodded.

"Then call out. Where's there baby?"

Alicia spoke between sniffles, "With… the nanny."

I slapped the table and stood up. "Perfect."

***

Alicia and I got our bodies beat, heated, and treated—everything minus the happy endings—by my favorite masseuse. He was a husky guy who went by the nickname, Villain (although he was attractive and not at all intimidating). He always wore his hair in two long cornrows. He had a smooth, deep, and sensual radio voice and had some kind of beastly character tattooed on both of his biceps. He took Alicia first while I enjoyed an organic facial. When it was my turn with him, I spent most of the session trying to convince Villain to pursue Alicia while she was in her vulnerability. Alicia needed to get acquainted with the idea of vengeance. A little "get back" always fixes a hurting heart—I knew this personally. Plus, I needed her distracted from cracking the mystery of Derrick's whereabouts. Only, Villain didn't seem interested in messing around with a married woman until I threw a couple of dollars his way. Before we left, he pulled Alicia to the side, and I waited for her in the parking lot. To kill some time, I called Marley to see how things went with Carmen. She answered on the second ring.

I rolled my eyes as soon as I heard Marley gush, "I love her!"

"What makes you love her? That's just like you to love someone you barely met. This is why you get taken advantage of by your behind nutty bridesmaids."

Marley's tone got low and dry as if my comment sucked the life of out her. "Why do you think they're taking advantage of me?"

"Because *they are*….and we're not gonna revisit that convo unless it's to tell me you booted them from the wedding.... So, what's so great about Carmen?"

Marley sounded ecstatic again, and the joy in her voice made me burn. "Believe me, Nola. She's perfect for my father. I don't mean to jump the gun, but she'd make the *perfect* leading lady."

I grimaced at the phone.

Marley continued endorsing. "She's been through the fire, and she came out unburned and even better! She used to be a coke addict, Nola. She started at fourteen. *Four-freaking-teen*, can you believe that?"

"Most crack fiends start young. They're all on the Judge Mathis show. Big deal."

"She got married to a drug dealer. He wound up beating her to bloody pulp over missing money. It was so bad that everybody thought she would die. But God…"

I pictured Marley smiling with her hands lifted to the sky.

"…He had other plans for her. Long story short, after a four-day coma, she gave her life to Christ, and she hasn't looked back since. She went to college. Got a couple of degrees. …Ugh.. She's my inspiration. I told myself, if she can overcome that storm, I can overcome anything."

I yawned.

"You've gotta meet her again, Nola. Maybe she'll inspire you too."

I wasn't convinced. "It's just a show, Marley. That woman is a Ratchet Rachel. She tried to fight me in a popular tea brewery, remember? What leading lady does that?" I unlocked the door for Alicia who was approaching the Range with a gigantic smile. "She's not right for your father."

Marley giggled through the phone. "Nola, if I didn't know any better, I'd think you were trying to push Carmen out of the way so you could have my father."

Exactly that

"Just kidding!" Marley shouted. "I know that you wouldn't dare."

I allowed Marley to run her mouth about Carmen while I drove back to my parents' house to drop Alicia to her car. By the end of that conversation, I learned Carmen's last name, where she resided, and where she worked.

CHAPTER 16

Silas's touch shot those familiar vibrations through my body again, but this time it was between my thighs. I didn't think I'd see him until the next Sunday, but surprisingly I couldn't resist accepting his invitation to brunch.

I suggested Hightower's, a rooftop diner located in Wilmington just off the Christiana River. It was one of my favorite spots because the view from the thirteen-story building was so pretty. I sipped the mimosa that Silas had waiting for me along with a bouquet of pink chrysanthemums.

"You're a very sexual person... How? You're a Christian."

Silas chuckled. His left hand continued to rub up and down my thigh, his right hand forked his omelet. "I'm flesh too. I'm a work in progress. And, I'd rather the word sensual over sexual"

He had called me as soon as I hung up with Marley earlier. I told him I needed time to get dressed before I met him there. He insisted that I come as is, but of course, I didn't listen. I slipped on a heather grey sleeveless suit dress with a cream cardigan, anyway. When I saw him, I realized that I shouldn't have dressed up after all. He wore only red basketball shorts, scuffed Jordan's, and a white tee. To be guy who has a real career and owns a beach home, he dressed pretty bummy and broke. Normally I would have left someone for dressing like that in a public, well-frequented place like this, but Silas was different. Therefore, I wasn't going anywhere. I swayed my booty over to the table, allowed his silky lips to greet my blushed cheek, and I sat cozily in the chair that he had already slid next his.

Maybe I was just pissed that Carmen had Marley's vote, and my chances of being Ronnie's leading lady were beginning to look slim to none. Maybe it was Silas's enticing touch, voice, and my body's attraction to it. Maybe it was both that sent me flying to the diner and kept me there.

I flat out asked, "Are you celibate?"

Silas tilted his head and shook it slowly,

"When was the last time?"

He smirked and scratched his ginger hair.   "You don't want to know."

"Last night?"

"You don't want to know because it's been a while - a couple of months."

I huffed. "That's nothing! Try a year and a half."

Silas raised both of his eyebrows. "Word?"

I nodded, and I felt his fingers press firmly onto my thigh. "Maybe a little over."

"I thought you didn't have to work today?" He spoke, but I didn't hear him. The intense grip on my thigh spoke louder. I asked him to repeat what he said, and that time I was able to focus.

"I don't..."

"Then why are you dressed?"

"Why aren't you?"

"I wanna see what you look like underneath all of this."

"And, you think a trip to your beach house and afternoon brunch at my favorite diner will get you that?"

Silas released his passion grip and patted my leg. "Not in that way. I mean there's more to you, and I wanna know it. It's in your eyes." He cut into his scrapple, then he squinted his eyes and pointed with his fork. "What's in your heart is different from what you put out."

I tossed my napkin onto my plate. "You're killing the vibe. How do you go from singer Ginuwine to Dr. Phil in one breath? Next you'll be Joel Osteen and tell me how good God has been to you."

Silas laughed, "What you know about Joel Osteen?"

I flagged my hand. "Not a thing. I woke up to him on the television a couple of times."

He nodded. "Anyway, like I said... I'm a work in progress. You have this distorted image of Christianity –that Christians are perfect."

I bit through a piece of cantaloupe and a drop of juice dripped on my chin. Silas wiped it with his thumb.

I said, "Aren't y'all supposed to be perfect?"

"We're all messed up," he replied never taking his eyes off my lips. "We all have weaknesses. Mine is you."

I laughed and pointed at Silas's devilish grin. "See that? That's the switch."

Silas lifted my chin and took my bottom lip between his. I closed my eyes and let him make his move.

His hands roamed. This time they went up my thighs and cupped my bottom. I lifted and crossed my leg to let him get a good squeeze, only because I was curious to know how far this Christian boy would go. Then, his tongue parted my mouth, and I gave it a gentle and inviting suck. The kiss was like warm milk. I was not too hot, not at all cold, but soothing and just right.

My phone vibrated our table, and I jumped to my feet when I saw Ronnie's name flash on the screen. I took the call a few steps away from table. He only wanted to discuss the budget for the catering, but I wound up maneuvering the conversation to find out what his plans were for the rest of the week. I leaned against the railing and gazed down at the river below while I listened as Ronnie ironed out his agenda for me. A couple of hospital visits to see members of his church, a banquet he had to host, and some preparations for Sunday's service. Everything was on his To Do List, except for me. I was a little disappointed that I'd have to wait to see him again. But at least it sounded like Carmen couldn't fit into his schedule either.

When I finally returned to our table, Silas had already paid for the bill, and our food was boxed and bagged. He didn't bother making eye contact with me. He kept looking down at his fingernails and flexing his jaw. Although a Stevie Wonder could see that he was annoyed with me, I didn't bother acknowledging it. *Silas wasn't my man.* If he had a problem with me dipping off to take a phone call for a couple of minutes, that was on him. I snatched my purse and doggy bag off the table, threw my sunglasses on, thanked Silas for the delectable meal, and swayed my booty out of there the same way I swayed in.

CHAPTER 17

"Ok ma'am, so the all-white Chrysanthemum floral arrangements with the Swarovski crystals are $53.13. Since you did want eight of them, we were able to apply the discount. Are you taking care of the payment now, or would you like to take care of it at pick-up?"

"I'm sorry, is that $53.13 each?"

"Yes, each. So that's $425.04 total. How would you be taking care of that?"

I bit down on my bottom lip and tapped my fresh couture designed nails along the counter. The move-out deadline that my parents slapped me with had been weighing on me. In the back of my mind, I knew I needed to get my spending together so I could move the hell up out from under them, but it was so tough. Where would I begin saving? If everyone around me knew me as the soror who could cover, if not all, most of the expenses, how could I turn around and utter the words, "I can't afford that"?

When my chapter sorors met me, Trav was my cushion. Up until I discovered his cheating, I didn't need to touch my own money. The rejection from him only reopened wounds that my therapist was only able to stitch. The neglecting and lies were the salt poured onto it. Now that my bad habit was wide open, and bleeding, I was running through my inheritance. I couldn't afford my lifestyle, anymore. The thought of that pained me.

I pressed the phone to my ear and groaned. I had a reputation to protect. Every year near the end of our retreats, I've always presented our Crystal Sorors with a gift to recognize their fifty plus years of membership within our sorority. Every year my gifts had gotten increasingly better. I needed something to top the Swarovski Chrysanthemum pins, and that something needed to be ready in two days. Nothing else could beat gifting the actual flower adorned with sparkle.

"I'll take care of it when I pick up," I told the florist.

"Ok great. We just need your card number to secure the deposit."

While I fumbled through my wallet, Dominic walked into the kitchen with his shirt off. "Nola, have you seen my *Thomas and Friends* t-shirt?"

I pressed my finger to my lip to signal Dominic to be quiet, and I began reading the numbers off my card credit card.

Dominic was persistent. "Nola! I need my *Thomas and Friends* shirt!"

The florist cut me off, "I'm sorry could you repeat that? I couldn't hear the first four."

I huffed and tried again, but this time Dominic was louder, so much louder.

"I NEED MY SHIRT! YOU DON'T UNDERSTAND, NOLA! I NEED MY SHIRT!

I quickly read her the numbers from the credit card and didn't bother waiting for the confirmation. I rushed off the phone to deal with Dominic. "Where's the manny?"

"I can't find him. I can't find him or my shirt. I'll be late to work!"

Dominic squeezed his fist and strained his face the way he always did before a meltdown. I wrapped my arms around his thick waist and spoke calmly.

"Baby, you have to relax. You will not be late for work." I looked at my watch. "It's only 9:15 a.m. You have to be there at 10:30 a.m., remember?"

The truth was that Dominic had no set time. His work hours were super flexible. He didn't even have to show up if he didn't feel like it, but he was a responsible boy. If you gave him a duty, he wanted to carry it out the best he could. Every day he looked forward to work.

The other day the storeowner said she'd teach him how to use the cash register, so his excitement to be there heightened. He had been begging her to show him how to ring up customers after the one costumer got clocked with a book.

"I'm gonna own that book store," he said with exuberant and confident eyes that night she offered to train him. "I'm gonna fill it up with train books".

I believed him, too. He was determined like that. With the proper counseling to teach him how to handle stressful situations, I believed that Dominic could be just as successful as my father or Derrick ... if not more.

After I got Dominic to calm down with a glass of orange juice, I went towards the laundry room that was connected to the garage. Derrick's all black Escalade was parked in my father's space yet it was empty, and that only meant one thing.

"What the ... oh heck no..."

The light from the laundry room shone from underneath the door, and there were stifled noises that weren't quite loud enough to be coming from the washer and dryer. I jiggled the knob. I could hear belt buckles clinging, and the stifled noises became quick rustling. I banged on the door like I was SWAT.

BOOM, BOOM, BOOM, BOOM, BOOM!

"This is messed up and straight up wrong! You got my brother freaking out, and you're down here getting your butthole treated???" I gave the door one hard kick. "Disgusting!"

One of them flung it open, and the manny came out and slid by me. He ran across the garage and into the house holding Dominic's *Thomas and Friends* t-shirt.

"You're fired!" I called to his back.

Derrick stepped out of the room tucking his white button down shirt back into his pants. I pointed my finger at him. "I don't want your money, so don't ask. I'm telling Alicia, and I'm telling daddy."

He smirked, "A lie like that could get you kicked out, Nola. Do you have a place to go on your absent income? According to our parents, you have no job and no plan. Where's a girl like you going to live? The hood? Section 8?"

"You are the devil. Do your dirt on your own time, Derrick, not Dominic's." On my way back inside the house, I made sure to spit on the hood on of his Cadillac.

***

That afternoon, the manny came knocking on my bedroom door with puppy dog eyes, wearing distressed styled burgundy Bermuda shorts. I was sitting on my bed with my MacBook on my lap checking my account balance. It was the first time that I noticed my parents hadn't deposited anything for me since the previous two months. *Was I cut off and they didn't bother telling me?* I was looking at only $30,645.86, and I wanted to cry. Anything less than thirty grand was pocket change with the way I spent. I had once blown that amount in nine weeks, and now I was supposed to stretch it to God knows when?

The look on my face probably made the manny ask me if it a good time to speak.

I looked up at him from my computer. "How much are my parents paying you?"

The manny stuffed his fingertips into his tight pockets, and shrugged. With his thick Columbian accent he said, "Two thousand, sometime three thousand monthly, depending on how long I stay with Dom."

"And you survive off of that?"

"I make it work. I save everything. I don't have family."

He lifted one of his hands and gestured behind him. "I don't have alla this. The money is paying for my GED, and I'm saving for a house." He sat on my bed and crossed his legs. "That's why I needed to speak to you. I can't lose my job, Nola. This is all I have. Before

Derrick introduced me to your family, I was waitressing at Outback Steakhouse. I was living with my drunk uncle, in North Philly, dodging bullets every other night. I was barely making it. Derrick came to the restaurant one night, and practically dusted me off and gave me this job. I have no real skills. I'm a high school dropout, Nola. I can't lose this job."

"If this job is so important to you, then why are you sleeping with a married man in a home that you work in? It's just messy that this isn't the first time I walked up on y'all. Doesn't seem like you care to me."

The manny pressed his lips together and titled his head.

The first time I caught him and Derrick in the act was a few months after I moved back here. My father was hosting a party for his firm to celebrate a major DUI case he had won. I like to call it A *Hooray-we-let-another-killer-back-on-the-streets* Party. Anyway, I was still depressed about Trav, so I drunk nearly everything the rented bartender had to offer. Alicia and I were by the bar giggling about the bad taste these women lawyers had in men, when I realized my stomach was feeling queasy. I handed her my glass and jetted upstairs in my white Louboutin pumps, running as fast as lightening. I had on a pure white Vera dress that would give me a heart attack had I ruined it.

I didn't realize how drunk I was until I reached the top of stairwell and flung the wrong door open. Derrick had the manny bent over in the walk-in linen. The manny's elbows were resting against the folded towels, both of their pants were dropped and hugging their ankles. They were so into it that they didn't even realize I was standing there frozen holding my mouth and my stomach. Maybe they didn't notice because the hallway was dark and no light had shone on them. The booming ol' school music from downstairs traveled up, so they probably didn't even hear me open the door. What they certainly did hear was me barfing all over the floor, all over my shoes, and all over Derrick's Tom Ford loafers when he tried to lead me to the bathroom.

The next morning, the manny was crying to me about how sorry he was, promising that he would never do it again, and swearing to God that they had broken up. Later that day, Derrick deposited $2,500 into my bank account and labeled it "Hush Money." I didn't need the money—I wouldn't have told anyway. Dominic needed the manny. But I definitely spent it on new shoes, a new bag to match, and clothes and train figurines for Dominic.

I looked at the manny who was nervously biting his bottom lip and shaking his foot. I glanced down at my MacBook, and the low balance of $30,645.86 smacked me in the face again. I needed a job. I could take his job, but Dominic needed him. And anyway, the amount that they were paying him would do nothing for me. However, if he thought he would get away with inconveniencing my Dominic this morning, he was crazy. There are consequences and repercussions when you mess with me or Dom.

"I won't tell my parents about you and Derrick, but you should take a two-week unpaid vacay."

The manny looked at me as if I was insane. "What?"

"Tell them you need to handle some things at school or at home or something."

The manny laughed apathetically. "I'm not taking an unpaid leave. Are you crazy? I have bills."

I slammed my MacBook shut and stood up. "You are sleeping with a *married man* in your *boss's house*, and you think you can get away with it? *That's trifling*! If anything you should be thanking me for not airing you out."

"Wow!" The manny shook his head and folded his arms. "I thought we were cool."

I sternly replied, "Two weeks, four weeks, or forever. You choose."

CHAPTER 18

Pastor Ronnie Robinson stood in his foyer with his dimply grin that I'd been dying to see all week.

"How do I look? You like it? You like my shirt?"

I folded my arms and smiled. "You look great."

He looked over in the mirror and smoothed his freshly shaven goatee with his hands. Then, he smoothed out his pastel pink, green, and grey button down. "Marley told me I had to wear your colors. I ran to Express and this shirt was hanging on the wall. I was in and out!"

He did a good job matching his shirt with light denim jeans and a pair of canvas sneakers. He was one up on Silas as far as style of dress, and I wondered if his shoe collection was just as impeccable as mine was. If so, we were definitely a match made in heaven.

I wanted to be the first member to arrive at Ronnie's, so I sent Bailey to pick up the flowers for the Crystal sorors, I talked Marley into carpooling a few sorors, and I arrived about two hours ahead of time. As I was pulling up, so was the company our chapter hired to provide the tent, tables, and chairs. At first, the driver of that van looked a lot like Ronnie's girlfriend, Carmen, and I felt my goosebumps rise. The last thing I needed was her interference. But it wasn't her. I sighed in relief while I parked.

When I got up to the front door, Ronnie greeted me with firm hug and a light tender kiss on my cheek. He smelled so delicious—a woodsy vanilla and spice fragrance that made me wanna wrap my arms and legs around his waist and lick is neck so badly.

Ronnie joked, "Now that I have at least your approval, let me introduce you to my member's church who volunteered to help me cater."

As Ronnie led me to his kitchen I tugged on the bottom of my olive colored high waist skirt and adjusted my satin coral blouse. Just to be safe that I wasn't exposing too much leg or cleavage. I needed to make a great impression on these members. They didn't know it yet, but they were about to meet their future leading lady.

The volunteers were three young men who looked about college aged. I smiled big and warm with the same smile I give my sorors, and I gave them each a hug by resting my hands on their shoulders, and leaning in for a cheek-to-cheek kiss. I greeted them like the deaconesses at their church always greeted me: "God bless you." Kiss. "God bless you." Kiss. "God bless you." Kiss.

One of them chimed, "Man! I'm glad I volunteered!"

The other two punched his arm and laughed.

Ronnie pointed at them, "y'all better cut it out." Then, he looked at me and smiled. "I hope they won't embarrass me in front of your sorors."

I playfully fanned him off with my hand. "Don't be silly…"

"I'm nervous. Y'all are my first professional clients. I want everything to taste good. I need everything to go good. I don't want y'all saying, '*uht-uhn this is not what we paid for!*'"

Ronnie's woman impersonation tickled me, and the fact that he was able to be vulnerable in front of me turned me on even more. "Relax. You will do phenomenally…. Let the Lord do His chore."

It sounded good coming out, but when Ronnie lifted his eyebrow in confusion and the young guys behind me giggled amongst themselves, I figured I didn't make any sense. I reinforced it with something simple that Marley would say and vowed to never overstep my biblical capabilities again. I pointed to the ceiling. "Leave it in His hands."

The awkward moment was saved by the sound of my ringtone. It was Bailey. I stood off to the side of the kitchen to take the call. She spoke quickly and frantically.

"Nola, I'm in front of the florist. She said the credit card on file declined! I would have taken care of it, but I don't have it."

"Bailey, slow down. That's number one. Just put the florist on the phone. The moron probably keyed the wrong numbers."

When the florist took over the call, I pulled out my card. The only one that hadn't been maxed yet. I began to read the numbers. Each time she said it declined, I reread them again... slower... and louder. It was on the fourth try that Ronnie stepped in. He took the phone from my hand and ran his credit card info instead.

"Thank you," I said to him after the purchase. "You didn't have to do that."

Ronnie handed me my phone. "Don't worry about it."

"I don't know why it wasn't working." *Besides the fact that I overspent.*

Ronnie looked me in the eyes. "It's good. You don't have to worry about it."

I need him to say those words to me for the rest of my life, I thought.

    ***

My chapter sorors gradually began to flood his home, and his backyard became a sea of pink and green hues. Being in the company of my sorors—the laughter, the smiles, the jokes, and encouraging words exchanged between us—effortlessly melted away my qualms. For that moment, I wasn't worried about the direction of my life, about how I was going to maintain the lifestyle I've always known, or how I was going to win Ronnie's heart. My brain temporarily got a chance to relax from plotting and scheming, and I was able to bask in the one thing in my life that I certainly accomplished –the love from my sisterhood.

Those women surrounding me would have taken care of me the best they could, had my pride allowed me to let them in on what was really going on in my life. I was broke. I had no career. And those floral arrangements presented to the Crystal Sorors should have gone towards the mediocre apartment that I'd soon be forced to live in once my parents kick me out. The BCBG outfit, Fendi sandals, and Dior perfume I wore probably should be sold on eBay. ...And the Nola...

the fancy Nola… the *"put it on my tab because I got it"* Nola… the lucrative career, so successful at such a young age, Nola… that they had grown to know, isn't Nola for real. The crazy part is that they wouldn't have cared. They would have loved me and supported me either way, *BUT I CARED*. I was already considered the incompetent one in my real family. I wasn't about to be that in this one. I used my fingertips to suppress the tears that were dampening the corners of my eyes.

My sorors began to gather to prepare a presentation for a soror battling breast cancer. She was about to be gifted a check of $2,700 from all of us. While they did that, I snuck away and headed to the house.

I charged up the stairs of the deck. "Where's Ronnie?"

Two of the young men shrugged holding aluminum trays of mini quiche Florentines and antipasto salad. One of them pointed in the direction of the kitchen.

My heart pounded at the thought of what I was about to do, but I needed to catapult my love interest. The sooner we'd date and fall in love, the seamless my transition would be from living with my parents and struggling finances, to living securely with Ronnie.

It was perfect timing. Ronnie and his sexy lips were standing by the oven. He had just pulled out dessert—tiramisu. I swallowed, took a deep breath, and went for the kill.

"Let me help you with that..."

"Nola, don't. It's hot!"

I shrieked and dropped the pan. The tiramisu splattered on his floor. I wiggled my singed fingertips. "Ow! Ow! Owwww!"

"Why would you... Are you crazy?! Let me look at it."

I extended my hand to Ronnie. The care in his eyes was enough to ease the pain from my minor burns. I pouted, "I feel so silly. I just wanted to help."

Ronnie took my hand over to the sink and ran it under the cold water. Tiny blisters formed on all of my fingers. While he grabbed his first aid kit, Marley walked in from the backyard.

"There you are. I was looking for you! "She slowly stepped around the mess on the floor and her eyes widened when she saw my blistered fingers under the tap. "What happened?!"

Ronnie took my hand and patted it with a dry cloth. "Your girl thinks she's invincible."

I nudged him with my elbow, "Stop it…. I was trying to give Ronnie a hand, and I ended up burning mine."

"Oh wow! I was just about to tell you that after dessert we were gonna wrap-up with prayer and head on to the farm."

"Yeah y'all should just go on without me. I'm not quite in the mood after this. I'm gonna stay here until the pain subsides."

Marley frowned. "Are you sure?" She moved in closer to get a better a look at my hand. "Doesn't look *that* bad…. Do you want me to stay back with you?"

I winced while Ronnie applied ointment. "No, Marley. You and Bailey both need to go without me. You have to take my place as Chair."

Marley nodded proudly, "Of course! Definitely..." She gently placed her hand on her father's shoulder. "Daddy, you ok with handling Nola? You need anything?"

"I got it baby girl"

The affectionate grin that Ronnie gave his daughter was similar to the ads you'd see for Colgate and Cheerio commercials. It made me resent my own father even more. That could have been us patting each other on the shoulder, smiling, and asking if assistance was needed. We could have been giving each other nicknames like "baby girl" or "daddy-o."

    ***

I was highly annoyed that our sorors kept thanking and acknowledging Marley for having her father host us. *It wasn't her idea; it was mine*. I was even more annoyed that she smiled pretty and said, "thank you" with a hair flip like I would have done. It began to feel as if Marley was slowly but surely becoming a miniature me, and I wasn't sure how I felt about it. Yet, President Gabrielle still presented *me* with a larger appreciation gift bag of goodies, as usual, so I didn't make a fuss of it. On top of that, all of the sorors were finally leaving me alone with my boo Ronnie, and that's all I really cared about.

When the last soror pulled off, I blew a kiss from the front door and joined Ronnie in his kitchen. "Let me help you with something, Ronnie."

"No! Heck no. You're accident prone. You sit over there. Waaaaaaaaay over there."

I laughed at the exaggerated expression on his face. "Don't be like that."

He was tidying up the little bit that the rented cleaners didn't get to, like the dishes in the dishwasher. While he put pots and pans away, I bent over and rested my elbows on the counter beside him, purposely brushing up against his arm. I heard him exhale as he walked around me, trying to get to the other side of the cabinet.

"What are your plans tonight?" I asked casually.

"Let's see. I put in sixteen hours of preparation all week for tomorrow's sermon. I think I have another four more."

"Twenty hours of prep for a, what, two-hour service? Sounds extreme..."

"It takes research, reading, and prayer."

"You think God will let you take a break?" I glanced at my rose gold watch. "It's only ten minutes until five o'clock. We can be back by 6:30 p.m." I couldn't take my eyes off the pastor's lips. I wanted to taste them badly, and I wanted them to be acquainted with mine.

He rubbed his smooth bald head and pulled his phone from his pocket, probably checking for any missed calls from his ugly girlfriend. "Where are you trying to go?"

I smiled. "That restaurant I told you about… the Moroccan one."

CHAPTER 19

We sat at a small table in the furthest back of the dimly lit restaurant. It was a full house, so Ronnie and I had no choice but to sit elbow to elbow and knee cap to kneecap on cushioned chairs. It was perfect.

"Which flavor do you want?" I pointed to the hookah menu.

Ronnie shook his head. "I'll pass on the hookah."

I raised my eyebrow and threw my neck back. "No you're not!" I handed our server the menu. "We're having the Passion Kiss flavor."

Ronnie smirked and cut his eyes to me. "You're a pistol. I'll have to watch out for you. I can tell."

I smiled. "I'm so good! I promise you. Relax, it's just a hookah. Very little tobacco. It's leisure."

After the waitress returned with our mouthpieces and hooked us up, she took our orders and disappeared through the throng of people. I puckered my lips on the tip and exhaled through my nostrils.

"Loosen up a little, Pastor." I motioned for him to take the hose, and to my surprise, he actually went for it.

The way he allowed the thick cloud of smoke to escape from his mouth, and then enter into his nose and back out of his mouth, made it obvious that he was no novice. I almost lost it! *No wonder he had no problem dating a former COKEHEAD!*

The pastor laughed. "Close your mouth."

I didn't notice that it was hanging open.

"I never said I didn't smoke hookahs. I said that I will pass." He did the mouth and nose trick again. "And, I do cigars every once a while."

I snatched the hose. "Show off!"

He threw his head back and laughed. That youthful smile melted me. His hand fell on my kneecap for a few seconds. After he moved it, I wondered if he'd done it purposely. I couldn't read him. He wasn't a direct and in your face type of guy like Silas. If anything, I probably had to initiate all the flirtatious moves and conversations.

I took a drag and exhaled, "So be honest. How serious are you and Carmen? You love her?"

"Depends. Which love?"

"Romantic, she's-the-one kind of love..."

Ronnie stroked his goatee, and answered, "We're taking it day by day."

I passed him the hose and watched him blow. *God, he's so sexy.*

He said, "You know, Marley always talked about you. She said you were good people."

"She's a good mentee."

"Mentee...?"

"I'm a good influence on the kid."

"Kid?"

"I'm about ten years older than Marley, Pastor. Anything she's experiencing now, I've already done that."

"Is that so?"

"Except for marriage... I haven't done that yet. I was close to it, but not quite."

He laughed, "You know, you're interesting Nola."

Now, back to Carmen "So if Carmen and I wanted to hang out with you on the same day, who are you willing to see?"

Ronnie said sarcastically, "Unrelenting eh... "

Our server placed our entrées on the small round table. Ronnie grabbed my hand, the unburned one, bowed his head, and said grace. Afterwards, he gave my hand a firm squeeze and said "Amen."

"Amen... So, which will it be?"

Ronnie readjusted himself and then he stroked his head, looking as if he was in deep thought. He squinted his eyes and looked at me. "Would you want to spend time with me, or is this hypothetical?"

"Choose."

He eventually said, "I'd go with whoever asked first."

Yeah, he's definitely not feeling that Carmen chick all the way. I tried to hide my smile behind the hookah mouthpiece.

***

On the way back to the car, an elderly woman who looked to be in her late sixties or early seventies approached Ronnie. I think she powered walk to catch up to us before tapping him on the shoulder.

"Pastor Robinson!" She had a doggy bag in her hand, and she wore a flared denim skirt. "I thought that was you. I spotted you from inside, but I wasn't sure."

Ronnie hugged the woman and kissed her on the cheek in the same way he had once kissed me.

With a single raised eyebrow, she brought her attention to me. "And, who is this little young lady? She doesn't look at all like Marley. Is this your niece?"

"This is a friend of Marley's."

I chimed in, "Her sorority sister." I extended my hand to shake. "My name is Nola, and you are?"

The hag rejected my extended hand and instead made a gurgling noise. Then she murmured, "Pleasure."

Ronnie spoke up. "This is Sister Bernadine Walker. She's on the usher board."

The old lady adjusted the straps of her 1997 looking Coach Bag and huffed. "Well. I should be going."

Ronnie followed Bernadine to help her into her Cadillac and swiftly returned.

I pointed in the direction of her exiting car. "That's the reason why I don't go to church... Church folks are so mean and unwelcoming... just dag on judgmental."

"Not all." Ronnie opened the door on the passenger side of his cherry red Lincoln SUV. I felt his eyes fixated on me while I climbed into his vehicle. He leaned on the door and said, "Listen, I want you to remember something…"

I looked up at him.

"Another person's actions shouldn't keep you away from God's glory. You deserve to experience Him in your life just as any of us. We're all sinners, and in God's eyes. We're all the same. No one person on this Earth is better. Just remember that."

I blushed inwardly. "I will."

"Look at you, Girl. You got me preaching on my day off." Ronnie smiled, and for the first time, I noticed that his top lip was slightly juicer than the bottom.

"Are you visiting us again, tomorrow?" his lips asked.

My eyes never left them as I nodded. "Of course."

CHAPTER 20

On Sunday morning, Carmen was sitting on the front pew next to Marley and her geeky fiancé Greg. Two things were wrong with that picture. *One*, Marley didn't even bother inviting me church, so I came alone. And I was late because I couldn't remember what time service started. *Two*, Carmen had on the same colors I wore—yellow and cream. At least my lay looked much better than hers. Her stripe maxi dress had nothing on my chevron knee-length dress, matching fascinator, and cream lace gloves.

I sat on the other side of Carmen, too. Yup. Sure did. She and Marley both did a double take when I sat down. Pastor however, smiled slightly from the pulpit and nodded a bit to acknowledge my presence. After pastor preached, the part came to invite us lost souls into a life with Jesus Christ. I rose quickly to reach the pastor's extended hand. A small card seemed to have fallen from my purse on the way to the front, and I watched from the corners of my eye as Carmen stepped on it with her $29.99 shoe and slid it closer to her.

I stood in the front of the church with five other people. Marley had her hands pressed together with a proud smile. Greg had his lips tucked in, and his eyes didn't seem to be focus on anything in particular. He looked like he would rather be somewhere else. Carmen's mouth was so tight, and her eyes were so bulged that she looked like she was trying to keep her inner ratchet from escaping.

"Is there another? Is there another? "Pastor Ronnie paced the alter with his arms extended.

I scanned the sanctuary and made eye contact with Silas and his shrunken shirt. He smile and nodded at me. After a few minutes had gone by and no one else joined us at the front, Pastor said, "Let's give God some praise." He turned to give us each a hug while the church erupted with claps and shouting. When he got to me, I wrapped my arms around his neck and lingered long enough to get Carmen's blood to boil.

Afterwards, a man and woman dressed in nappy navy blue suits lead us to a small room, sat us at a long table, and passed us each a booklet labeled "Welcome Packet." While everyone went around the table introducing themselves, I kept my eyes on the glass doors waiting for Ronnie to walk in at any moment. He was supposed to walk in at any moment, right?

"What about you, Sister?" The woman with the navy suit smiled. The brass label on her jacket read, *Deaconess Michelle Camper*.

I didn't realize it was my turn to speak so I asked, "What about me?"

Deaconess Michelle Camper never stopped smiling. "Tell us a little bit about yourself."

"Oh!" I sat up straight and projected my voice, as a Leading Lady should. "My name is Nola. I'm in Real Estate, and actually, I'm a good friend of Pastor Ronnie Robinson."

Everyone nodded and looked impressed.

"Ok great! We love it when friends of the church family join! So, tell us, did you join for Salvation?"

I chuckled. "I'm not sure. I remember going to church a couple of times when I was younger, but I don't remember anybody splashing Holy Water on my forehead."

I cut my eyes to a young girl who snickered and whispered something under their breath.

The Deaconess nodded slowly. "Ok, well let me explain the process to you. The salvation prayer that you just recited was the first step in your walk with Christ. The Baptism ceremony is something we also do, and you will also begin new membership classes—Those are four weeks. After that, you will receive the Right Hand of Fellowship, which is how you all will be officially welcomed in. And finally you will take your spiritual gifts class to see how God can use you within the church."

I tapped my lace-gloved fingers along the table and tilted my head to the side. "Deaconess Michelle Camper, that sounds like a lot of work to join a church. Is there a way we could shorten those four weeks to two since I'm personal friends with the Pastor?"

She laughed, "Our walk with Christ IS work, Sister."

***

When we left the conference room, the church lobby was almost empty. Pretty much the entire congregation was gone except for a few stragglers. I approached two teens and asked them if Pastor Ronnie Robinson had already left. They shrugged their shoulders. I asked them where his office was and they pointed in the direction of a hallway. The hall that led to his office was empty, and I began to feel like I wasted time. I didn't care to join the church and do all that class stuff, I just wanted a one-on-one with Ronnie but on his level - a church level. Had I known they would have pulled me away from him, I wouldn't have gone up front to join.

Luckily, the office door was wide open. I entered the room, and faced a secretary sitting at her desk. She was the only occupant of that space. There was another door to the left of her. Since the secretary was looking down into the desk drawer, I walked right up to the ajar door and pushed it open.

Carmen was sitting in a chair facing Ronnie's desk, and his eyes lit up when he saw me. "Nola! What's up?"

"Great sermon today, Pastor," I said with the sweetest smile.

"Thank you, Nola, and thank you for joining the church family." He stood up and walked around the desk to give me a hug, along with his famous pastor's kiss to the cheek.

Carmen could have broken her neck with how quickly she turned around. "Oh, you just missed Marley," she had the audacity to say.

Although the words clung to the corners of my mouth, for dear life, I managed to spit them out anyway. "Good morning Ms. Carmen."

She flashed half a smile and turned her back.

As the Pastor made his way back to the desk, I scanned his office. Plaques, certifications for achievements, pictures of pastors prior to him, and a couple of pictures of him and Marley were hanging on his walls. Behind him was a large window that allowed him to view the parking lot. I spotted my car and wondered if he saw me whisk off with Silas last week. Then, I wondered how thrilling it would be to have the pastor bend me over in front of that window. Fogging up the glass with our passion, while looking out at everyone, yet no one being able to look at us.

"How are your fingers?" He broke me from my fantasy.

I pulled off my glove and showed him my fingertips. "Unattractive right?"

Carmen looked at them and scrunched her face. It took everything within me not to knock the back of her head with my brand new and still wrapped in plastic bible.

Ronnie said, "They'll heal in time... So what's up?"

I had to think fast. "I wanted to talk about the membership packet... but it's private."

Carmen reluctantly excused herself. She walked over to Ronnie, kissed his head, and picked up a purse that looked like it came from Boscov's. I snuggled my booty where she sat and placed my designer purse on Ronnie's desk.

"She's so mean and unapproachable. You know Marley can't stand her?"

Ronnie grimaced, "Marley told me she loved her."

"Marley doesn't want to hurt your feelings. She can't stand that woman. She told me the other day. I don't blame her, especially after that coffee shop incident."

"She should have just told me..."

"You know your daughter. She isn't outspoken like that, but she tells me *everything*. She vented that Carmen seemed wrong for you. I believe it..."

"You believe it..."

"You're warm, compassionate, and gentle, and she's tough as nails. She doesn't like to smile, and she's filled with animosity. I sat next to her to make amends, and she completely rejected me. You saw it! I know you saw!"

Ronnie rubbed his head and sighed, "I need to speak to my child."

"Yeah sometimes our loved ones see what we don't see. Or, in your case, *DO SEE*, but in too much denial to face it."

"What does that mean?"

"You don't even like Carmen. You just need a reason to get out of it without looking bad."

"Come again?"

I leaned in closer and spoke slowly, "You... don't... like... her."

Ronnie chuckled and leaned back in his seat. He folded his arms right below his orange striped tie. "And, what makes you say that, Nola?"

"The way you look at her. There's no spark, no fire. It's nothing like how I've caught you looking at me."

Ronnie sat up and adjusted himself in his seat. He glanced down at his navy and silver Movado watch. "I need to wrap up. What about the packet?"

I almost forgot about the excuse I used to get Carmen out of his office. "I don't think I'm cut out for the Christian life. I'm so flawed. Sometimes I curse, sometimes I drink wine, and sometimes my temper gets the best of me. I thought about it, and I'm not gonna join and do that whole four weeks of classes thing."

"Nola, listen. Nobody is perfect. We all have our battles with our sinful selves. That's why we need Christ. Not because we're perfect, but because we're imperfect. We need Him to help keep us righteous. Don't be discouraged, you can do it. Temper, wine, and curse-words is nothing compared to the sins most of us struggle with. If we can do this, you can do this." Pastor spoke smoothly and compassionately.

I asked, "What are you struggles?"

Ronnie laughed. "That's a whole 'nother time and place to talk about that. We'll discuss it some other time. Just remember, this walk with Christ, it ain't easy. There will be tests, there be trails, and there will be setbacks. Nevertheless, trust God and trust the process. It ain't easy, but living with Christ is enjoyable. Trust me. I'm excited for you, and so is Marley. She was waiting for you, but she and Greg had to run a few errands before meeting me for brunch." Ronnie glanced at watch again. "It looks like it'll be dinner."

He began rustling with his papers on his desk.

I said dryly, "A couples' dinner this time. How sweet..." I grabbed my purse and stood up.

Looking down at his papers, he said, "Actually, I'll be the third wheel. Carmen has to head home to get ready for work."

***

I shamelessly followed Carmen home. I waited for her and Ronnie to walk out of the church together, and for her to pull out of the parking lot. I tailed about three cars behind her red Toyota Camry all the way to the Northeast section of Philadelphia. I parked across the road once she pulled into a driveway of a surprisingly nice two-story home located in a cul-de-sac. I snacked on M&Ms and a Pepsi while I watched a young guy with a chest covered in tattoos open the door for her. She was also greeted by a Rottweiler. She was in the house for about twenty minutes and then out again wearing scrubs.

I scurried across the street when she pulled off. I knocked on her door. The guy with the tattoos and their horse-height dog came to the door.

"Hi, is Carmen here?"

The guy stepped outside and looked to the left and then the right. "Uhh, you just missed her."

"Aw, man. Are you her boyfriend?"

The guy smirked, "Nah I'm her son, you cute. Who you?"

I extended my hand for him to shake. "I'm Morgan from the women's ministry at church. I wanted to get her to sign up for our retreat, but she didn't come today. I'll come back tomorrow." I turned to walk away, but then I stopped.   "Listen, I'm embarrassed to ask this, but can I use your bathroom?"

"Yeah. You good, Ma... Come on." Her son stepped to the side. "And, don't worry about him. He cool," he said referring to their beast.

A whiff of marijuana hit me as soon as I stepped in their living room. It was so strong that I was surprised I didn't immediately catch contact.

"So you a church girl, huh? I didn't know they made them as pretty as you. I guess I need to start going!" The guy salivated as his eyes slowly crawled from the crown of my head to the tips of my toes.

Although I felt disgusted, I smiled and said, "You're not too bad yourself. Those tattoos... Mmmm sexy. I would take your number but your mom would wonder how I met you."

He shrugged, "So. She cool. She won't care."

"I don't want anybody in my business, if you know what mean. I tell you what... don't even mention I was here."

He nodded his head rapidly, looking like a toddler who was offered a chocolate chip cookie but only if he behaved. "Yeah, yeah, yeah. That'll work. That'll work."

I stored some random number in his phone. After he directed me upstairs to their bathroom, he and his dog sat on the couch and resumed whatever video game he was playing.

I walked into the bathroom, slid off my shoes, and then tiptoed into Carmen's bedroom. I dropped a little gift for her in the back of her panty drawer, and then tiptoed back into the bathroom, closed the door, and flushed the toilet. When I walked out of the bathroom, I was startled to see their horse that they called a dog. He barked, and I jumped back nearly breaking my ankle as a tripped in my heels.

"Excuse me!" I yelled to the guy who still downstairs. "Can you get your dog???"

The dog barked again, and this time he growled and inched closer. I was so scared that I stood frozen, knowing that I could easily run back into the bathroom and slam the door shut. Carmen's son finally came hustling up the stairwell.

"Killa! What up with you, man?" He grabbed the dog by its collar.

I put my hand on my chest and exhaled. "You told me he was cool. He nearly ate me alive! You can't invite people over when you got a wild beast as a pet!"

The guy looked at me like he wanted to snap back, but he instead shook his head and lifted his free hand. "Look, I apologize. You said you had to use the bathroom. You free to go right now."

I slid past the dog and hurried down the stairs.

As I crossed the street, Carmen's son shouted, "Yo! Im'ma call you, Yo!"

CHAPTER 21

Soror Marley begged me to come to her job for lunch. Said she needed to talk to me about something important.

The only thing I wanted to hear was that she kicked her knock-off toting line sister's outta her wedding. That was the only news I was hoping to hear as I slid on my new paisley printed tunic dress designed by Lily Pulitzer. I told Marley I'd head over after I finished "work" with the internship. The only "work" I had for the day was dropping Dominic off to his job, and then picking up his medication, all before having to reassure him multiple times, that the manny would be back in two weeks, and that I was gonna do things just as good, if not better. It almost pissed me off that my Dominic lacked trust in me, but I remembered that I needed to charge it to his head not his heart.

The receptionist at Marley's work place pointed to a glass door when I told her I was looking for a Marley Robinson. I was surprised to see that behind the door, was Marley... And only Marley. Sitting at the only desk. I was expecting to meet with her at a cubicle. Never did I imagined she worked from a gorgeous office with a gorgeous view of the city. Nor was I expecting it to be so neat, with four gorgeous tropical plants adorning each corner, or the gorgeous wall art that reminded me of Silas's work.

"When did you become office status? Or, are you office sitting?" I walked over to a mirror hanging on the wall and made sure my obnoxiously large bun was still neat and smooth.

"Office sitting?" Marley laughed. "They don't do that. And, last year I told you that I was promoted to VP."

"Oh" I fanned my hand and sat in the chair across from her. "I was distracted with nonsense last year. I can barely remember what I did for my birthday... So what's up?"

"Did you and my dad go to some restaurant, the night of the retreat?"

128

"Yeah...," I said nonchalantly. "Is there a problem?"

Marley's eyes grew wide. "No! No!" She waved her hands. Her new engagement ring flickered against the late April sun and greeted me. It was a big gorgeous one, just as Greg promised. "It's just… You know… *Weird.*"

I had to peel my eyes off the, what looked like a 2 Ct., solitaire diamond ring. "No. What's so weird about it?"

Marley belted out a nervous chuckle, "Well…"

I grew annoyed. I knew she wanted to tell me to stay away from her father. That was obvious. But, if she wanted to come at me, she needed to come correct and not stall. Since she struggled, I took the opportunity to grab hold of the steering wheel and drove the conversation home.

"What's weird is your immaturity – and to be a young woman who is so academically advanced! Wake up and realize that we are *adults*. Ok?

"No, it's just—"

"--I'm twenty-nine. You're twenty. I don't know how you missed this, but there actually comes a point in our lives when we should be capable of conversing with *anyone* regardless of age."

"I understand that. I—"

"I'm offended! If it's embarrassing to see me engage in casual conversation with your father, that's *your* problem not mine. Grow up a little, Marley. Ok?"

Discussion parked. Keys snatched out of the ignition. Bye, little girl.

Marley sighed and threw her elbows on her desk. Her diamond-studded bangles clapped along her wrist as she ran her fingers through her hair, flipping it from one side to the other. "I'm sorry, Nola. This wedding stuff… It has my brain all…. When Sister Bernadine said she saw y'all out... forgive me if I'm wrong, I just had to ask because I needed the understanding. The idea *does* make me feel uncomfortable, and plus I assumed you were stepping on toes.

He's with Carmen, yet I'm hearing he's out at dinner with you, and then the next day you joined the church. …It doesn't help that I'm so protective of him."

I nodded. "So is that the reason you didn't invite me to church yesterday? Because, you want me to stay away from your father? Wow. How petty..."

"No! No... No... No. The only reason I didn't invite you was because I knew Carmen was coming. I was trying to prevent anything awkward."

I rolled my eyes but decided to drop everything. I couldn't keep fighting with Marley if I was going to need her blessing to marry her father eventually. "Girl, the wedding has you overthinking and stressed. Get some sleep," I said rising from the chair. "No hard feelings."

On my way to pick up Dominic, Marley called me. I sent her straight to voicemail and listened to her message after I parked in front of Dominic's bookstore. She was speaking through tears, begging me to forgive her. She also mentioned something about feeling convicted for questioning my involvement with her father and that she would try not to assume such on me again.

I laughed as I pressed DELETE.

CHAPTER 22

I was sitting on the couch checking my Facebook when I first spotted Carmen's Camry circling our block. The second time she rolled around, I jumped up and took plenty pics from the living room window with my phone. At one point, she stopped in front of the house, and then finally, after a few minutes, she sped off. Moments after I sat back down the doorbell was ringing. I hesitated to answer it. I didn't think Carmen would knock on the door.... I had to prepare myself. *What if she came back to fight? Did I need to grab a weapon first?* The doorbell ringing was relentless, so I swung the door open with the first thing I saw in hand – my Jimmy Choo with the gold stiletto heel.

To my surprise, it was just Alicia wearing a black tee and gray sweatpants. She pushed past me and plopped on the couch.

"Girl, you were two seconds from having this heel pierced into your forehead. Why are ringing the door like that? You know no one is home. It's not like my car is parked out front."

"I knew you were here, Nola." Her tone was melancholic and she waved her hand lazily. "Derrick told me about your situation months ago. I noticed that a grand was missing from our account. He told me about you needing it."

Derrick hasn't given me any money since the first time I caught him, but from the look on Alicia's face, I knew that now wasn't the time to burst that bubble. "I have other things going on in my life too, you know... Anyway, what's up? What's wrong?"

Alicia threw her face into her hands, "I slept with Villain, your masseuse."

"What?!"

"I cheated on my husband. *Twice*... over the weekend."

"What?!"

"And, we didn't use protection."

131

"Alicia, what?!"

"Derrick left on Saturday for a so-called emergency two-week business trip… a two-week business trip? Yeah right! I called his job, and you know what they told me? Yes, he is away from the office for two weeks, but it isn't business."

By this point, Alicia's face was soaked with tears and a snot bubble hung from her nostril. I handed her a Kleenex, and she blew loud enough to wake the dead.

"I was so mad, Nola! So, I left Hannah with the nanny, and I went to a bar and never came home. I haven't been home since. While I was at the bar, I called Villain...and ... well... now I'm here."

"So you're in Saturday's clothes?"

Alicia blew her nose and nodded.

"It's Tuesday..."

"I know," Alicia sobbed. "I know..."

While Alicia wallowed in guilt, my cell buzzed in my hand. It was a text from Silas: *"One minute you're hot. The next minute you're cold."* I had no idea what that was supposed to mean so I deleted it. Then another one popped up: *"Even the Bible says be either or..."* I deleted that one too and directed my attention back to Alicia.

"Ok. First, we need to get you showered and outta these clothes. Second, you need to go to your baby immediately! I know she's missing you."

While I was in my closet picking out a dress for Alicia, I could hear her sobbing from the shower. I pained for a little bit as I wondered if the mistake she made was my fault. Immediately, I balled that thought up and trashed it. *Heck no... It was definitely all Derrick's fault*. It was his web of lies and I was tangled in it. I laid the dress on the bed and went outside to call him, only for him to forward me to his voicemail.

"You jackass. Both of you are jackasses. I didn't make him take a two-week suspension so you can go cheat on your wife! Now she's here, a mental wreck all because you're a dirty, lying, pretending, TRADE!"

As soon as I ended the call, my phone chimed. It was Silas. I had venom left so I bit him, too. "If you want to see me, say you want to see me! Stop sending me these stupid ass cryptic text messages!"

His voice was low, calm, and purely seductive. "I want to see you. All I want is forty-five minutes... uninterrupted."

I couldn't refuse.

CHAPTER 23

Friday morning, I had my arms wrapped tightly around Ronnie. I rested my head on his chest. "Thank you for taking out time for me." I inhaled his aroma.

"It's fine. I'm glad you didn't mind meeting here." His hand fell on my back as he rubbed in circular motion. "You sounded frantic on the phone. What happened?"

I released him and tucked my hair behind my ear. "It's about Carmen."

He stepped back. "What about her now?"

"You'll want to sit down."

Ronnie folded his arms. "Just tell me."

"It's not good news."

"I'm a big boy."

"Sit down... *please*?"

Ronnie walked over to his desk and slouched in his chair. He threw his arms up. "So what's up?"

He was aggravated, and it turned me on. I wanted to smile, but this wasn't supposed to be a smiling matter, so I held it together and slid my phone from the back of my jean pocket. I pulled up the pictures of Carmen's car and handed my phone to Ronnie.

I sat across from him as he scrolled through the pics. "She's been stalking my home. The other day, I came home to my front door cracked and my diamond tennis bracelet missing."

Ronnie zoomed in and out of the pictures, making sure that it was definitely Carmen. He slid the phone back to me.

"Wow... I don't know... I don't even know what to say. And, you said your tennis bracelet is missing?"

I nodded. "And that's not all, Ronnie."

I dug into my purse, pulled out four envelopes, and dropped them on his desk. This time his eyebrows nearly touched as he scrunched his face.

"I don't take harassment lightly, Ronnie. I've been getting these all week. I figured I'd show you before I take them to the police."

I spoke while he shuffled through the opened envelopes addressed to me from "*C.*"

"They're vulgar, and full of expletives. I mean, what she wrote in there scared me so bad that I felt I needed Jesus's protection. Read them. It's terrible!"

He pulled out one of the typed letters and stroked his goatee while he read. "Are you sure these are from her?" He looked disgusted as he read the others.

"I know everything is typed, down to the labels on the envelope, but I can assure you that they are from her. I've never had any problems like this prior to that tea brewery incident. The fact that I caught her in my neighborhood...how couldn't it be from her?"

Ronnie sighed and rubbed his face. "Wow... I'm at lost for words. I'm sorry you had to go through this." He folded the last letter and stuffed it back inside. "I know you're fed-up and scared, but I promise you that you won't have to go to the police. I will handle it. Ok? I promise."

I folded my arms. "I don't know, Ronnie. That woman... something is off about her..."

"Listen, she's not as crazy as she's trying to make it seem. She doesn't want to go down that road. Trust me." He reached for my hand and gave it a gentle squeeze.

    ***

I knew it wouldn't be long before the news of Carmen's harassment got to Marley. She sent me a text begging me to call her, and when I called her, she begged me to come down to her gown alterations to talk. I brought Dominic along since it was just about time

135

for him to clock out. Plus, I knew he would love seeing Marley in her gown.

She came from behind the curtain in a big fluffy Pnina Tornai with a sweetheart neckline and beaded embroidery along the bust. She was beaming so hard that her smile almost reached her ear lobes.

Dominic bounced in his seat. "I like it! I like it, Marley!"

Marley spun slowly, "Do you, Dominic?" She admired herself in the mirror. "Do you like, Nola?"

"Who helped you pick it out?"

The style of the dress and designer was too fashionable for Marley's taste. Her taste was more of a David's Bridal brand – never a designer like Tornai.

"I found it online. Do you like it?"

"Is it real?"

Marley slapped her leg. "Nola! Yes it's real, silly. It came from Kleinfelds."

"Kleinfelds?!"

"And, my father spent a grip."

Never have I guessed there would be a day that I'd feel jealous of Marley Robinson. Marley - my little hot mess mentee who never had a clue and stuck to me like glue. Now she was standing before me in a gown that *I should have worn* down the aisle some weeks ago, rocking a diamond ring that I should have had on *my left finger*, and just leaving an office that *I should be working in.* My stomach turned, and I suddenly felt dizzy and nauseous.

Dominic pressed his forehead against mine, and said, "Smile, Nola. Isn't Marley pretty?"

I moved Dominic out of the way and ran to the restroom before my lunch splattered on Marley's gown.

By the time I came from the bathroom, Marley had changed back into her regular clothes, and she was sitting next to Dominic who was schooling her about Diesels from his iPad.

"You alright, Nola?" Marley stood when she saw me. "I have saltine crackers in my purse, and I have of a bottle of ginger ale in my car."

"I'm good."

"Was it Carmen?"

"What?"

"My father told me all about it. Is her harassment stressing you? Is it causing you to get sick?"

"Oh!.. Yeah... I think so."

Marley wrapped her arms around me and squeezed.

"Awh Nola! I should have believed you when you first told me about her. I'm sorry you had to go through that. I've been a terrible friend."

"You'll do better."

"Well, we won't have to worry about Carmen anymore." Marley stepped back and clapped her hands as if she was dusting them off. "My dad is through with her. He was livid!"

Suddenly I felt better.

"You wanna know something crazy?" Marley continued, "When he had her come down to the office, she was wearing a tennis bracelet like the one you described to my dad. She had the balls to tell him she thought it was a surprise from him!"

Marley shook her head. "My dad said he's willing to serve as a witness if you're gonna press charges."

I was flattered but I had to quickly decline. "If she needed a bracelet that bad, she can have it."

"After my dad told her that it wasn't from him, she switched it up and said it must have been her son who gave it to her."

"She was bad for him. I told you that. Listen to your soror. I know best." *Now all I need to do is get rid of your ugly bridesmaids.*

***

After we left the boutique, Marley wanted to drag us to dinner, and she let Dominic choose. We ended up at a quaint Italian restaurant in Rittenhouse. I brought him here a while back. He loved it because it was a small, chill, dimly lit, and relaxed environment. Wasn't too overstimulating. I liked it because they made authentic Italian food, and they had Italian servers with thick accents, so they were definitely the real deal.

When we walked into the restaurant, the hostess grabbed menus and looked directly at Dominic. "Hello, sir. Just 3 today?"

Dominic just smiled and nodded, and she led us to a table near the back.

We were chowing down on fried calamari when Marley mentioned Silas. She wanted to know how things were going with him.

Dominic spoke with calamari in his mouth, "What's Silas?"

Marley babbled, "He's Nola's soon-to-be boyfriend, and maybe soon-to-be husband!"

I put my hand up. "Don't tell him that. He'll take you literally... Dominic, Silas is my friend from church."

Dominic looked confuse. "Hmmmm"

"Yeah, I know I haven't told you about him. He's not that important."

Marley chimed in, "Well, he thinks very highly of you! We were talking about you after bible study Wednesday... Oh! ... You should come to bible study with us next week. After that, the four of us can double date for dinner."

I shook my head and declined.

"Why not?"

"Because, I'm not interested."

"In what? Dating?"

I frowned. "Marley, chill out. I don't need you arranging my love life. I got it under control." The only double date I was interested in was Ronnie and me with the blanket and his bed. That's it.

Dominic poked my arm. "Don't be angry with Marley, Nola."

"I'm not baby. She's just a pest! Tell your girlfriend to relax."

He lowered his head and blushed, and Marley playfully blew him a kiss.

The waitress returned and slid Dominic the check. A common mistake anytime he and I went out to eat. And I'm sure if the people sitting at the bar next to us wondered, they probably also thought that the tall husky guy, with curly hair, a fresh shape-up, and dapper yet casual attire was a lucky guy who scored two pretty ladies to treat to dinner. Dominic had often been mistaken as my boyfriend when we're out in public, judging from his height and style alone. It was when he spoke that bystanders would realize that it was most likely not the case.

Marley pulled out her Michael Kors wallet and grabbed the check. "Look! They slid Things Remembered and Pandora coupons in here."

"Talk about right on time." I grabbed the Things Remembered coupon and put it in my purse. "I was just on their site looking for something for your father."

"My father?"

"Yeah..."

"What would make you wanna do that?"

"Because he's great, and I appreciate him."

Marley chewed on the inside of cheek and looked like her mood was broken. She sat quietly from the time the waitress came to grab the check to when she returned with the card and receipts.

CHAPTER 24

"How you get my address?"

"A 'Hello' would be nice."

"You look creepy."

"Creepy?"

"How you get my address?"

It was around 8 p.m., and Silas was standing on my doorstep holding sunflowers, wearing burnt orange cargo pants, a navy and white striped polo shirt, and a goofy smile. I dropped the flowers in an empty vase I found in the kitchen cabinet and poured myself a glass of wine. When I got back to the living room, Dominic, who was focused on assembling train tracks, already had Silas skimming through a manual for a train model set that I bought for him earlier.

"Man, what's a big burly dude like you doing messing around with trains anyway?" Silas flipped the through manual scratching his head.

Dominic sighed, exasperated. "Just read step four."

"I can't find step four. This thing is all over the place."

Silas passed it to Dominic. "Ay, why are you assembling trains on a Saturday night?"

I interrupted, "Marley sent you, didn't she?"

"Yeah." Silas looked up from the box the train came in. "She said you said you could use some company. Said something about you having a draining week."

I was about to send Marley a long text, telling her about herself. But, because Dominic looked like he was enjoying Silas's company, I cooled down and sipped my Riesling while they built the train.

Silas nudged Dominic. "It's Saturday night, man. You should be out with your homeboys."

Dominic never his took eyes off his model. "If I should be out with homeboys, why aren't you?"

Silas was stuck on how to respond, and I giggled from my glass.

About hour and a half later, the neighborhood train model was completed. I smiled as the two of them shook hands and patted each other on the back. Then, I watched as Silas looked at Dominic with confusion as he grabbed a few toys from a wicker chest and scurried upstairs with them under his arms, after I instructed him to take a shower.

"What? You never met anyone with special needs?" I asked while picking up the plastic and cardboard that been wrapped around the parts to the model.

Silas stammered, "Yeah... I just didn't know... couldn't tell. Why you let me badger him about it being Saturday and going out?"

"Dominic can handle his own. He answered your questions didn't he?"

Silas took the garbage bag I was holding and held it open for me. "What's wrong with him?"

"Nothing is wrong with him. He's perfect in my eyes. He's my therapist, my diary, and he's a great conversationalist." I tied the garbage bag, and pointed to the closet for Silas to store it in there. "It's just that he grew taller, he got stockier, but his mind never grew past age ten."

Silas said, "Wow."

I nodded slowly.

"I'm familiar. My uncle owns a few centers for children and teens with those kinds of disorders. I used to help him out in the summer when I was in school." Silas plopped down in my father's favorite recliner. "Dom had me fooled. I wouldn't have known."

He tapped his fingers along the arm of the chair. "Nice place, by the way. You gonna give me a tour?"

"No. it's not mine."

"Are you housesitting?"

I folded my arms and huffed.

Silas interpreted my body language. He smiled, and sat up. "I'm not trying to frustrate you, and I'm not trying get all up in your business. I just wanna know you better... and get a glass of water to drink, if that's alright with you. You haven't even offered me any since I been here."

"You're asking for too much."

"*Water* is too much?"

"I'm about to put you out."

I could hear Silas laughing under his breath as I walked away. After I handed him a tall glass of iced water, I went upstairs to check on Dominic.

He was already out of the shower and putting on his pajamas, and he was sobbing. I couldn't remember the last time I've seen Dominic cry, that's how uncommon it was. Even when he was overstimulated and frustrated, he didn't cry. My heart pounded through my chest as I cupped his damp face.

"What happened? Did you hurt yourself?"

"I can't... I can't" Was all he mustered between sobs.

"You can't what Dominic? What happened? Did you hurt yourself again?"

I helped him push his arms through the sleeves of his A|X t-shirt. He had both of his fists clenched tightly.

"Did Silas hurt your feelings with his questions?"

Dominic kept his head lowered as he sniffled. "No."

I sat next to him on his bed, put my arm on his back, and rested my head on his shoulder. "You're making me sad. I wanna make it all better. I wanna make you happy, but you won't tell me what's wrong. *Please*. You'll make me cry, too. Tell me..."

Dominic resisted.

I continued to push. I needed him to be okay. I didn't want him in that dark place again. I needed his smile, his warmth, and his strength. If he was broken, who else could I rest on? "Tell me what's wrong."

Dominic lowered his head and sobbed harder. My body heat rose, and it felt like fire was beneath my feet as I raced down the stairs and charged Silas. "YOU NEED TO GET THE HELL OUTTA MY HOUSE!"

Silas jumped to his feet. "What? Why, what I do?"

I shoved him. "GET OUT!" I screamed to the top of my lungs. "GET THE HELL OUT!"

He defiantly followed me back upstairs. "No, I'm not leaving. Tell me what I did wrong."

"I'm calling the police!"

"What did I do?"

When I got back in Dominic's room, I slammed the door behind me only to have Silas open it back up.

"What's wrong with him?"

I ignored Silas as I tried to get Dominic to stand and follow me to my room since my door had a lock on it. When I grabbed both of his wrist, I noticed that blood was leaking from both of his clenched fist.

"Dominic! Did you...?" I panicked. "Oh my God, he's bleeding!"

While Silas rushed over to pry open Dominic's hands, I hurried to the bathroom to grab what was left in the first aid kit. By the time I returned, Dominic's hands were open, and a bloody porcelain locomotive that was broken in half was sitting next to him on his bed. While we bandaged him, between tears, Dominic told us that he accidently dropped it.

"Are you sure that's exactly what happened?" I looked deep into Dom's eyes searching for truth.

He nodded slowly.

"Then boo, we can get you another one. There's no reason to be sad," I said tenderly. "I'll go get you another one first thing tomorrow."

"It's the last one," Dominic said sadly.

I looked at Silas helplessly.

"I can get that one fixed," he offered.

The tears had slowly come to a stop, and the thick fog of somber finally lifted. Silas tucked Dominic in bed while I was in the kitchen cleaning off his train and then packaging it into a Ziploc for Silas to take.

"So you live with your family."

I groaned, "Are we back on this?"

"Why?"

I snapped back, "Why, what??"

The frustration I felt about Dominic's two cuts and not knowing if he had done it purposely, must have taken over me. Before Silas could respond, I let him have it... probably too much.

"Because I'm a bum! Is that what you want to know? I have no job... *surprise*!!! In fact, I don't know where I'll be living by the end of the year either. I've been black balled by my ex. My savings account is empting, and my parents are tired of financially supporting their healthy grown-behind child who can't seem to get it together. *That's why*. Now that you know my business, are you satisfied?"

After a brief silence, Silas simply said, "Wow."

I leaned against the counter and avoided eye contact with him. "I'm a disgrace and nobody knows..." I motioned to an 11 x 13 family photo that was hanging on the wall. We took it when I was fourteen. Everyone matched with dark hair and big smiles except for me. I was the light-haired girl off to the left who had a slanted smile on her face and wore plaid instead of the hunter green sweater, because my father "accidently" spilled juice on it.

"*They know*," I said. "My father used to tell me that every single day, from when I was about age eight up until I went to college. 'You're a disgrace,' I mocked his tone of voice, and then laughed to mask the pain that still lingered whenever my past was poked and prodded, even after all these years. "When I complained about it, or about anything for that matter, I was told to be a 'Victor not Victim.' Do you see how confusing that is for a child?"

Silas didn't answer. He just stared at me blankly and rubbed his forehead.

"You asked," I said. "You told me you wanted to really know me… there it is. I'm a bum. I'm a disgrace"

"You're not a disgrace."

"… Only when I'm pretending not to be one."

CHAPTER 25

Tuesday night, I convinced Pastor Ronnie to meet me at this restaurant known for their sesame wings. It was located just a few minutes from his house. He was trying to wrap up some stuff at his church office, but he relented when I kept begging and pleading. I love a man that relents.

I had already downed two Coronas and was working on my glass of Riesling when Ronnie was approaching the table. He wore a fedora that matched his dark slacks, which hugged him to perfection. With the brim of my glass resting against my Poisoned Pink colored lips, my eyes fell to the print below his waist that appeared and then disappear, and then reappeared as he took each step strolling closer. It was amazing how this man still managed to be centerfold sexy even after being cooped up in the church chambers all day.

His dimple flashed and his juicy top lip curved as he smiled. "You dragged me here and started without me."

"It's been a tricky day. Trust me when I say that I needed it."

I stood up and tugged on the bottom of my nude bondage dress before I fell into his opened arms. The feel of his body pressed against mine made it hard for me to release him.

Like the gentleman he was, he helped me back into my side of the booth. "What's up? Rough day?"

"Very rough," I said. I gulped the last of my wine and wiped the corners of my mouth. "Yesterday my brother returned from a getaway with his boyfriend and came home to find his wife in bed with my masseuse."

I covered my mouth to belch quietly. "Needless to say, I need a new masseuse and I a need chiropractor. I've been helping her move her things all morning."

Ronnie took off his fedora, shook his head, and raised his eyebrows, obviously confused. "I'm not even sure I followed you correctly."

"Trust me. You heard right.

"Pray for them."

"What?"

"I know it's the typical, preacher response, but prayer works. Pray for them. We can pray from them right now. Give your hand."

I laughed. "What? No. I'm not talking to God. I've been drinking."

"Give me your hand. It's alright." Ronnie took my hand into his and lowered his head. "Most gracious God, we lift up Nola's brother and his wife, dear God. We ask that you cover them with Your spirit of healing, dear God. We ask that you cover them with Your spirit of forgiveness, dear God. We ask that You untangle them from the hands of the enemy, dear God, and that they will flee from sexual sin and restore their marriage, dear God...."

As Ronnie continued to plead with God on my brother's behalf, I looked around to see if anyone was watching us.

Ronnie said, "Amen!" and lifted his head. I was staring at him as if he had lost his wits." Why are you looking at me like at?" he asked, while sipping his water with lemon.

"Because you just invited God and His spirit in and - not to disrespect you or Him - I'm slightly inebriated. Not only that, they're playing twerk music over our heads."

"I got news for you, shorty…"

Shorty. Mmmm. I like that.

"He was already up in here. He's everywhere." Ronnie flipped through the menu. "How'd you find this place, anyway?"

"Reviews from yelp.com..." *Using a five-mile radius filter, from your address.*

After our waiter took our orders, took our menus, and refilled my glass, Ronnie's phone chimed. He lifted it, "Marley."

"Don't answer it!"

Ronnie stuffed his phone in his pants pocket. "Why not?"

"She'll ruin the mood. The vibe. And we're vibing… Aren't we?"

"Yeah, as long as I don't burst out into prayer…"

I reached over the table and playfully slapped Ronnie's arm. "Stop it!"

His dimple flashed.

I switched gears. "How have you been holding up? You know… after the break up…"

Ronnie shrugged and fumbled with a straw wrapper. "What God has for me, He has for me. What He doesn't, He doesn't."

"But, were you mad... Sad…?"

The waiter briefly interrupted our conversation to place a big dish of sesame wings in the middle of the table along with a plate of celery and Ronnie's side of steamed zucchini and squash. When she walked away, Ronnie answered my question.

"I was disappointed, but I'm getting over it."

"Well, I have something to speed up the recovery process." I took a bite of a wing, and then wiped my hands and mouth with the napkins. I reached under our table, and pulled out a large silver gift bag. I sat it on the table and pushed it towards him. "Go ahead and open it!"

Ronnie dug inside the bag and pulled out a wooden case that contained sterling silver grilling utensils. With that youthful smile that always made me melt, Ronnie read aloud the engravings on each of them. "Grill Master Ronnie… Chef Ronnie Robinson... Phenomenal Cook."

He neatly put everything back into the gift bag and took my hand. He helped me wiggle outta my seat to stand and give him another hug. "Thank you, Nola. I like 'em. That was thoughtful."

I inhaled his scent without any intentions of letting him go. Then my favorite Beyoncé song, "Get Me Bodied" played over the restaurant's speakers. I let go of his hand and clapped. "Mmmm mmm! This is my song, Ronnie!" I swung my hips to the rhythm. "I haven't heard this one in a minute! Dance with me!"

Ronnie shied away. "No. I'm good. Enjoy."

"No... No... No... Dance with me! It's clean music. Come on. Dance with me!" I took Ronnie's hand and whirled myself. Then I dipped and swayed my hips. Finally, he got into it with a two-step and seconds later he was grooving.

The both of us laughed hard as we followed Bey's commands to "do the Uh-oh, pat our weaves, and stop and cool off." Ronnie cleverly put his masculine spin on the moves and a small crowd formed and cheered us on. By end of the song, my belly was aching, and my cheeks were burning from how hard I laughed. Ronnie really opened up!

He was sprawled in the booth with his hand on his chest cracking up. "You... You have a way of making me feel young again."

My phone vibrated the table and without paying attention to the Caller I.D., I answered and pressed my finger in my other ear to hear clearly.

"Sounds like you're having fun."

"I am!" I laughed.

"Where are you?"

"New Jersey!"

It finally clicked that I should see who I was talking to before I shared my full whereabouts. When I saw Marley's name, I scurried to the ladies' room.

"I didn't get that. What did you say?"

"I asked what's happening in New Jersey."

"Wings and beer..."

Marley pried, "Oh. Who are you with, Silas?"

I took the phone off my ear and grimaced at it as if she could see. "Yeah. Maybe I am."

"No... You can't be with Silas. I just saw him at ShopRite..."

I smacked my thigh. "I'm out with my mother and Dominic. I wanna get back to them. Do you need anything?"

"I need to run a couple of errands for the wedding tomorrow. Can you come with me? I need your expertise."

"Yeah... Sure," I replied quickly.

"I'll be at your place at 8 a.m. We can do bible study and dinner with Greg and Silas after we run errands. "

"Okay, that's fine," I rushed.

Marley lingered, "So you don't work?"

"What? Oh! No, I'm off."

"OK… Well, 8 a.m."

I ended the call and checked my head full of loose curls. I reapplied my lipstick and joined Ronnie at the table He. as he was going in on his plate of wings.

After dinner and my third glass of Riesling, I was wobbly. Ronnie and I walked arm and arm through the parking lot. My heels click-clacked against the asphalt with an occasional slipping sound each time I lost my balance. I giggled and snorted. "This would be a terrible time for someone from church to see us."

Ronnie said, "Yeah. Tell me about it."

We stopped at his Lincoln.

"Listen, I'm gonna drive you home."

I nodded, "Great idea."

When he started up the car, the Bluetooth rang through the speakers, and Marley's name flashed on the touch screen. Ronnie immediately declined the call and shook his head. Under his breath, he said, "This would be too tough to explain right now."

I looked down at his phone resting in the cup holder. *Marley 5 Missed Calls* blinked on its lock screen. Two stoplights down the road, I tapped Ronnie's leg. "I have to pee badly."

"I'll make this U-turn."

"You can't," I said. "I have this phobia about using public restrooms."

Ronnie turned his head to look out his window, and then he looked to the right. "I don't see any woods anywhere. What are we supposed to do?"

"How about your place?"

"My place? You gonna make it?"

I shook my legs. "Yes... Yes, I'll make it. Just go. Hurry."

***

I slipped off my Jimmy Choo shoes as soon as we walked into Ronnie's house, and my bare feet scampered along his marbled flooring and into his powder room that was just off to the left of his foyer. After I tinkled, I took a couple of minutes in the mirror to make sure I didn't look as tipsy as I felt. When I opened the door, a trail of brewing dark roast coffee led me to his kitchen.

Ronnie already had a mug waiting for me on his island. I sat on the barstool and added cream and sugar. "I'm not really a coffee person," I said as I took a sip.

Ronnie turned from the counter with a mug in his hand and sat on the stool next to mine. "You're a tea person, but tea won't kill that buzz."

I smirked. "I'm not buzzed."

Being this close to Ronnie in his home at this hour was exactly what I've been wanting since I first saw him at Worship Way two months ago. I didn't want this moment to end. So, I took slow, tiny sips and asked long, open-ended questions in between. Questions like: how he felt about fasting? Who inspired him to preach? And where were the majority of his college friends located? I asked absolutely anything that had absolutely nothing to do with anything.

After a while, his cup was completely empty, his answers became short and dry, and he yawned every three minutes, glancing down at his watch. So, I shifted gears to spark some excitement.

"You're my ideal man."

"What? Where did that come from?"

"The tip of my tongue."

"It's the alcohol."

"It's sincere."

"I'm not your type, Nola. A woman like you need a fast paced guy who is young and full of life."

"You just described yourself. You're young at heart, you're gorgeous, and you know how to have fun."

"You're stunning yourself," Ronnie replied as his eyes traveled from my lips down to my crossed legs and pedicured toes.

When his eyes journeyed back up, I locked eyes with him. "I like you. I have a feeling that you're feeling me, too. I like how you love God and how compassionate you are. I even like how you adore Marley. No, actually I love that..." I spoke his to lips "And, I love your style. I love your sense of humor. I love your scent. And I love your smile..."

Ronnie leaned in and his scent wrapped itself around my body. He kissed just the corner of my lips, and quickly stood and put his mug down on the counter.

"Don't say anything else," he commanded, looking only at my sinister grin. "I tasted Riesling on your lips."

I laughed to myself.

"It's late. If you want to stay, I can take you to your car in the morning. I have a t-shirt you can sleep in..."

I suppressed my smile, and tried my best to hide the excitement that was building up inside of me. All I could think was, *"Yeah. He wants me."*

CHAPTER 26

Before I opened my eyes, lifted my head, or moved any muscle, I danced to all of love's possibilities. As Ronnie's thick, plushy comforter wrapped around my body, his soft pillows and Egyptian linens caressed my every angle. The morning zephyr glided through the opened windows whispering, "Every morning should be like this." As the risen sun kissed my eyelids, begging for all of the beauty to not just be felt, but seen, I finally obliged.

A to-go cup of FeliciTEA's was on his nightstand to the left of me. Scribbled on it was: "*It's about time you're awake. Hope this is the right kind*" I took a small sip. It was room temperature, but nonetheless the right flavor. I was impressed. I grabbed my purse that was on the floor by me and took out my pocket mirror, lip liner, and lip-gloss. The essentials so he could see that I was just as beautiful with barely any make-up on. Then, I teased my curls and created that messy, yet sexy wave look that men love.

In just his t-shirt, I met Ronnie in the living room. He was reclined with his feet kicked up on his leather ottoman. His arms were crossed, and his eyes were focused on sports highlights. He was dressed in black gym pants and a white tee that had his church name on it, which altogether made him look his age. The first time I saw him dressed completely down. But at least I wasn't turned completely off. He was still delicious to me, and I wanted to straddle him.

I nestled my bottom into his soft leather couch with my legs folded beneath me and my knees pressed against his thigh. He smelled shower fresh with a hint of light cologne. I took in his aroma, inhaling it, and breathing it deep into the corners of my memory box. I wanted to be able to smell him when he wasn't round. I wanted the mere thought of his presence to trigger and awaken my senses.

I asked, "So where did you sleep last night?"

"Where you were supposed to…" He spoke dryly and his eyes never left his 60" flat screen.

"I thought I was in the right room." I dusted imaginary lint off his shoulder to snatch his undivided attention. He didn't bite the bait.

"Is that right?" Ronnie shifted, leaving a few inches of space between us. It was then that reality slapped me with the certainty that the man didn't want me there. We sat in the most agonizing awkward silence that no human should ever have to endure, until I stood and shook my cup.

"You mind if I hit your kitchen to warm this up?"

Still avoiding eye contact, Ronnie motioned his head to the right. "Yeah… help yourself."

"Thanks." I smiled at the side of his head and then turned to jet out of there immediately.

He spoke to my back. "You still have on my shirt."

I smirked. *But, you can watch me walk away?* "I do, and it's pretty comfortable."

I turned to face him. His eyes crept slowly from my toes to my thighs, then from my thighs to my chest, and from my chest to my eyes… then, he shied away.

He scratched his scalp and said, "You should get ready to go."
***

"She's about to drive me up the wall," I groaned as I gripped the stirring wheel and threw the gear into park.

I was just about to call Marley and tell her I was getting dressed. I'm glad I didn't. She had beat me home, and even worse, she was parked behind Derrick. My dashboard read 10:34 a.m. There was no telling how long they'd been there together or what they talked about, and that gave me an unsettling feeling. I pulled a brush from my glove compartment and pulled my hair into a sleek bun. Then, I attempted to mask last night with bronzer, blush, and lipstick just in case I needed to make it seem like I ran out early this morning to do something.

Marley was on the couch with her purse on her lap and her legs crossed at her ankles, holding a glass of orange juice that Derrick probably had given her. The both of them were sitting on opposite sides of the couch watching the Wendy Williams show. Marley parted her lips to speak, but as soon as I said, "Good morning," with my apricot colored smile, Derrick jumped up and took me by the wrist.

He led me onto the back patio, slid the door closed, and stuffed his hands into his pocket. "Listen, I need your help."

I blurted out, "What if he's gay?"

Derrick's eyebrows wrinkled, and then smoothed when he caught wind of who I was talking about. "He's a Christian," he said.

"He rejected me. He could be gay."

Derrick shrugged. "He's probably not interested in sleeping with his daughters' friend."

"We're not friends. She's my soror. Not every soror is your friend. It's just like family. Not every cousin is your homie."

Derrick laughed. "Is that what you tell yourself?"

"I slept in the man's bed. I was standing there in nothing but his t-shirt and he didn't budge. Imagine Boris Kodjoe in your living room wearing nothing but boxers."

"First of all, you are not the female version of Boris. Let's not get ahead of ourselves."

"Move," I tried to push past him. "I need to explain why I'm late."

Derrick held my arm. "It's taken care of. Sit down."

I tilted my head and glared at him. "Whadduyou mean it's taken care of?"

"I told her you had to run something to mom at the hospital."

I gave Derrick the side eye, "What made you do that?"

"Because you've been gone since I met Miguel here early this morning, and she's been waiting since he and Dominic left out."

"Again, what made you do that?"

"I need your help. She's filing for divorce." Derrick pounded his fist along the railing of deck. "I gotta explain something to mom and dad. There's extra loot in your account. I know you could use it. Just..." Derrick lowered his head and in almost a whisper he said, "Just keep quiet about... you know."

"Of course, I will," I said sarcastically. "There's only room for one f-up in the family, and I have that slot occupied."

Derrick lifted his head up. "It can pay for the first six months of rent, if you choose somewhere reasonable to live."

The look of desperation on Derrick's face actually tickled me. I was seconds from pulling my phone from my purse and snapping a photo to save for when I needed a laugh. I sat on the bench, slipped off my shoes, and rubbed my ankle. My poor feet hadn't recovered from last night's dancing or the couple of times I almost slipped.

"Oh! While you're at it, set up a chiropractic visit for me. You owe me. That move killed my itty bitty body."

Derrick huffed, "You're being dramatic... Anything else you want me to do?"

"I'm just glad Alicia finally left you. Good for her."

Derrick glanced at his Rolex. "Anything else? I need to get to work."

"Do you even care that she left with your child? Or are you and the manny that preoccupied with yourselves?"

"Watch your mouth, Nola. It's not too late to cancel the transaction."

I flagged my hand at him and rolled my eyes. "You're just one screwed up, individual." I pointed to my chest. "I'm not the screwed up. *You're the screwed up one*. I'm your hero."

"You're scheming to sleep with your friend's father. For what? To marry him and gain financial security, Nola? Let's not get high and mighty now that you're about to get some holy penis."

I grabbed my shoes and stood up. "Oh so what, your lace panties are in a knot because I spoke the truth?" I pushed pass him. "You need me, Derrick. I don't need you.

I slid the patio door open.

Derrick spoke to my back, "Consider the transaction cancelled."

I gave him the finger without bothering to turn around.

"And, if anything gets out, Marley and all your soror friends will know what's up - *everything that's up.*"

***

Marley sat on the edge of my bed paging through a NORDSTORM catalogue, while I browsed for a dress in my walk-in closet, wearing nothing but my bra and panties. After sharing hotel suites for our sorority conferences over the years, walking around in a towel or even dressing in front of each other was about as normal as a mother drinking from her sweaty teenage child's soda bottle without a qualm. The sisterhood that comes with sorority is just powerful like that. It could also make a mere three months of friendship seem like there was a lifetime already invested. That's the reason why I fell in love with it. The women of this sorority didn't need to know my past or my vulnerabilities. They only need to see what I've shown them, and what I've continued to let them see. They adored who they thought I was, and although they would have accepted the real me with arms wide open, I felt better allowing them to believe what they saw - especially Marley.

"Lord, I gotta have these," she said in what almost sounded like a prayer.

I peeked out and looked at the cobalt sling backs that her bejeweled fingernail was resting on. Then, my focus fell on her full set of nails that had looked none other than my stylist Delilah's signature designs. *When did she go see Delilah? Why didn't tell me? She better had put my name down as a referral!*

157

Marley looked up and smiled. "Can I use your laptop? I wanna order these right now!"

At first, I was hesitant. *Now you're an avid shoe shopper?* "Yeah... go 'head. "I pointed to my desk.

When Marley stood and smoothed down her white pants, I couldn't help but notice the extra pounds she gained – especially in areas that complimented her figure. Her neat spiraled curls swayed as she sat in my chair and jiggled the mouse to take the monitor off sleep mode. I slipped back into my closet and decided on pants. My cargo camo joggers hugged my booty perfectly. I had to show Marley how to really rock a pair of pants, and remind her who the real fashion queen was.

"Nola, why does this coupon have your address?" Marley called.

I asked from the closet, "What are you talking about?"

"This So Smooth Spa Day coupon… It says it's a free spa treatment located at So Smooth Spa on its apparent grand opening date, but the address is yours."

When I realized that Marley was looking at the template I created to plant the coupon falling out of my purse, for Carmen to steal, and bring to the house, I nearly tripped over my pant legs and fell on my face. I must have leaped over my king bed with how fast I reached over Marley's shoulder and minimized EVERYTHING.

"My parents... They had a theme party here. They really get into it. They had me making all kinds of props." I shocked myself with how quickly I came up with that. I closed my laptop and sat down to tie my black strap sandals. "You know what? I just remembered that I have pair of shoes just like those. I wore them only once. They're by a different designer, but they're the same style and same color. And you know I only mess with high quality. You can have them."

I could feel Marley's eyeballs starting at me in disbelief. "Are you sure?"

"When have I ever been stingy with my things?"

"You don't have to do that, Nola. You should probably sell them on eBay. Get extra money out of it."

"And why should I do that?"

Marley stumbled on her speech, "Because... You should... save since..."

"Since what? ...Marley just hush."

Her shyness always frustrated me. I wanted to shake her sometimes, grab her by her arms and say, "Girl, be bold!" That right there was a prime example that no matter how much she tried to alter her style, she could never be Nola Victor.

I stood up, flicked my hair from my shoulder, and teased the curls so that it would get wavy. "There's a time for shopping and there's a time for saving," I said while putting on my black baby tee. "Don't act like I don't hook you up. If you feel you're too good and mighty to take my cobalt sling-backs, don't take them. Just don't forget that I'm the reason you look the way you do."

Three times, Marley looked like she wanted to say something but stopped. She let the conversation drop and went into the closet to find the pair of shoes.

"Hurry," I rushed her while I put on my shades and slid my purse on my arm. "We were supposed to get started hours ago."

CHAPTER 27

It was awkward sitting on the first pew, sandwiched between Marley and Silas while Pastor Ronnie Robinson facilitated bible study class.

I couldn't even recall agreeing to sit front and center with the man who I've lusted for, while the man who I hoped to marry one day, stood directly in front of the both of us. It wasn't until Marley mentioned during lunch, with a mouth full of California spring rolls, that I promised Silas and I would be pairing with her and geeky Greg for a "Christian couple night".

Marley was so excited about our Bible Study double-date, that avocado flew from between her teeth and landed on our table while she talked. I guess I also agreed to going to dinner with them afterwards. That wasn't going to happen. I needed to stay back and confront Ronnie. I needed to ask about his cold behavior towards me this morning, and why he avoided eye contact with me the entire study.

Silas pulled me to the side while we were in the church lobby. It was right after I fed him, Marley and Greg some BS story about my menstrual keeping me from joining them for dinner.

He looked like he had it rough at work before he came here. His circle patterned tie dangled around his neck, his suit jacket had a coffee stain by the pocket, and his shirt was wrinkled and hanging out of his pants. The only neat thing about him was his freshly shaped-up red hair and his beaming white teeth.

"Hey," he smiled. "How's Dom?"

"He's cool… Thanks for asking about him."

"That's my lil homie."

Cute. I giggled.

"Listen. Give me your email address. A couple of positions opened up at our company. I'll send them to you"

"Which positions?"

"There's one in the Marketing and Communications department, and there are a few in Finance. They're entry level or willing to train."

"Entry level? Uh uhn. No. Not enough money. Not interested." I was about to walk away.

Silas held my arm. "Aye, it's not like you in a position to be choosey."

I snatched my arm away. "Excuse me?!'"

Silas placed his hand on my mouth and looked around to see if my tone had alerted anyone. In almost a whisper he said, "All I'm saying is that you need to take what you can get."

I looked at him like he had lost his mind, because he obviously had. "I never asked for your help, and I sure as hell didn't ask for your input."

Silas backed up. "You're tripping, man."

My facial expression didn't change. "Who the hell do you think you are, telling me what I need?"

Silas flexed his jaw and slowly shook his head. Then, he stepped closer. His chest was getting so close to my face that by reflex I lifted my hands and pressed against him.

He spoke through grit teeth, "I could really go in on you right now, Nola. But, since we in God's house Im'ma let it go and walk away."

With that, his torso bumped my body as he walked away from me. He slapped hands with Greg and nodded goodbye to Marley who were both standing by the doors gawking at each other. Marley immediately rushed over as soon as Silas exited.   "Everything ok? Silas looked upset."

I probably should have mentioned that her friend Silas had a temper, came off aggressively, and was showing signs of being low-key crazy... On the contrary, I found it very sexy and attractive that I could bring him to frustration that easily.

"He's taking it hard that I can't come tonight."

Marley semi-pouted, "Aww!"

Then, she quickly switched gears. Without easing into it she flat out asked me, "So, how was last night? I know that you stayed out somewhere because of the dress you had on this morning. You wouldn't slip that on to run to your mom's job."

Marley looked like it pained her to wait for my response, so I waited. I took a long pause and pretended as if I was afraid to let her know, just to teach her a lesson about being nosey.

Finally, I said, "I was with Silas."

Marley looked like she started breathing again, and replied, "Oh!"

My eyebrows gathered on my forehead. "Where did you think I was?"

Marley turned pink and laughed nervously, "It's silly. Never mind that..." She tilted her head towards the exit and asked, "You heading out?"

I held my stomach. "Go without me. I need to hit the ladies' room."

Marley caressed my arm before she left with Greg.

"Hope you feel better."

   ***

I watched Marley and Greg leave the church parking lot, and then walked right by the ladies' room and into Ronnie's office. He looked like he was about to break outta there. He was by his desk stuffing folders into a bag, and his fedora was already on his head. I lightly tapped on his door. He looked up briefly to say, "What's up."

There was still tension there, so I kept my distance and leaned against the entryway. "Nice study, tonight," I said to break the ice.

Ronnie shook his head and smirked. Even with a smirk, his dimple flashed. "You know, you don't have to come back here and feed me your false encouragements every time I preach." He never looked back up as he spoke. "90% of the time, I know I'm good."

Ronnie walked over to his bookshelf, grabbed a book, and stuffed that into his bag, too - all without making eye contact with me.

"What are you talking about?" I asked, looking at the profile of his face.

He spoke quickly and brashly, "You know what I'm talking about. I've been teaching for twenty years. I have a knack for distinguishing who's really paying attention. You haven't listened to one sermon since you started visiting here. Yet you always deem it necessary to tell me, I've done well."

I struggled with finding the right words to say. He had me, and I couldn't deny it. I never paid attention him. I was too busy thinking about more important things like how long it would take him to fall madly in love with me. "What's wrong with you? Why are you being so hostile?"

Ronnie zipped and buckled his bag. "I think you're taking it that way."

"No I'm not. You haven't looked at me all night, and you didn't look at me this morning. You've been short and agitated. What's the problem?"

The pastor and I paused as a group of stragglers came walking down the hall and pass the office.   When the hall sounded clear, Ronnie spoke up. "I'm not talking about it here."

"Ok fine. I'll wait for you in my car."

I marched out before Ronnie could say anything else. Fifteen minutes later, the lights inside the church went out and Ronnie and some other man were walking out and locking up. The man slapped hands with Ronnie and walked to a Jeep parked on the side street. When Ronnie looked like he was starting towards his own car, I tapped my horn and waved my hand out the window. I parked only about four spaces away from his car. How could he miss me? I immediately caught an attitude. His act was getting old.

Ronnie came to my car, opened the passenger door, slid the seat back to accommodate his legs, and sat down. His sweet cologne took the pleasure of overpowering my lilac scented car freshener. "Let's make this quick. I have early morning plans."

"It's like you woke up this morning and suddenly decided that I was an inconvenience," I spoke sweetly trying hard to mask my 'tude. "I thought we were friends. I thought we connected and were getting along great."

Ronnie took his time to respond as if he was being sure to select his words carefully. He looked straight ahead and said, "Silas... he's really feeling you. Marley talks about you two all the--"

I lifted my hand and cut him short, "All the time? Silas and I aren't even around each other enough for Marley to have something to talk about all the time."

Marley was beginning to aggravate my soul with her blocking.

Ronnie finally looked at me when he asked, "You're not dating him?"

"I'm single."

I felt his tension ease up. I sighed. Then I broke the silence.

"Hold up wait. Is that why you've been acting weird? Because of Silas?" I laughed. "Are you the jealous kind? You act like you and I are seeing each other... or are we?"

Ronnie shook his head and laughed. He bashfully looked away, which was kinda cute. He looked at me again. "It was crazy walking upstairs into my bedroom to see you under my covers with your hair stretched over all of my pillows."

He paused and looked away as he rested his elbow on the armrest. He pressed his thumb onto his chin. I could tell he was holding back something he wanted to say.

I softly said, "Just tell me..."

"You reminded me a lot like Margo - my wife." He then sat up and spoke clearly. "It's like I was excited... happy, you know. I felt full and I wanted you. I wanted to hold you... but not *you*... Margo."

He stopped and looked at me from the corner of his eyes. "You think I'm crazy, don't you?"

Still burning after he stung me with the words, "…but not you… Margo," I just shook my head.

He went on, "Then, just that like that…" Ronnie snapped his fingers. "I got upset. I resented you being there."

"Wow" was all that I could say.

Ronnie continued, "I prayed about it, and I realized two things. One, I'm still mourning my wife. Two, I may not be ready to date yet."

I swept everything he had just said under my car rug.

"You seem stressed. Let's go get ice cream."

Ronnie slowly shook his head to decline. "I have an early morning."

"It's just ice cream," I pressed. "God's not gonna get mad at you for taking a few moments to chill and eat ice cream."

Ronnie took moments to think about it, and I sat on the edge of my seat waiting. I was preparing for a letdown. Just before I could get frustrated and shout, "JUST FORGET IT!" he finally asked, "Where are we going?"

***

We ended up at Coldstone Creamery just over the bridge in New Jersey. It was my suggestion. Our ice cream outing turned into a television in-ing at his place. Surprisingly, it was his suggestion. We started out on opposite ends of his couch watching a Modern Family marathon. Both of us had our feet up with his stretched towards mine and mine stretched towards his.

During a commercial break, I crawled over to him and collapsed my head onto his chest. His arm fell on my back, I held tight onto his waist, and we slept like that until dawn. The next morning wasn't awkward at all. To make sure it stayed that way, I got up, brewed him some coffee, and got out of there before he woke up.

***

165

"No. I don't feel like it. I don't wanna do anything today."

I could hear Dominic fussing when I walked through the front door. His deep voice carried from the kitchen.

"I don't even wanna be a grown up anymore. I want to be child forever like Nola."

I caught the tail end of his statement at the doorway. The manny sucked his lips in and blushed when he saw me. My father was in there as well. He was sipping from a mug and smirking.

"Good morning… And, I'm not a child, Dom." I greeted him with a kiss on the cheek. "I'm an adult like you."

Dominic sounded confused when he asked, "You are?"

My father dropped his mug in the sink. "You are a very smart man, Dominic."

Then he patted Dominic on the shoulder, wrote the manny a check, and left out for work, walking right by me as if I were invisible.

The manny stuffed the check into his tight pants pocket and reasoned with Dominic. "Okay, you don't have to go to your program or to your job, Dom. Everybody deserves a break. We can just hang here or go to a quiet museum."

Dominic blurted, "I wanna go to the train station."

"You can handle that?" the manny asked him but looked at me. I shook my head in disagreement. The manny scratched his head.

"Let's think about that. For now, let's just relax here."

Dominic agreed and left the manny and me in the kitchen. It was actually the first time we were alone together since he got back from his getaway affair with my brother. Since Alicia's fight with Derrick, I had a feeling that the manny was purposely trying to avoid me. He was always exiting any room that I entered or keeping his head down when we crossed paths in the hallways. I was looking in the refrigerator for a bottled water when he spoke to me.

"Listen, I just wanna tell you that it's over 'tween me and Derrick."

I spun around quicker than a Tasmanian, "Really??? Since when? Why?"

The manny flagged his hands. "Girl he had the nerve to dump me. He said I was ruining his life." He rolled his eyes and sucked his teeth. "No, I haven't ruined your life, yet!"

I giggled, but then got serious. "No, don't do anything to mess up your job here. It won't be fair to Dominic."

"I'm just so mad," he said as he looked up at the ceiling like he was fighting back tears. "You won't see him around here much anymore, since I was the only reason he came to visit anyway... No offense."

"What? None taken! You think I didn't know? They praise that man like he's Jesus, but as soon as he left for college he never looked back. He never called or anything until he brought you here."

The manny nodded, "This is a closed chapter... And, I mean it this time."

CHAPTER 28

"Oooo… this is our song! Remember?"

"Uhh yeah?"… It's hard to forget it when it's played on every DJ's dance mix

Bailey grabbed my arm, swayed her hips, and said, "Then let's go stroll."

"No! I don't wanna sweat my hair out."

President Gabrielle and her husband Adonis threw themselves a vow renewal ceremony at a lovely banquette hall located in North East Philly. The guests were required to wear formal attire. They invited the entire chapter, other sororities, and fraternities from the region, as well as her church family. Of course, I had to splurge on the absolute best, so I purchased a lace Jovani gown with tulle and beading. Once again, Delilah came through with making my tresses look regal and my nails superb. My hair was pinned to the side with cascading curls that fell below shoulders, and my nails matched my dress to the exact hue.

"Girl, bye." Bailey released her grip. "You're not gonna sit pretty all night. Let's dance!"

"Where's Marley? Wasn't she invited?" From my seat, I tried to look through the throng of people partying in their gowns and tuxedos, as if it were prom fifteen to thirty years ago all over again.

"Of course she was invited." Bailey whipped out her pocket mirror and teased her natural curls. She always wore it big - really big. Had she pressed it, she'd probably look like the black Rapunzel. "She's probably running late. You know she's busy with wedding stuff." She closed her mirror. "You better get up and dance before Soror President thinks you're bored."

The truth was that I wanted to get up. I wanted to circle the place, mix and mingle, and even stand arm and arm with Gabrielle who adored me. I wanted to dance, and I wanted to eat, but I couldn't. I wanted to wait for Marley. I had a feeling she was trying to pull one of my numbers and arrive fashionably late. Why wouldn't she? She was already using my stylist, imitating my swag, and even picking up my habits. The last thing I needed was for someone to catch me with a curl out of place or my lipstick smudged, while she's waltzing in looking like Princess Diana reincarnated.

Bailey gave up on begging and hit the dance floor without me, but that didn't stop President Gabrielle from finding me moments later. She looked absolutely gorgeous in a gold sparkling gown that had a long train. Her hair was styled in a sophisticated up-do. Her arms were stretched out as she came towards me.

"Noooooola! There you are!"

I rose and kissed her on the cheek.

"I want you to meet my closest family friends!"

Gabrielle took my hand as she weaved me through tables and around the dance floor. I smiled, nodded, and received loads of kisses on the cheek as she introduced me as "a young and emerging real estate mogul who is about her business, and something to watch out for." Various people gave me their business cards, and Gabrielle pressured me to give my number to people who were interested in doing business with me in the near future. My palms and underarms were beginning to get sweaty as I answered questions about my non-existent classes and my non-existent internship. I was rescued when Gabrielle's husband interrupted a conversation by pushing his way through our mini circle and landing an unexpected passionate, yet aggressive kiss on her lips. It caught us off guard, but I used that opportunity to back a few steps away and slide out of the circle. I watched from outside the circle as Adonis whispered something in Gabrielle's ear and stepped off. She excused herself from her friends and approached me with a slanted smile.

"The hubby needs me at our table."

I smiled, "Aww. I envy you two. You're just perfect."

"There's no such thing." Gabrielle's smile faded and she added, "I'll tell you a little secret that I told Marley last week."

She looked behind herself and then back at me. Her eyes locked with mine, and she spoke low enough for only me to hear "Behind what seems like perfection is a beautiful lie threatening to erupt."

I grimaced. What was that supposed to mean? And, what made her tell Marley that?

Gabrielle glided off to join Adonis. They locked hands and kissed again before posing for their photographer. I was balling up business cards and tossing them in my clutch when Bailey approached me again.

"Check your phone for an email!" she cheered.

"Why?"

"Marley's bridesmaids sent an evite to her surprise bridal shower. It's so cute!"

Bailey pulled it up on her phone. There was an animation of a champagne bottle popping out the word. "Shhhh..." along with confetti. Underneath that, glittery words appeared with the event's description, location, and time.

I smirked, "Looks cheap."

Bailey nudged my arm.

"Don't be mean."

"I'm being real. I would never send an evite for a bridal shower. That's so tacky. It's a wedding - a once in a lifetime big deal. You're so supposed to go all out for the bride and send actual invitations not this crap."

I pushed Bailey's phone away.

"If I ever get engaged again and make you my bridesmaid, you better not!"

Bailey laughed as she tucked her phone in her purse.

"Well if you do plan to be engaged again, you better snatch your future husband while you're here. These men have it going on."

"They have nothing on my boo," I spoke confidently.

Bailey's jaw dropped as she playfully slapped my arm.

"Why didn't you tell me? Shoulda known... A woman like you could only stay single but for so long. I wanna meet him."

"You will at the right time." I smiled as I thought about entering formal events like this, while arm-and -arm with a dapper dressed Ronnie.

The dinner was over after an hour. Marley never showed up and neither did her evite. *Those ratchet birds didn't send me one.*

I kissed Bailey on the cheek and waved goodbye when valet returned with her car. While I waited for them to return with mine, I spotted Gabrielle's white Audi pulling from the VIP parking area. She was in the passenger seat and Adonis was driving. They looked to be in an intense argument as Gabrielle's hands wagged in Adonis's face. As I watched them argue, I heard a couple behind me speaking lowly, in almost a mumble.

The man said, "Look. Those two are at again."

The frustrated woman replied, "Gots to be kidding me. Told, you. He's no good. I wish she'd forget what the bible says and just leave."

The rest of the crowd, who obviously didn't catch the altercation, clapped, cheered, shouted "Woohoo!" as Adonis screeched off.

CHAPTER 29

"Hello, Jerks! Don't just stand there. Help!"

The three college boys that were in line looked stunned as they walked over to me. They were stunned that I just snapped on them for staring at me as if I was a circus freak, and probably stunned at the fact that a woman dressed in a formal dress was alone at FeliciTEA's at 9 p.m. I couldn't blame them. I loved FeliciTEA's dearly, but being there on a Friday night *was* pretty pathetic, especially for a woman in her late twenties. I just wasn't ready to head home. Had I known Gabrielle's Vow Renewal ceremony would end so early, I would have tried to make plans with Ronnie.

After the guys helped me free the bottom of my gown which got caught underneath the door, my eyes instantly fell on a man who was rising from a table all the way in the back. His back was towards me and he had a baseball cap on his head, but from observing his posture, I knew it had to be Silas. I picked up the tail of my gown, walked over, and tapped him on the shoulder.

"Leaving so soon?"

The guy, who certainly wasn't Silas, nor was he easy on the eyes, turned around and pulled his headphones from his ears. "I'm sorry. What was that?"

I pointed to his chair. "Oh... oh, I asked were you leaving. I wanted the table."

"Oh, yeah. Yeah." He grinned and stuffed his books into his bag. "It's all yours."

I sat down and watched while he walked away. I wanted to call Silas just for the hell of it. Just 'cause I missed his hunched walk. Just 'cause I missed the way he sweated me. However, I quickly remembered he was pissed, and I canned that idea. After a cup of mango green tea, I decided at least to call Marley. I was curious to know why she didn't show up at the dinner tonight. To my surprise, she sent me to the voicemail after just two rings. Usually, she wouldn't let my call get past one ring.

***

I couldn't sleep that night. Maybe I had too much sugar in my tea. I kept having nightmares about Dominic, a train, and his bloody hands that were gory compared to the other night. In the dreams, Dominic was running and sometimes skipping through a meadow. He was laughing and pointing towards a train in the distance. While he pointed, his hands got bloodier and bloodier. Eventually, large chunks of his hands began to fall off.

I shuddered as I jerked from my sleep for the third time. My room was pitch black aside from the little bit of light that peeked beneath my door. A nightlight we plugged in the hallway for Dominic. This time I tiptoed down the down hall to check on my baby brother. He was sleeping peacefully. The cuts on his hands still healed. I kissed him on the forehead and climbed back into my bed. The dream returned. Dominic was running through a meadow laughing and singing my name. He sang my name in a blissful baritone key as large chunks of his hands, once again began falling off. With each chunk fallen his voice got higher, and higher. When he hit a soprano note, I jerked from my sleep.

"Nola! Damnit!"

When my eyes got into focus, I saw Alicia standing over me with her arms folded. Saturday's sun was up and birds were chirping.

"What? Are you dead already?"

I pulled back my comforter and jetted down the hall to Dominic's room. It was empty and his bed was made. I walked back into my room. Alicia had her hands on her hip. Her lips were pressed together tightly and her eyes were like daggers. I returned the exact look and asked where my baby was.

"They were leaving as I was coming. Nobody's here but me and you." She rolled her neck as she spoke. "We need to talk."

I ran my hands through my hair and stretched. My eyes felt heavy, my voice was groggy, and I was still shaken up by my eerie dreams. The last thing I wanted to do was have a conversation with Alicia, who was already pissed off, by most likely Derrick again. I pointed my thumb to my door.

"Well, you need to wait for me downstairs so I could at least brush my teeth and get outta this t-shirt." I was wearing one of Trav's old tees. It fit me like a sloppy dress designed for the morbidly obese. It was a V-neck, so if I wasn't careful, a boob would surely pop-out. There were a few tiny holes in the sleeves, but I loved the shirt. It was comfy.

Alicia wasn't having it. "You think I care about your t-shirt?"

She had been dropping hints the entire time, but it wasn't until I heard of her tone of voice that I realized her wrath wasn't for Derrick. It was for me. "You think I care about your teeth? You're about to get bust *between* your teeth."

At first, I just stood there, trying to make sense of what I had just heard. Then, I laughed. I couldn't help it. When did little good-wife   Alicia become thugged out? Fueled by my laughter, she pointed her finger to my face. "I could have knocked you out stone cold while you slept, but I told myself, 'I'll be a woman about it and let her speak her piece.' So, Im'ma ask you one question and one question only." Alicia stepped forward. "Did you pay Villain to go out with me?"

Not only did the woman have the audacity to confront me in my home in my bedroom, while I wore nothing but a beat-up T-shirt, she questioned me like she was a boss. Maybe I would have responded differently if she hadn't done that, but because she did, I let my words slice her.

"Yeah I paid him, *and* I had to beg him. Why are you mad? Nobody told you to smash Villain. And it's not my fault that my brother got bored with your washed-up vagina."

CLOCK! Alicia's fist connected with my face.

174

My neck snapped back as I fell backwards against my dresser. My vision was blurry, but I had enough sense to swing with one hand and use the other one to reach for something to hit her across the head with. She managed to grip me by my hair and I felt myself being yanked from one side of the room to the other side like a rag doll.

Seemed like the more I scratched her hands and punched on her arms, the tighter she locked onto my hair. She was on top of me on the floor of my bedroom entryway when I saw a pair of tan A.P.C. shoes and navy slacks approach. Alicia's weight was lifted off me. I sat up just in time to see my father guiding her downstairs. She was crying and yelling, "She tried to sell me like a prostitute! She treated me like a prostitute! ... Your son is a cheater and your daughter sold me like a prostitute!"

My bedroom was a wreck, and my favorite t-shirt was blood stained. I was in my mirror examining the cut on the side of my swollen eye and dabbing it with toilet tissue, when I felt my father's presence at my door. "Dad, I think I need you to go to Walgreen's for first aid. I used the last of it on Dom."

"Take yourself."

I looked at him. His chest was puffed up, and he was red with fury like he was the one involved in the fight. "What? How? I can barely see."

"You're that bitter of a person. You ruined your life and now want to ruin marriages? Take yourself." He seethed, "and you deserve every bit of what was given to you."

My father turned away, but I followed him down the hall and into his office. "No, I didn't ruin my life. *You* ruined my life."

"Get out," he commanded with his back turned.

"You ruined my life when I was four and you pushed my head into the toilet bowl, remember?"

My father swung around and pointed his wrinkled finger in my face. "Lies!"

"I was trying to lift my head back up, and you made me knock my tooth out when you forced my head back down against the porcelain. You made me lie to the doctors and lie to the family. You made me tell them that I tripped. You think I was too young to remember?"

My father's wrinkled face and flabby jaw trembled. "I said get outta my office!"

"You ruined me at age five when you left me at the gas station in the middle of that snowstorm."

"You snuck outta the car."

"That's what you told mom, but we know the truth. I remember the truth. *You left me.* You sent me in the store to buy a bag of chips, and I watched you from the window. You left me!"

My voice cracked. I felt myself about cry, but I held it together. "And then, when you picked me up, you told me not to cry because I was a 'Victor, not a victim.' You ruined me at age six, when you made me wipe Derrick's piss with a paper towel every time he had a bad aim. You ruined me with the constant name-calling and limitless confusion with the 'I love you, but I can't stand you' comments."

"Who's gonna believe that? No one will believe that."

"Then, after the mental torture, you always showered me with gifts and money just to keep me quiet. Or, maybe you were paying me to forget? Your money definitely can't erase the multiple times you almost killed me but failed."

My father's voice boomed throughout the house as he yelled, "I SAID GET THE HELL OUT!"

CHAPTER 30

Less than thirty minutes later, I was on Silas's bed. He was the only one who picked up my call. I only had enough time to slip on a plain white T-shirt and jeggings before he arrived. My hair didn't stand a chance, and at that point, I didn't care. He ran to a pharmacy by his home, scooped me up, got us some Thai take-out, and drove us to his laidback, regular house out in the Mt. Airy section of Philly. I was surprised that he came. Thought he was still mad at me. Instead, he spoke to me as if our altercation never happened. He was only concerned with my fight with Alicia and the following details.

When I got in the car, he touched my cut and kissed it. Kind of like a father would do. I smiled. The frustration and boiling anger I felt for Walter Victor lifted from my spirit and evaporated above our heads. That's when I knew that Silas and I were good. I didn't know what to expect when I hopped in his Infinity, but I was desperate and prepared for an argument. Nothing was worse than being trapped inside the house with my father. When Silas pressed his lips against my bruised eye, I knew he wasn't going to bring up Wednesday. Not a drop of grudge tainted this man's tall muscular body. Then again, how could it when his mother is wickeder than Maleficent? He has forgiven even her.

He had two dozen fully bloomed white carnations waiting for me in his bedroom. He split the flowers into two vases on each side of his bed, where we sat directly in front of each other while he aided me.

"It looks like she got you with her wedding ring. You gonna press charges?" Silas asked while he dapped me with peroxide.

"Yeah, right. Walter Victor is her key witness."

"I'll make it better." I watched Silas's mouth moved and his jaw flexed as he pressed down on the gauze.

He was taking good care of me, but it was hard for me to feel completely appreciative; I wanted Ronnie. I wanted his hands. I wanted to be with *him* on his bed not Silas's. The only reason we were up there was because his downstairs area was being renovated. Otherwise, we'd be on his couch where it would be less tempting... I suppose.

He wadded up the bandage wrappers, tossed them in his trash basket, left me in his room for a few minutes, and returned with a light pink boa and an easel. He also brought with him that familiar slanted sinister grin from Hightower's Diner. "I want your body. I want it raw."

I nearly choked, "You are THE raunchiest Christian I know!"

He set up his easel and canvas and opened a large kit that looked like rolling luggage. It was filled with pastels, colored pencils, paints, and all other kinds of art junk.

"Not in a sexual way," Silas reassured as he aligned his supplies onto his tray. "…yet."

He tossed me the boa. "Take off your shirt."

Something about the look in his eyes and the command in his tone turned me all the way on. Still, it wasn't enough to get me to be his artistic subject - not with a bruise between my lid and brow the size and shape of Madagascar. I resisted.

"Is this what you say to get up a girl's skirt? 'Let me paint you a portrait?'"

Silas raised his eyebrow and looked serious when he said, "Usually I don't have to say anything."

"I don't want you to draw a picture of me. Look at me. My hair isn't fixed. Plus, I look like Spot the pup."

Silas laughed. The sound of it tickled me. Once he got ahold of himself he said, "Nah... You look... real. I like you better this way."

I stood up, turned my back towards him, slid off my shirt and bra, and wrapped the boa around my bare shoulders and breast.

"Turn around," he commanded softly.

I started towards him. As got I closer, I could hear him breathe. I felt him watching me as I ran my fingers along his kit, closely admiring the hundreds of colors. An unopened bottle of metallic silver body paint attracted me the most. It stood out from all the pastels and all the dull colors. It was desperate for attention and longing for appreciation and respect. Unlike the rest, it couldn't blend in even if it tried. It was surrounded by so many hues, yet alone. I pulled it out and dipped my fingers in it. It was smooth, exotic, soft, yet bold. It was dark yet bright, and it shined as it coated every one of my fingertips, wrapping itself around fluidly dependent on my touch.

Silas took my wrist, and wedged his fingers between mine. Now the metallic silver coated him too. He wrapped my arms around his neck and gently kissed them as he guided me to straddle his lap. With my breast pressed against his chest, I could feel his rapid heartbeat through his shirt. He sucked in my bottom lip, then slid his tongue in with ease like liquid. Our body heat rose, and so did self-control. There was metallic silver on his face, my waist, my tights, his pants, his bare chest, and my bare thighs. Then it transferred to his sheets as I laid with his pillowcase gathered between my teeth. There was a metallic silver mess all over our sweaty naked bodies all afternoon and into the evening. We only rested to catch our breath and start again.

***

The jarring ringtone I used for Ronnie caught my attention while I was on top of Silas. My phone vibrated against the vase of carnations and when I reached for it, Silas locked his hands on my waist.

"Yo... Whoever it is…they can wait."

I looked down at him and tried so hard to regain focus, but I couldn't - not when Ronnie was ringing my phone. It was as if something clicked and I didn't even want to be there anymore. I felt ashamed, dirty, and guilty. I released Silas's grip and climbed off. I grabbed my clothes, my phone, rushed into his bathroom and answered just in time.

"Ronnie."

"Nola, sorry I missed your call earlier. It got hectic for me all day. You won't believe I'm checking my phone for the first time since this morning."

I smiled at the sound of his voice. "You're fine."

"You good?"

I looked at my naked self in the mirror. I had a bruised eye, matted hair, paint and sweat on my body, and moist passion between my legs. *No, I'm not alright.* "I had a little situation earlier. I'm cool now."

"Alright cool. By the way, I'm in your neck of the woods."

I almost rose my voice, "Are you??"

"The God's Tabernacle Worship Center."

"Oh. Never heard of it," I said while slipping on my jeggings.

"I'm guest speaking tonight. Come out. It starts at six. And, anyway, you owe me for forcing me in that wing joint."

I glanced at the time on the phone. I had only about 1 hour and 30 minutes to get decent and cute. That was not enough time.

"I really wish I could I'm just tied up. How about we grab a bite to eat afterwards? Your pick and my treat..."

Ronnie took a moment before he responded. "I don't think I can handle a late night. I have Sunday worship service in the morning."

His rejection burned me. "Right... I understand."

Silas was sitting on the edge of his bed with just his boxers on, and his face was buried in his hands. He picked his head up when he felt my presence. "I feel bad..."

"Me too." I feel like I cheated.

"God's conviction... It's real isn't it?"

"Yeah, sure is." Whatever that means.

CHAPTER 31

"I'm sorry, what? Who did you say this was?"

I took the phone off my ear and looked at the phone number on the screen. It didn't look familiar, and it didn't help that the hooded dryer I was sitting under made it difficult for me to hear.

"Can you hear me now, Sister Nola? I said this is Deaconess Michelle Camper from Worship Way Baptist Church. You joined over a month ago in April. And well, it's June now. We haven't seen you in any of the new members' classes. I don't believe I've seen you at church in the mornings either. I was just checking to see how you were doing, if you had any concerns, or if there's anything you may need help with."

Although the deaconess's tone was very warm and affectionate, sounding as if she did genuinely care where I've been, I was pretty sure that she was simply list checking for the books. I've had to do the same for our chapter when members would take a hiatus. Nine times out of ten, I could care less about the soror's absence. Surely, they had a pretty good reason for why they've been m.i.a. It wasn't my business to care nor was it to pry. I only wanted the numbers.

Delilah walked over and patted my perm rods. My hair must have been dry, because she invited me back to her station.

"You know what Ms. Deaconess Michelle Camper, I've been so busy with work that the classes slipped my mind. I do apologize," I explained while I gathered my purse and magazine and sat in Delilah's chair. "Are those classes really required? I just don't see how I could fit something like that into my crazy schedule."

I needed my weekends free. Pursuing Ronnie while keeping Silas busy was beginning to feel like a full-time gig plus overtime. It had been two and a half weeks since that day Silas and I were intimate. Since then, avoiding him became more difficult than dodging the credit card bill collectors who just recently figured out my parents mailing address and telephone number. Lucky enough they hadn't done any pop-ups, unlike Silas who had become infamous for that. So far, his gestures had been sweet, though, which made it increasingly difficult to snap on him for his random house runs. I couldn't turn down a man who doted tickets to the zoo for Dominic and me or reservations to a paint and wine class. Unfortunately, a few days ago, he popped up and I was with Ronnie at a cigar lounge in Philly. My lips were cuffing a Bolivar, and Silas's lips were probably poked out and pouting as he read my text message: "I'm out. Not coming home anytime soon."

"Well, Sister Nola, to be an official member of Worship Way, the classes *are* required. Afterwards you will receive the right hand of fellowship, and then move right into joining a ministry. I can't force you to take these classes. I can only recommend them." The Deaconess's voice was still warm and friendly. "How about this... You're paperwork reads that you live in Wilmington. So do I. If you would like, we could meet and do this one on one and get you caught up. I really want you to experience the full fellowship with the Lord, Nola. It's nothing like allowing God to use you and guide you. You don't want to be a person who only shows up to church. Be a part of the family."

Deaconess Michelle's persuasion crept over my shoulders and hugged me from behind as Dominic would when he wanted to whisper his appreciations for me in my ear. The word "family" made my heart smile, reminding me that if I wanted Ronnie to be my husband, he would become my family along with his entire church. I would be their Leading Lady - representative of all the Worship Way women. I would be their go-to. Deaconess Michelle didn't know it yet, but I didn't need those classes to be officially a part of the family. What I needed was a certain signed document and a shiny 3.5 ct. diamond ring. I turned down the offer, and the deaconess gracefully ended the call.

"Goodness. What is with you and your girl being on the phone with church people when y'all sit in my chair?" Delilah was halfway through unraveling my rods. "How can I be nosey about what's going on in your life if ya'll always the phone?" She smiled at me through the mirror and flipped her fire engine red hair.

"Marley?"

Delilah nodded.

"How often does she come here anyway?"

"Just about as often as you… She brought one of her bridesmaids a few days ago… the heavyset girl. She invited me to the surprise shower."

I swung around to face her. "And you better not go!"

"If you don't turn your butt around! I almost snapped my fingers on this perm rod." Delilah spun my seat.

"They're messy, Delilah." I went on, eyeing her through the floor length mirror. "Hating heifers…"

"Marley hired me to do their hair for the wedding."

"Hell no!" I shouted loud enough to be heard over the blow dryers and the classic R&B mix playing from the hanging flat screen. A few ladies sitting in the waiting area behind me, lifted their heads up from their magazines.

Delilah slapped my arm with her comb and giggled.

"Cut it out! What's wrong with you? That's your girl."

"It's those nasty bridesmaids. They didn't invite me to the shower."

A look of disgust swept Delilah's face. "Why not?"

"They hated on me from the minute they met me. They're the miserable type who can't stand being around people who are better than them."

"That's petty."

"She'll have to find a new stylist for them. I'll pay you if she gave you a deposit. Just trust me. They'll trash your reputation and give you a bad review over one uneven curl."

"Oh I don't do uneven anything. I slay!"

"Delilah, you know what I mean. Don't do it, and you definitely can't go to the shower."

"That's petty that they didn't send you an invite." Delilah fluffed and teased my hair intensely as she continued, "I know you're going anyway."

"Of course I am!"

"And, I wanna go too! I like Marley. She's a sweetheart, and she got it going on to be so young! Man, if I was where she is when I was twenty… Girl! I'd be a killing. I mean, I'm a killing now, but let me tell you. This wouldn't be my only shop."

"Excuse me? Where's your loyalty? I've been coming to you for how long? 10 years!"

Delilah laughed, "What does that have to do with anything?"

"You're not going. Plus, I don't want you in the middle of that drama. I'm protecting you."

Delilah snapped her head back and puffed her cheeks trying hard to restrain laugher. Little did she know, she was beginning to piss me off and with each giggle, a dollar was being deducted from her usual hefty tip.

"Fine," she gave in. "I'll just take her out to eat."

"That won't even be necessary. She easily forgives. She's not tough at all."

Delilah passed me a hand mirror and turned the chair so I could assess the back of my hair. She hadn't listened to a word I said.

"We went to Derek's the other night." Delilah looked like a light bulb went off in her head. "I'll take her there!"

I scowled, "You both been hanging out?"

"Only once…. No, no twice. Yeah, twice. Both were after her appointment. She's my last client for the night and that poor girl's stomach is always growling by the time we're through."

I rolled my eyes and continued checking my hair, keeping my thoughts to myself.

Hanging out with my stylist now. Marley was on the roll. What else was she going to take, my baby brother?

CHAPTER 32

Brrrrrrg. Brrrrrrg. Brrrrrrg.

"Hello?"

"Well, well, well! Finally, you pick up my calls. What are you doing?"

"Waking up… I thought you were my alarm."

I quizzed, "If you were alert, would you have picked up?"

"What time is it?" her voice was raspy.

"7 a.m."

"God, I hate Mondays," she whispered under her breath.

"I called because I wanted to know what you were wearing to your bridal shower Saturday."

"My bridal shower is Saturday?"

I smirked. "Oops!"

***

We looked like two strangers in a waiting room. My father and I. Except we were in the kitchen. Two complete strangers not interested in speaking or getting to know one another for a couple of minutes. Just there to get what we wanted. He wanted a coffee. I wanted a toasted bagel.

A "hello" would have been foreign and most likely would've caused confusion if not fluster, especially since we hadn't made eye contact since the day I fought Alicia. While resting against the counter, I stole a couple of glances only when I was positive that his eyes were glued to his tablet. He was scanning CNN's website. I watched how his white bushy eyebrows would bunch together then collapse. I watched how the wrinkles on his olive-toned face would define as he chuckled under his breath after reading a headline. Then, I wondered how a woman as beautiful and optimistic as my mother could remain in love with a man who was so gruff, who used to be physically abusive to her, who's fifteen years her senior, and a bully who never smiled at their daughter unless he was telling some offensive joke.

There was silence in the kitchen aside from me rattling dishes, and opening and closing the refrigerator door to pour myself a glass of orange juice. A few times, I purposely slammed the cabinets loudly just to see if I could divert his attention for even a second. It didn't work when I was a child, and I had not an ounce of shock when it didn't work this time. Ironically, what did work was the shuffling sound of the manny's feet as he speed-walked to the sink and quickly turned on the faucet.

"What's going on?" my father asked before I could.

The manny was rinsing a cloth. As he squeezed it, the draining water turned red, then light pink, and back to clear. I was already running out of the kitchen towards Dominic's room before the manny could produce a vowel. My heart was pounding when I busted through Dominic's door. He was picking at a bandage on his leg.

"You hurt yourself."

Dom shook his head.

"Be honest."

Dominic looked at me and smiled. "Don't worry, Nola"

My father and the manny were seconds behind me.

"I let him get ready for work," the manny explained. "I decided to come check on him and his leg was bleeding. He said he tripped. There's a lot of blood, but the cut is small - nothing major." He shrugged. "Seems fine to me..."

My father nodded at Dominic. "He's a Victor - a strong boy. Right?"

"Right, Dad."

My father rubbed Dominic's head and patted the manny's shoulder before exiting. "Thanks for taking care of my boy."

I followed my father out into the hallway and into his office. He was snatching his suit jacket off his chair when he finally acknowledged my presence. "What is it?"

"I think Dominic's having dark thoughts again."

"Don't be ridiculous."

"Do you really think I'd be speaking to you if I wasn't serious?"

"We changed his medication over a year ago. If it were a side effect, it would have shown up before now. Besides, one cut to the leg doesn't constitute suicide. He's a happy boy now. He's been happy since I hired Miguel."

"How would you know he's happy? You're never here."

"Get a hobby, Nola. Dominic is fine."

"This isn't the first time he hurt himself. It's the second incident in weeks. It's just how y'all said it happened the last time… Started random… then suddenly became frequent."

"Last time the cuts were so deep that he had to be hospitalized. *You* weren't here. Remember? This was when you were playing Ms. Most Accomplished," my father replied hatefully.

"Don't be a jerk. Don't make it seem like I wasn't around. I visited every weekend, or every chance I could. You know that."

He smiled, satisfied that he got under my skin. He knew the right words to use - any that pertained to Dominic.

Walter Victor slid on his jacket with ease" "You're bored, Nola. You're bored with yourself and you are with your life. Get a job before what's left of your mind evaporates."

   ***

"There's something I need to tell you about myself," I said.

"There's something I need to tell you, too."

"Really? What?"

Ronnie bit into one of the turkey, provolone, and pesto sandwiches that he made for the both of us. He chewed a bit, and then swallowed. "You first."

I took a breath. "Well..." I nervously played with my curls as I fought against the fear of harsh judgement, misunderstanding, and worse... rejection. "My father is a jackass to me. My mother is as naive as Little Red Riding Hood about it. I despise my older brother who I said before is married and on the down-low, and my younger brother has a neurodevelopment delay. Yet, he has more sense than all of us, and he happens to be my only best friend. Usually, I have lunch with him. Today he ditched me for this girl who broke up with him because she grew tired of his obsession with trains."

I studied Ronnie's eyes for a reaction.

I felt comfortable so I went on, "I'm not working, and I have no idea where my life is headed. I'm just treading. I'm not swimming, but I don't feel like I'm drowning either."

I sat back on the bench and looked out at the river ahead of us. It was gorgeous out, and the perfect weather to greet July. The skies were clear, the sun respected my bare shoulders, and I didn't have to fight with the wind to keep my dress down.

"My father and I kind of got into it this morning."

Suddenly, I was an open book.

"He, of course, mentioned me being unemployed. The way he speaks to me, I feel smaller than an ant sometimes. Deep inside, I'm smaller than ant. I show up like a lion, but that's just my defense mechanism. I'm no lion."

For a moment, there was silence until he broke it.

"You have no purpose or passion."

I almost snapped. "What you mean by that?"

"What I mean is, you either lost it, or you haven't defined it. You have to ask yourself, 'what's my purpose?' Ask yourself, and ask God."

I couldn't help but laugh. "What am I supposed to do, ask and then wait for some deep vibrating voice to fall from the sky and reveal the answer?"

Ronnie didn't laugh or smile. He just motioned for me to come closer. "I'll show you where His voice comes from. I'll show you how to listen."

I looked at him and grinned. "Are you being flirty?"

189

"Seriously, come here."

I moved our sandwiches from between us and scooted over to let our arms and knees touch. Ronnie positioned himself so that he was facing me. He locked eyes with mine, reached down to my hand, gave it a gentle squeeze, and then brought it to my chest.

"Right here... Listen with your heart."

I wanted him to kiss me. Couldn't keep my eyes off his lips. I would have leaned in and stolen a kiss. However, Ronnie's phone chimed on cue, and he was on his feet taking the call.

"Hello... What's up Baby Girl? Really? Really? Wow..."

That's all I could hear as he paced further down the path looking down at his black woven Nikes and sometimes looking up at the clear blue sky that was filtering through trees. I knew it was Marley. He always called her Baby Girl, and he always went a distance when he took her calls.

As I played with my fingernails, I pondered how we would break news to her. Reveal the truth that he and I often made time for each other. This happened almost every single day, even if it was for twenty-five minutes in the Brandywine Park on a bench like now. I wondered when he'd finally tell her that some nights he'd call just to hear my voice and wish me a peaceful night. When would he tell her that when he hugs me, it's as if he doesn't want to let go, and then he squeezes the sides of my waist, passionately right before we separate. Every time. Every single time.

On Sundays, after their brunch, my car is pulling in minutes after she is cruising out. I'm the one who helps him with the dishes while he winds down for the night, preparing for the next day. That's my way of giving him a taste of my wifely capabilities. I wondered if he'd tell her that he plays in my hair, too - especially while we're watching TV or taking a drive. Honestly, I've always believed that Marley should know. Part of me hoped that she'd pop up at his place and catch us... catch us falling in love. She ought to be fine with it once she sees the way he looks at me.

"Weekly rant." Ronnie was standing in front of me stuffing his phone back down into the pocket of his slacks.

"Wedding planning will do that to you."

Part of me envied their bond and the fact that she was able to call her father just to rant, and he would willingly lend his ear. He never rushed her off or belittled her nominal struggles.

"Does she ever mention me?"

I had to ask. Aside from this morning, I hadn't heard from Marley in weeks. I'd see her at church of course, but she barely spoke during service. She only spoke short whispers and nods to Greg. They never stuck around after church. I imagined that she rushes off to New Jersey, eager to beat her father there... maybe to prepare brunch? A part of me believed she was avoiding me altogether. But why? It's funny how people change. I remember when I used to duck and dodge Marley and her annoying click-clacking kitten heels after chapter meetings. She always wanted to tag along. She wanted to hang out, and she couldn't get enough of me. Now it all took a 360-degree turn.

"Echo... she throws her little inside jokes here and there. Other than that, not really... What makes you ask that?"

Ronnie sat back down. His arm was stretched behind me but resting on the back of the bench.

"What inside joke?"

Ronnie did a short chuckle, smirked, and then another short chuckle. "It's nothing. I don't even get the joke to be honest. You're asking about her like y'all haven't spoken."

I didn't let up. "What's the joke?"

Ronnie threw his head back and smiled, "I'll tell you, but I told you that I don't get it. It's just funny how she says it."

I stared blankly, waiting.

"She says, 'Don't front like a Nola.'"

"Huh??? What's that supposed to mean?"

Ronnie lifted his arms. "I don't know. I figured it was an inside joke between y'all. I told you it didn't make sense."

I left it alone. "What did you have to tell me about yourself?"

Ronnie looked confused at first. He almost forgot what I was talking about for a second. When it came back to him, his eyes lit up.

"I'm feeling this lady. It's something about her. She has a beautiful spirit. She loves God. I can tell she loves God, but I can tell she needs to know Him better."

I blushed. "I know what you're saying." I broke a piece of my sandwich and popped it in my mouth. "And now I know what I need to do... So when are you gonna tell Marley?"

Ronnie looked puzzled. "Tell her what?"

"About this…our little friendship."

Still puzzled, he said, "I honestly didn't think to... Didn't think it was necessary..."

"You don't think she'd care?"

"Why would she?"

I nodded. "My sentiments..."

There was a pause before, he said, "I hope that you and I are on the same page."

"We are!" I smiled. "Trust me. We definitely are."

CHAPTER 33

While I was in route to Silas's that evening, I called Deaconess Michelle Camper to arrange that meeting. We met at FeliciTEA's the following Wednesday afternoon. I dragged her there because I was craving their mango green tea, their tea biscuits, and the atmosphere. I was mentally drained and needed the serenity that always met me there. I wouldn't have made her take the thirty-five minute drive into Central Philly if they'd just open a FeliciTEA's in Wilmington. It would have made my life a bit easier, I'm sure.

Since I beat her there, I choose a table in the back, but before I took a seat, I had to check myself in the mirror one last time. I wore a new suit just for her. Although, I felt a little bit insecure rocking it. I bought it just a few hours prior on clearance at The Loft, since it was all that I could afford. The other night, my account balance almost made me cry, and almost made me want to resort to stripping - or worse, go crawling to my brother for a loan. A balance of $15,000 wasn't going to get me out of my parents' house and into something nice and furnished without having a steady income. It darn sure wasn't gonna get me that Herve Leger dress I've been eyeing for Marley's wedding. What would be left of that $15,000 wasn't gonna get me bi-weekly visits to Delilah's, new dresses and skirts for the chapter meetings, nor the money I needed to pay for the chapter dues, and the deadline was approaching. I couldn't be an inactive soror and have everyone in my business. That would just made me look bad… real bad.

I tore the plastic wrapping off my bible, feeling somewhat ashamed that I hadn't opened it when I bought it months ago. I was feeling nervous, too, as if it was a job interview. In a way, it was. First impressions mean everything, and I needed Deaconess Michelle Camper to love me. If she loved me, they'd all love me, and my job as

Ronnie's wife could go smoothly. The way I saw it, the church would have my back if Marley tried to give me grief.

The Deaconess strolled in wearing dark denim jeans, a lavender blouse and killer lavender heels that I couldn't peel my eyes off. I think I greeted them before I greeted her. Her hair was styled in a shoulder-length asymmetrical bob with so much body that she looked like she was auditioning for a Pantene Pro-V commercial as she walked.

I stood. She hugged me tightly and rubbed my back.

"Hi, Sister Nola!" She stepped back and admired my suit. "That's sharp boo! Where you headed after this?"

"A conference." It was the first thing that came to mind. I was embarrassed that I overdressed, but I played it off with a smile and slow twirl so she could get a better look.

As the deaconess dug in her all white oversized Dooney and Burke tote, I made small talk. I asked her how traffic treated her, and I apologized for taking her out of the way to meet me here. She was unbothered.

"A good friend of mine works out here. At least I could pay her a visit." She smiled big. "So it worked out."

She had a light about her as if she could be friends with all personalities. She was one of those people who effortlessly balanced the tightrope line between "Very Approachable" and "Not to be Messed With." She was friendly yet feisty. I could tell all of this from the shoes she wore, the bag she carried, the blinging watch she wore, her stiletto styled nails, and the eyes that adorned her nearly wrinkle-free face. She placed two workbooks and two bejeweled pens on the table. Then she reached into the tote and pulled out two bibles. I picked up mine and waved it proudly.

"I brought my own."

"Girlfriend, that thing has never been used. You'll have a tough time keeping it open. Plus, when you leave here you'll throw it on the nightstand and never pick it back up."

"How do you know it's brand new?"

"Child, look at it. It's crisp!"

She slid hers across the table. It was pink and had a rose and pearls graphic art design on it. *Woman Thou Art Loosed* was printed across the top. "This bible has gotten me through! Let me tell you."

She closed her eyes and shook her head, which caused her hair to sweep gently across her bronze, and rose blushed cheeks. She looked like she went on a quick trip down memory lane. When she returned, she opened her eyes and went on.

"It's a study application bible, and it has daily devotionals" She reached over and flipped through the pages. "See? It's no standard KJV. You won't have to worry about getting lost or getting bored. It's yours now. Take it."

I picked it up and hugged it. "You are so generous, Deaconess Michelle Camper."

"Call me Deaconess Michelle or Deaconess Camper, and take that suit jacket off, honey. You are making me sweat! I know I don't look my age, but my body knows how old I am." She fanned herself with her booklet while I removed my jacket exposing my shoulders, bust, and cream camisole.

We were supposed to follow the outline of the booklet, discussing *The Holy Trinity, Salvation, Fellowship with Christ: The Word, Prayer, and Tithes*, and *Ministry*. Moments into our cram session, she had me feeling completely comfortable and eager to learn more about God. My nerves were gone, and I felt like I'd known her my entire life. We did just as much talking as we did reading. It didn't feel like a class at all, but a woman to woman chat on life and God, and entwining the two.

We were moving along pretty quickly until we reached the topic of prayer. We lingered there because it was where I had the most questions and needed the most understanding.

"Shoes, a dress, a purse that needs to go on clearance before I make the purchase... I can go to God about that?"

"Girl, anything." Deaconess Camper sipped her tea and smiled.

I flagged my hand. "Whatever. Jesus doesn't have time for that. He's busy saving starving babies in third world countries."

"It's not about what you're asking for. It's about conversation and establishing a relationship. If going to God about material things is what sparks conversation between you two, then so be it. I can assure you that in no time, your desires will shift, your prayers will no longer be shallow, and your relationship with The Almighty will strengthen, because that's just how He moves. He will turn it around. He'll transform you." The deaconess gently pounded the table, "Mmmm Mmmm Mmmm. He's so good!"

I lifted my teacup and sipped, just as a signal to remind her that we were in a tea brewery... not church.

"And, he's an on-call God. On time and on-call. You can go to Him whenever you want, however many times you want, and wherever you are. He will be there because like we just learned, God is--"

"—God is omnipresent." I flipped a few pages back to my notes and read: "Proverbs 15:3 'The eyes of the Lord are in every place, beholding the evil and the good."

Deaconess Michelle nodded proudly, "You got it, sweetie."

"He's also omnipotent. Luke 1:37 "For with God nothing shall be impossible."

"Go 'head and show off if you want to."

I laughed. "And..." without having to read it, I said, "He's omniscient. 1 John 3:20 "For whenever our heart condemns us, God is greater than our heart, He knows everything."

"Amen... Amen"

"He sounds like the ultimate father."

"He is, The Ultimate Father."

"Wish mine was more like Him.... He's such an ass Deaconess Camper."

Her eyes bulged, but not in a judgmental, condescending way.

196

"I'm sorry for my language."

"Take your time, and speak your heart."

I said, "When I was growing up, people used to think that I was lucky because he's so famous around Delaware. He's been on television a couple of times, and he's well respected. They considered me blessed. They don't know how much of a burden it really is to be Walter Victor's daughter."

I paused to bite into my biscuit. Reading the Deaconess's facial expression that was all twisted up, I reasoned with her. "Don't worry I'll get into details some other time. This'll spoil our meeting."

She mouthed my father's name.

"I'm sure you've heard of him. Let me tell you that my father has always been a ball of anger, except in public. In the courtroom, he comes off likable. It's his wrinkled face, grey hair, and corny sense of humor that seems to win jurors over." I sipped my tea. "I know this because I've watched him in action once."

His name must have registered with her, because she looked at me as if something clicked. "Your father is Walter Victor… Walter Victor the criminal defense attorney?"

I made air quotations, "Delaware's best."

She looked mortified. Her mouth wouldn't close, and she placed her hand on her chest.

"Let me guess. He got your offender off the hook?"

She wouldn't make eye contact with me anymore.

I felt bad for her. I spoke carefully. "I'm so sorry for whatever it was that happened. From the look on your face, justice wasn't served."

Her hands shook as she packed her tote and stammered, "I… I really need to go…"

"What? Why?"

I stretched my arms to stop her.

"Wait, wait, don't leave! Whatever it is, we can talk it out – unbiased. Don't let your experience with him come between us."

She began shaking her head and jumped to her feet. "I can't do this. I'm sorry. I just can't do this!"

Before I got a chance to stand and try to calm her down even a little bit, Deaconess Michelle was outta there.

CHAPTER 34

After the deaconess abruptly left, an uneasy feeling lingered all of that evening and at random times throughout the week. Saturday morning rolled around and her look of horror still haunted me while I did my face for Marley's bridal shower. There were a few times I'd pause in the middle of getting dressed and contemplated reaching out to her. Nevertheless, every time I picked up my phone, I lost the courage to press the contact button. A part of me feared the unknown. Maybe I'm better off not knowing... *but what if it's something that could damage my reputation? What about my bible classes and earning respect from the church?*

I arrived at the shower in a somber mood that I thought I'd shake by the time I got there. I was thirty minutes early since I had to crash it. They hosted it in a rented conference room at some hotel I've never noticed located in Downtown Wilmington, small room big enough for only about sixty people. The hotel staff had no clue that it was supposed to be an invitation only event, so I was happily escorted down the correct hall.

I sat pretty with a resting bitch face, wearing a peach linen romper set, gold chunky jewelry on my neck, wrists and ears, and gold strappy sandals. My curls had loosened and graced me with sexy beach waves, and my makeup was regal. I made it a point to floss for Marley's bridesmaids. I wanted them not only to be pissed that I showed up anyway, but to hate me even more for how disgustingly gorgeous I looked. Judging from their outfits last time, they'd be no contest, probably rocking summer frocks and Target flip-flops.

The bridesmaids started arriving about fifteen minutes later. The short skinny one associated with Trav was the first to come. The rest of them arrived together. Each of them did a double take after seeing me sitting at a table opposite of the entrance. They whispered and laughed obnoxiously amongst each other, but neither of them had the balls to approach me or try to escort me out. Instead, they tried their best to keep their eyes from my direction while they decorated with tacky Dollar Store paper streamers that no one uses for anyone after their second birthday party.

The centerpieces consisted of foiled wrapped paperweights, confetti, and heart shaped Mylar balloons that made it difficult to determine the color scheme or theme. *Who doesn't choose a theme? It's a bridal shower for goodness sake!* Of course the heavyset one, Trisherica, was in charge of preparing the spread of potato salad, Pathmark fried chicken, tossed salad, baked macaroni and cheese, a couple of other sides for the pathetic menu, and a tray of various cookies and sliced cakes that were wrapped in plastic like we were at a bake sale. And, it looked like the money they could have used for a caterer and event planner was spent on bottles of top shelf liquor and Simply's Strawberry lemonade.

Sorors were the first guests to arrive, considering that we take timeliness very seriously. Gabrielle and Bailey gravitated to my area of course. From my peripheral, I noticed that the two of Marley's line sisters, Trisherica and Shardae, looked too intimidated to come introduce themselves. Figures…Class never mixes with trash—that's just the raw reality of it…soror or not

When Marley made her grand entrance, she should have received a nomination for an Oscar with how well she played the "surprised" role. I even overheard her telling her bridesmaids how wonderful of a job they did with the planning. *Lie. Extreme lie.* Marley worked the shower like a celebrity. Our sorors gathered around her, fawning about how good she looked, and even asking her for makeup and fashion tips. I, on the other hand, was bored, hot, and underwhelmed. Therefore, I was the first one of us to escape.

"I'm gonna go."

I hugged Marley from behind while she sat at her personally decorated table chowing on red velvet cake. She wiped icing from her mouth and smiled. With twinkling eyes she said, "Aww. Here let me walk you out."

As much as I didn't want to admit, she looked gorgeous in her white goddess style maxi dress. She had her hair braided in an up-do, and the entire ensemble made her look taller, something like a super model, and like a Nubian Princess.

"Thank you for the monogrammed candle holders. I'm gonna use them for our first romantic in-house dinner." Marley walked me through the lobby of the hotel. It just so happened that Trisherica was already occupying it with a plastic red cup full of alcohol in one hand and her cell in the other. "Thanks for coming. I hope you had fun."

I raised my eyebrow and laughed.

"Why are you laughing?"

I nodded my head in the direction of her inebriated line sister. "Your girl didn't invite me."

Marley shook her head. She didn't want to believe it.

"Invited everybody except for me. *Shady*. She even invited Delilah. *Delilah*. My stylist."

"Your address changed. I gave the addresses months ago. I must have given them the wrong one."

"You are so naïve, Marley. When will you wake up? She didn't mail out invites. She sent tacky little evites, girl! Perfect for a tacky little bridal shower."

Marley tilted her head and softly asked, "Why are you always so rude? Maybe that's why you weren't invited. Your attitude sucks sometimes, Nola."

"You're backing her up?"

Marley lifted her hands. "I'm only giving the benefit of doubt."

"They ganged up on me few months ago." I pointed to Trishaerica with my thumb. "Whether you choose to believe it or not, *she* purposely excluded me...which I should have been grateful for. Everything was a mess, the food was blah and cheaply put together, yet there is a table in there with $200 worth of liquor. You don't even drink!"

Marley folded her arms and said nothing.

"Had you not been so distant and acting different, I could've done better than this."

"Would you have been be able to really, Nola?" she asked with lucid sarcasm.

"What's that supposed to mean?"

Right then Trisherica stumbled and wobbled over wagging her phone in the air. "Is this chick bothering you, Marley? 'Cause I got an ass-kicking reserved just for her."

She sized me up, and I backed down. I wasn't a fool. Home girl was huge. She would've mopped me! I turned around and headed for the doors. About three steps forward, I felt cold liquid smacking my back and dripping down to my legs. The bottom of my hair was damp and the stench of daiquiri groped me. NOW she had gone too far. I dug in my purse for my stun gun.

***

"Nola, what gonna be when you grow up?"

I was just pulling my head from under the bathtub faucet when Dominic asked. He handed me a towel and patiently awaited my answer. I stood up and patted my hair with it.

"Dom I think I like it better when you quiz me on trains. The life questions are tough."

I tossed him the towel, stood in the mirror, and frowned. I finger combed my hair trying hard to make sense of the curly disaster. My hair was supposed to last me two weeks. "Ugh! I shoulda stun-gunned that hoe!"

After Trisherica caught sight of my blinged-out stunned gun, she lost it and charged towards me. Unfortunate for her, because she slipped on the alcohol she had just thrown on me. Unfortunate for me, because I was excited that I could finally put the stun gun to use, but it wasn't needed. The floor took karma into its own hands, and Trisherica was knocked out cold.

"Nola I like you like this." Dominic was in the mirror smiling behind me. "You are beautiful."

I melted. "You think I should wear it like this more often?"

He nodded.

Diing… Diiing… Diing… Diing

"I'll get it!" Dominic's eyes lit up as he charged downstairs for the door.

"No! Let the manny get it," I called to his back. It was late evening, and since no one was expecting company, I assumed it was the pizza delivery guy. The manny always ordered himself pizza.

"Nooooola!" Dominic's voice carried from downstairs. "It's Silas!"

I huffed and wrapped my hair in a dry towel. When I got downstairs, Silas was holding white roses. I was annoyed. The last time I was with him, I told him that he needed to cool it with the pop-ups. Yet here he was again, an apparent addict for my wrath.

"What, do you have an infinite flower garden in your backyard?"

"Just take them."

I snatched the roses and tossed them to the manny who was curled up on the sofa pretending to mind his business. He smiled and sniffed them.

"Silas, look." Dominic lifted a box and shook it. "New model steam engines from England! Come help me assemble."

I stepped aside.

***

The manny and I shared the sofa watching Martin reruns while Silas and Dominic worked diligently. Dominic was so happy. Silas was the first guy I was involved with to interact with Dom. Then again, Silas was also the only guy actively interested in spending time with him. Somewhere in the middle of the third Martin episode, my phone vibrated in my hand. I just knew it was Marley offering me a well-deserved apology, but it wasn't. It was a text from Ronnie that read: *"Hey, how are you?"*

"Good. Martin Marathon with the family. You?"

"Trapped in the church office…"

I casually rose and carefully stepped over Dominic's train tracks and Silas's stretched out legs. Upstairs I pressed my hair as best as I could and brushed it into a ponytail. I threw on some denim shorts and one of my sorority t-shirts, and about fifteen minutes later, I crept back downstairs, out the door, and into my Range.

    ***

I waved the bag. "Brought you donuts."

Ronnie spun around from his bookshelf. Smiled…but he wasn't excited. "What are you doing here?"

"Surprise! It sounded like you could use some company." I sat in the chair across from his and opened the bag. "I got glazed and chocolate glazed. I wanted to get powdered, but you know how messy that gets. Oh and there's two plain ones in case you're that type."

Ronnie was still standing by his bookshelf. "Nola, thank you, but you didn't have to do this. The text was just a casual checking up on you thing. There was no subliminal message."

"It's fine. Don't worry about it. I wasn't doing anything anyway." I pulled a few napkins from an extra bag. Ronnie reached over me and began stuffing them back in. "What are you doing?"

"I'm headed out… wrapping up. This is why I say your visit was unnecessary."

"Unnecessary?"

He didn't respond. He just busied himself with packing up.

"Where you headed?"

"A frozen yogurt joint, and I don't wanna be late." He said it nonchalantly while zipping his laptop bag.

"Frozen yogurt? You're passing on donuts for frozen yogurt?"

I watched Ronnie's face for sign that he was joking. When it didn't come, I asked, "What makes you go there?"

"It's a date."

"A date?"

I felt like I was being pranked. I wanted to look around to see if I would spot a flashing red button to clue me that I being recorded.

Ronnie slid his bag over his shoulder and walked towards the light switch. "Ready?"

"So you're serious? You're really going on a date?" I was still sitting, feeling blindsided, smacked, confused. And hurt. "Why?"

"Why not? I'm single."

Ronnie was pretty much holding the gates of the Friend Zone open so that I could march my little behind inside, and I refused to go. I tried everything within me to hold it together while I asked the next two questions.

"Who is she? And how'd y'all meet?"

As we walked to the parking lot, Ronnie told me that he met the woman last week through Marley...*I could kill her*. When we got to our cars, something got a hold of me and I lost inhibition. I stood in front of his car door and protested.

"You're not going."

Ronnie laughed. "Come on... Move."

"I'm not letting you go."

His smile faded as soon as he realized I was serious. "I don't know what's going on with you, Nola, but you gotta move."

I folded my arms. "I don't believe it. This entire time... The hanging out, the dinners, the brunches, the long talks... I thought we had something going. I was mistaken?"

Ronnie rubbed his head and looked away. "Listen, I gotta go."

"Answer me!" I shoved his chest. "I was mistaken?"

Still not a word.

"I'm not moving until you answer me. Whoever she is will be stood up."

Ronnie went for my hand.   "You're acting crazy."

"Don't touch me."

He shoved his hands in his pocket. He was dressed so sexy. So edible. A red, yellow, and orange-checkered button down shirt. Distressed jeans. Tan canvas sneaks. I wanted him. And I burned because I couldn't have him. "I honestly don't know what made you think we had something going—"

"You gotta be kidding me."

"—I thought we were two friends passing time—"

"That's bull. You know that's bull."

"—if I blurred the lines somewhere along the way, I deeply apologize—"

"You apologize?"

"—I would never date my daughter's best friend—"

"Soror."

"—against her wishes."

I wasn't buying it. He couldn't even look at me. "So you never felt anything deeply for me?"

The pastor backed up and took two steps to the side while stroking his chin. I imagined him trying to conjure up some lousy explanation.

"Look at me!"

When he did, his eyes fell directly to my lips. And then my eyes. And back to my lips.

"Nothing? No feelings whatsoever?" I begged for an answer.

He hesitated first. Then he said, "I'm sorry, Nola."

My eyes fell to the ground right along with my crushed feelings.

Ronnie stepped forward and extended his hand.

I swatted it. "DON'T TOUCH ME!"

I hopped in my Range and burned rubber out of there.

   ***

"What are you still doing here?"

I slammed the door behind me, jolting Silas from his nap on the sofa. The living room was dark aside from the glowing television screen. Dominic was likely in bed, and it was evident that the manny was gone. The space where he parked was now occupied by my father's vehicle.

Silas wiped the corners of his eyes and then stretched his arms. He yawned when he asked, "Where'd you run off to?"

I snapped my neck. "That's none of your business."

Silas nodded. "You're right." He slapped his knees and rose.

"Last time I checked, you weren't my man." I spat as he walked by me and headed for the door. I was still infuriated with how played I felt by Ronnie, and I needed Silas to be my punching bag. "And if you keep popping up here, and trying to spend the night, you will NEVER be my man."

Silas bit the bait. He turned and faced me. "I wasn't trying to spend the night. I was making sure you got home safe. It's called being a gentleman. A man of honor. Something ungrateful chickens like you wouldn't recognize."

"I will never be grateful for something I never wanted in the first place. You're a bug –an irritant who's always in the way. Take a hint and take a hike!"

Silas waved his finger at me and faked a chuckle. "You… you are a miserable little girl. You know that? I thought you had something going for you, but you're just a typical brainless beauty who'll end up single and a bum."

I kept my composure as I sucked in his ammunition. He was trying to hit me where it hurt. Nevertheless, I knew how to hit him harder.

I stepped to his chest and fired. "I'd rather be single than be addicted to abandonment like you. I rejected you how many times? And you just keep running back. Keep vying for my attention like the little boy *you* still are. I'm not your momma. She never wanted you and neither do I!"

"You *BITCH*" Silas's mouth foamed with fury. "You silly *BITCH*."

I said nothing. Couldn't say anything if I tried. I was too shocked. Shocked that *he* would take it there... Disrespecting me in the worst possible way. *He* of all people.

"You lazy, fake *BITCH!*" As he spat each word, he began to look nothing like himself.

I tried to push him from my face. "Stop," was all I could muster.

He mushed my head.

Then he kept at it. Calling me all possible B-words until he suddenly backed up off me and walked out of the house. I stood in the doorway stunned.

Silas sat in his car without starting it up. His arm was resting out of his window, and his head was resting on his fist. When the shock wore off, I immediately felt bad and walked towards his car, my heart pulling me like a magnet after metal.

I said nothing when I opened his car door. Just grabbed his hand and led him out. My eyes apologized, and he knew this, picking me up and carrying me up to my bedroom.

We were tangled in my sheets. *"I'm sorry"* smothered by passionate kisses and heavy breathing. *"I forgive you"* demonstrated with each thrust –each stroke.

CHAPTER 35

I wanted to crawl under my bed and hide from God when Silas left.

Then, as if I could hear the deaconess's voice whispering in my ear, I remembered that with each rising of the sun, God brings us new mercy. Since Silas was out of there just before dawn, I hurried to my knees hugging the bible that Deaconess Camper gave me.

I whispered, "Um, hey God. My name is Nola, I know You already know who I am, but I never formally introduced myself. I'll be honest, I don't know what to say. No. I know what to say. I don't know how to say it. Well, the deaconess said prayer is conversation, so I'll just let it flow out so I don't waste up Your time. Here goes: I sinned. Right here. On my bed. I don't know what got into me or why I did that. Or, why I feel I have to tell you this. All I know is I don't feel good at all. It feels like I committed a crime. God. I'm no criminal! Please get rid of this feeling. Please sprinkle some of that mercy on me. Ok? Thanks. This was easy. I can do this more often. Ok bye. Well, not bye, but… You know what I mean!"

I stood up and exhaled. When I turned around, I nearly jumped out of my skin seeing Dominic at my bedroom doorway.

"What were you talking to?"

"I was praying to God, Dominic. Why are you up?" God, *I hope me and Silas didn't wake him.*

"I had to use the toilet."

I breathed, "Oh ok."

"I want to meet God." Dom stepped in my room and sat at the edge of my bed.

"You really do?"

He nodded.

"Ok. Well, sit here." I had Dominic sit in my desk chair while I shuffled through the pages of my New Member's workbook. When I found the page that I was looking for, I said, "Now repeat after me…"

Dominic echoed the statements, "Lord I admit that I am a sinner… I admit that You are our Lord and Savior… I believe that You died on the cross for my sins…. I believe that You rose from the dead…. I confess and repent of my sins…. Please take control of my life…. In Jesus' name…. Amen!"

I hugged Dom tightly. "Now you know Him. All you have to do is believe deep in your heart. That's what a really nice lady told me."

"I believe, Nola."

I handed him a bible—the unused one—and helped him bookmark the book of John. "Ask the manny to help you read this section. When you are done, I'll help you find a church that won't bother you. I'd bring you with me to my church today, but it's *too* loud."

Dominic smiled. "Okay. Can't wait."

***

"Tell your neighbor: drugs, alcohol, and cigarettes ain't the only addictions."

The church echoed Pastor Ronnie's sentiments.

"And, I see some addicts up in here today." He slapped his podium and walked to the side. The congregation roared with laughter. Even I couldn't help but chuckle.

The entire sermon, he had me tuned in. For the first time, I wasn't focused on how good he looked pacing along the altar, and it probably was because I sat on the balcony with other tuned-in worshipers who loved to slap high-fives or tap your shoulder saying, "Amen, Amen," when he said something really good. I guess it was beneficial that I felt too salty to try to sit up front.

"Praise God. Listen, Listen." Pastor wiped his forehead and returned to the podium. "We become so hooked on... *addicted to...* what the *flesh* desires, that we begin to think it is making us happy. But, in the long run it is *destroying* us sometimes physically, sometimes mentally, but most *definitely* spiritually. I didn't make this up. It's in the bible. Romans 8:5-6, 'For those who live according to the flesh set their minds on the things of the flesh, but those who live according to the Spirit set their minds on the things of the Spirit. For to set the mind on the flesh is death, but to set the mind on the Spirit is life and peace.' Therefore, that *tail* you was chasing last night,—"

People began to rise and shout, "Preach pastor!"

"—that *car* you was profiling in last night,—"

"AaaaaaMEN tell 'em!"

"—those *big face* 'hunits you were glorifying last night, not about to *guarantee you* the kind of PEACE that MY GOD can!"

"Preach, Preacher!"

"Some of us carry so deeply a void in our hearts, and we are allowing our flesh to fill it up with the wrong things," he went on. "Listen to me,"

The church quieted down. Some were still praising and whispering, "Hallelujah." A woman next to me was rocking side to side with her eyes closed. Under her breath she kept murmuring, "Thank you for your deliverance, Father. Thank you. *Thank you.*"

"People, vanish. Clothes, fade. Cars wear and tear. Money gets snatched. Food perishes.... But God..."

Pastor Ronnie paused to praise, himself. The congregation clapped and praised, too.

"God... God is everlasting. His love endures. Now THAT is something to get hooked on. Let us pray..."

***

I met Silas in the lobby right after service. He hugged me tightly and told me that he had a surprise waiting for me at his place.

He was hoping I'd leave with him right then, but I wanted to linger. This time for Deaconess Michelle. Silas kissed my cheek and told me to call when I'd be on the way, and I sat patiently in a chair for the deaconess to come out of the sanctuary.

It didn't take long for the lobby to clear. Deaconess Michelle was nowhere to be found. Something stirring deep inside the bottom on my belly had me needing to know why she jilted me at FeliciTEA's, so I wasn't about to let that stop me from finding her.

I walked right past the secretary lady and tapped the Pastors door. His eyebrows rose when he opened it and saw it was me. "Sorry if I'm disturbing you. I just wanted to ask if you had Deaconess Michelle Camper's address. She was helping me through New Members classes. I haven't been able to reach her. Thinking about paying her a visit."

"Come in." The pastor stepped aside, and then closed the door after I walked in. "I usually don't do this, but since I know you, I trust you wouldn't do anything crazy with it."

The pastor pulled a folder from his file cabinet, copied her information on a sticky note, and then handed it to me.

"Thank you!" I turned to walk away, but I didn't move. I had to ask first. I turned back around to face him. "How was your date last night?"

The Pastor folded his arms and shrugged. "I didn't go…"

"Oh." I turned to leave.

My hand was touching the doorknob when he said, "As you can see, Marley and Greg didn't make it to church this Sunday."

"I see…"

"They can't come for brunch, either… I uh, had this spread prepared. I don't want it to go to waste… You should join me."

CHAPTER 36

A monarch butterfly fluttered by as I sat on the edge of Ronnie's ground pool, nibbling on Canadian bacon, scrambled egg, and provolone cheese sandwiched between a flaky croissants.

"How do you like it?"

"I love it"

It was just like my daydream from the first time I came to Ronnie's house. Minus the grill. Minus the magazine. With my maxi skirt hiked to my thighs, I tapped my toes underneath the cool water, intrigued by the rippling effect it created against my toe nail polish. Ronnie lounged in a chair behind me wearing Ray-Ban mirror aviators, a t-shirt and shorts set he changed into after I insisted we eat brunch poolside.

"It's home baked."

"What?"

"The croissants. I baked them. Last week."

"You got talent."

"Not my only. I used to swim competitive, too."

I pointed my finger at him. "No Swimming!"

Ronnie stuffed the last bite of his sandwich into his mouth. Then, he grinned.

"I didn't come out here to swim. Just to enjoy the weather and your backyard."

As soon as I turned my back towards him, SPLASH!!!! Ronnie dove into the pool. Shirtless—Aviators still on. The sunrays reflected and glistened off his toned body as he swam towards me. I exhaled, breathing out the raunchy thoughts that brewed inside of me, trying everything within me to be on my best behavior.

"Get in."

I watched my head shake in the reflection of his sunglasses.

"Get in."

"I will not."

Ronnie grabbed my wrist and pulled me in any way!

I popped up and hopped out quicker than a jack-in-a-box. "Are you outta your mind?" I was livid. My nose and cheeks collected droplets of water as my freshly pressed hair coiled and drenched.

Ronnie flashed a grin. "I didn't think your hair would curl like that." He got out of the pool and retrieved two towels from a bin nearby. "You're adorable when you're mad."

What had gotten into him? I didn't know whether to slap him or suck his bottom lip dry. I snatched the towel.

He snatched it back.

I snatched it again.

He grabbed my wrist, this time leading me back to the house and upstairs.

"Take off your clothes."

My eyes widened.

"I'll dry them for you. There're shirts in the drawer in there." Ronnie pointed to the guestroom. "Go change. I'll wait out here for you."

A 10x16 photo of Margo, his deceased wife, hung on the wall above the dresser. In it, she wore a pink sundress and posed with a pink chrysanthemum. She smiled sweetly at the photographer. I found one of Ronnie's button-downs, threw it on, and met him back in the hallway.

He took my hand and kissed it. Slowly. Softly. I smiled. "What is all this about?"

"If only I could practice what I preached today."

"Am I your addiction?

Holding both of my hands, he backed me against the wall and lifted me by the waist. I wrapped my arms around his neck as he carried me to his bedroom. Both of our bodies collapsed on his bed. Wedged between my legs, he kissed my neck, and my heart pounded as he then kissed just above my breast. Then, finally, our lips touched.

Finally.

Both of us exhaled, and the temperature rose. A haze of anticipation released and morphed into a thick cloud of sexual tension surrounding our intertwined bodies, and then I felt him rise through his shorts.

"Mmmm mmm, Silas." ...My eyes shot open and my hand covered my mouth. But it was already too late to catch the words that slipped out.

Ronnie pulled himself off me. "Silas? Silas?...Wowwwwwww!"

"Daddy?!"

Ronnie and I both jerked, startled by the sound of Marley's call from downstairs. I scurried into the guestroom closing the door behind me.

"Why is Nola's car parked outside? Why is Nola here?"

Stuck in the guestroom with Marley's flower barring mother staring over my shoulder, I could hear Ronnie struggling to explain brunch, the pool, and my wet clothes... minus the steamy details... and my Silas slip. I threw my hands on my head. *Why did I make that slip?* For minutes, I tried to come up with something crafty to tell Marley. After I ended up with nothing, I simply buttoned Ronnie's shirt up to the collar and made my way downstairs. Luckily, his shirt was long enough to meet at my thighs.

The entire house fell silent as I casually walked by Greg who was completely baffled, Ronnie—who was rubbing his temples, and Marley—whose lips were so tightly pressed together that I thought her face would explode. I grabbed my purse and sandals from the kitchen, and then walked right back into the foyer where they stood.

"Are you seeing my father?!" Marley barked. Greg placed his hands on her shoulder. She shook it off.

He said, "Marley, your—"

"—Greg, don't!"

I looked at Ronnie. "Im'ma go."

Marley followed me outside. "I asked you a question! ARE YOU SEEING MY FATHER?"

"Get away from me, Marley," I warned without turning to face her. "I'd do you like I shoulda done Trisherica."

She tugged my arm and I swung around pressing my fingernail into her forehead. "DON'T TRY ME, MARLEY!"

By now, Greg and Ronnie were descending down his steps. Greg was hustling over. "No. You won't do this. Not while you're carrying my son." He moved her back, Ronnie helped.

"She's pregnant?" I looked at all three of them. "You're pregnant? That's why you're having this microwave wedding? 'Cause your pregnant?"

Marley tried to break away from their hold. "Every day I've seen you for the manipulating, fake, and selfish person you are!" She then barked at the guys. "Let go of me! I'm not stupid. I'm not gonna do anything."

They freed her, and it was right then that I noticed Marley's protruding belly beneath her tunic-styled shirt.

"Good bye, Marley." I slid my purse back on my arm.

"The chapter knows about you Nola. EVERYBODY knows about you. You just haven't seen me in a while because I'm tired of playing along!.. And, what makes you think my dad would want someone like you anyway?"

"Baby girl... don't," I heard him say.

I gave Marley my back and approached my car.

She went on. "You can't keep a man, you have no career, and you live at home with your parents, bumming off of their money."

I paused. It took everything within me not to knock her teeth to the ground. I blew air from my cheeks and swung back around. "Little girl you are Nola Jr. I created you. *That's* why your father would want me. We have that in common! Now, how about you wobble and slither your spineless behind back up into the house with your corny fiancé, and speak to me when your lips aren't lacquered with my hand-me-down lipstick.

I hopped in my car.

"Stay away from my dad, Nola!" I could hear as I reversed out of the driveway. "Don't even come back to my church!"

CHAPTER 37

No sooner than I turned out of Ronnie's driveway, my cellular chimed through my Bluetooth. I pressed the pickup button. "Yes?"

It was my mother. She was frantic. Sobbing, and nearly incoherent. "Nola! Nola...you have to come... Come to Christiana Hospital quick!"

"Mom, calm down. What's wrong? Is it daddy? Did he put his hands on you?"

"No," she cried. "It's Dominic. Nola, he was struck by a car."

I flew to Delaware in under fifteen minutes almost causing three accidents. Two of them would have been on the Commander Barry Bridge. The other would have been in the hospital garage.

I rushed through the doors and down the halls, nearly knocking people over. My mother met me in the waiting area and grabbed onto me.

"I wanna see him!" I demanded. "Where is my baby brother? I wanna see him!"

"You can't. They're performing emergency surgery," she cried on my shoulder.

"Who did this to him?!"

The manny, whose eyes were bloodshot red, came over to rub both of our backs. "Your father and Derrick are speaking to the detectives now."

"It was hit and run?" My heart was pounding so heavy that I thought it'd jump out of place.

My mother blew her nose in a napkin. "No, the driver stayed at the scene."

"Then why are we speaking to detectives?"

My mother sniffled. "The driver says Dom walked into traffic. She and a few witnesses are calling it suicide."

Four hours later, we got to see Dom. He was in a coma. Both of his arms were amputated. His face was completed distorted from multiple fractures. Two hours after that, Dominic died. My best friend was gone.

***

I stayed in bed for two days. I didn't shower for three. News about Dom spread like wild fire, after it was covered by local reporters. It made headlines: *Delaware's Notable Defense Attorney Walter Victor Mourns Autistic Son After Alleged Suicide*. I kept my phone down to avoid it all. It was constantly ringing. The last phone call I accepted came from the manny who called to tell me he was moving to Texas with a guy he met online. After that, every call got ignored. I had voicemails and text messages loaded with condolences. Most of them were from sorors. Some of them from Silas, and even one of them was from Marley. They had the funeral four days after Dom's death. I didn't go. I felt like it was my own.

***

"Nola? Is that you?"

I was in FeliciTEA's completely zoned out before I heard the familiar voice. I slowly rolled my heard in the direction of it. Sharron, the concierge from my old condo across the street, was standing over me smiling.

"I barely recognized you!" It was my hair, which was braided in two cornrows. It was my face, which was bare—not a touch of make up on. It was my hideous outfit—black biker pants and an oversized olive colored t-shirt. "I haven't seen you in so long! Can I sit?"

I took my legs off the sofa and scooted over. I barely recognized her either. She was slimmer, and she wasn't wearing a flamboyant wig. Instead, her hair was braided into long individuals. Plus, she wasn't dressed in her uniform.

She sat. "You don't look good." We didn't look at each other; just straight ahead thru the oversized window. "I'm not even gonna play like I don't know what's wrong. I saw it in the paper this week while I was working. My heart sank when I saw your name printed. Funeral's today, right?"

I nodded.

I felt her staring at my profile. "You still don't cry, huh?"

I shook my head slowly, then dryly said, "Nope."

She patted my knee. "Well, I'm glad I ran into you. You were there for me when you gave me that ring. I never told you, but I was facing eviction. On top of that, student loans were snatching almost every penny I earned. I needed the money desperately, and you didn't even know it. I knew it was God moving through you, though."

I looked at Sharron. "Why didn't say anything? I would have bought you… given you whatever you needed. You saw the way I spent."

She shrugged. "Pride and protecting perception. I'm known as the super joyful concierge. Working in a residence full of ballers, the last thing you'd want them thinking is that you're a mooching charity case."

I nodded, all too familiar with the feeling.

"Anyway, since you blessed me all of those times, I'm gonna bless you. You were there for me, I'm gonna be here for you. Befriend you." She playfully tapped my shoulder with hers. "You look like you could use a friend."

Sharron and I hung out in FeliciTEA's and talked until the sun began to go down. True to her word, she lent me her ear to vent about everything, without interruption like a real friend would. She nearly choked on her tea when I told her about the STD, trying to pursue the pastor while sleeping with Silas, getting beat up by Alicia, and my altercation with Marley, but she didn't judge once. And that made me feel good. If I could have, I would've kept her all night, bought her dinner, and made her sleepover so I could talk until her eyelids collapsed, but she had a scheduled engagement.

She slurped the last bit of her tea, and then squeezed me tightly. "We'll catch up some more soon. I promise. Maybe get our nails done. Pampered a little bit? This weekend?"

I accepted her invitation.

Sharron grabbed her tote from Victoria's Secret and threw it over her shoulder. She turned and walked away, but then she came back. "Why don't come with me?"

"Where?"

"I work at a recreational center now for youth in West Philly. You should come check it out. The kids are amazing. They always cheer me up."

I shook my head. "Uht-uhn, I'm sorry, not looking like this. Plus...I don't know if I can handle seeing young people yet. It'd make me miss Dominic."

She didn't press me. "Next time then."

CHAPTER 38

"What are you doing here?"

The deaconess looked behind me like she was checking to see who brought me. Her hand was on her chest and the look on her face told me that she was surprised. Hell, I surprised myself when I drove by my exit on the way from FeliciTEA's.

I was guided by the adrenaline of wanting to know why she left me so abruptly. In fact, I grew pissed that even with all that transpired from that last time I'd seen her, I STILL hadn't shaken the look on her face and the eerie feeling it brought me. I banged on her door with every intention of demanding her to woman up and explain, so that I could bereave my baby brother.

"I want answers."

"How did you get my address?"

"Answer my question, and I will surely answer yours. Who are you, and why do you know my father?"

"Lose the attitude. You want something from me, then you come to me with respect. Otherwise, you could march your tail off of my porch and back into your car."

"What are you, his mistress? You got a grown baby by him? Is that what it is? You a reformed hoe?"

The deaconess slammed her front door on my face.

I stormed off her porch and hopped in my Range. I started up the car, but I couldn't put it in drive. I was too angry. My hands shook. My temperature was risen. Mostly likely, she was Walter Victor's side chick. *That's why she was being a coward.* I was angry for my mother. *The poor, faithful, soft spoken, formerly battered woman had been putting up with this monster for 32 years and he pays her back by sleeping around? I could possibly have half siblings!* I couldn't wait to tell my mother. But, first I needed details. I took a deep breath and exhaled slowly.

This time I rang the doorbell. "I'm sorry for the way I came at you just now." I pressed my hands together. "I just really need to know what's up. It's been bothering me."

The deaconess stepped aside and invited me in. I followed her through the living room and into the dining area. "Have a seat."

I folded my arms. "I'm fine right here. Just get started."

"Would you like something to drink? I have lemonade."

"You are kidding me? I have no idea who you really are, yet you want me to sit and sip some lemonade with you? No, thank you. You're probably the enemy."

"Cookies?"

I grabbed my face. "Lady! Would you please stop?!"

"You have your father's temper. The way your eyes squint and your nostrils flare."

"So you're his mistress."

"I am his mother." The deaconess turned around and dug in the drawer of her china closet. The cabinets of the closet were covered with photographs of her and her apparent deceased husband, judging from the obituary that was posted up there as well.

"What the hell are you taking about? My father's mother passed when I was a baby. What kinda game are you playing? Who the hell are you, and why the hell did you run out like that?"

"Watch your mouth!" she scolded from over her shoulder.

"Then 'fess up and quit BS'ing me!"

"I am your grandmother." She turned around and handed me a photograph. "*This* is your father."

In the picture was a man who posed next to her. He was about her height. Short. Stocky. Medium brown skinned with a long beard and long locs.

"You're mistaken. I'm sorry you've lost your granddaughter, but I'm not her."

I tried to give her back the photograph, but she refused it. "Sit down and we will talk about it."

"No. You're crazy." I slammed the picture on the dining table and tried to leave.

She held my arm. "Your mother is Danielle Victor. Your father is Walter Victor. You have an older brother named Derrick Victor. I'd never lie about this Nola. God is my witness. I would never mess with you like this!"

I snatched my arm.

"I didn't want to believe it either. That's why I ran. She… She told me she terminated the pregnancy." Deaconess Camper reached for a box of tissues sitting on top her cabinet. She dabbed her damp face and continued, "I ran home, pulled up your paper work, saw your birthdate, and calculated the numbers... I fell on my knees, and I just cried and prayed ... cried and prayed."

I said nothing. I didn't know what to say. She was a wreck and convinced.

"They loved each other." Deaconess Michelle slowly sat at the table and blew her nose before she continued.

"Forbidden love. She was married to his lawyer... Elton had a drinking problem. Always in trouble for DUIs, and Walter was always there to handle it. Every time." She sniffled. "I told him so many times, 'Elton, this is so wrong. You can't steal that man's wife after all he's done for you,' but he was so stubborn, so determined, so in love."

I sat across from her. "I'm from Bowie..." It was statement but it came out sounding like a question.

"Conceived in Wilmington." The deaconess looked directly at me. "He'd bring Danielle around all the time. And sometimes little Derrick, too. She'd have dinner here and spend nights. We'd go shopping together. She was so happy. Full of life, very talkative. She and I would talk at this very table about anything and everything. From men to the stars in the solar system. A bright young woman. They'd have the funniest debates, she and Elton." Deaconess paused to giggle and wipe tears.

I wondered how she could she be talking about the same person. The Danielle I knew never debated, was usually timid, and had become a "yes" woman to my father.

She went on. "Then, one day everything went from risky to a complete nightmare. She got pregnant. Elton was excited and told me as soon as he found out, but your mother panicked. Two days later, the police were banging on my door, pushed me out of the way, and they arrested him. They charged him for rape."

There was a knot in my throat, and I swallowed hard to remove it. I looked down at the photograph laying between us. It was then that I realized that the man... Elton... was wearing a khaki prison uniform.

"Elton pled innocent, but they had evidence. Bruises on her arms, seaman samples..." The deaconess paused to hold it together. "He wouldn't have raped her, Nola. He would never violate her or hurt her. And, he would never lie to me."

"So you're saying my mother is a liar."

"They moved. Disappeared. She told me she terminated the pregnancy, and almost thirty years later, you are standing right here."

I felt my temperature rising... my breathing almost of out of control. I closed my eyes and spoke clearly and slowly. "Deaconess Michelle… Please watch what you are saying to me..."

"You look just like him. Your eyes, your..."

I raised my hand to stop her. "My baby brother just died... My best friend... he is DEAD. I have no one. I have absolutely NO ONE... And, you are telling me... four days after his death ....that my father... isn't really my father??"

I opened my eyes to see the deaconess sliding me the box of tissues. I touched my cheek. And I caught the first tear to fall since I was little a girl.

CHAPTER 39

My mother turned away from the counter, still gripping the knife she used to chop the chicken breast. "What did you ask?"

I kept my eye on the knife. "That a weapon?"

"Of course not." She sat it down and wiped her hands with a cloth.

"I asked does the name Michelle Camper ring a bell."

My mother couldn't look me in the eye. "I know where this is going."

"Well, she lives right here in Wilmington, just less than fifteen minutes away. How could you not think I'd run into her?" I had my questions loaded and ready for fire. I had been preparing them all week only because it took exactly a week to get my mother and father home at the same time. A when I heard her preparing dinner, I knew right then was the best time to confront her: Cornered in the kitchen.

"We'd never cross paths. Her lifestyle is completely different from ours."

"How? She's a deaconess at Marley's church... and she used to be your friend!"

My mother peeked her head out the entryway of the kitchen. "Lower your voice... Your father had a very stressful week... This is last type of discussion he needs to overhear."

The look on my face did the talking when I thought, *who gives a flying rat's ass about that man you insist on calling my father* But, I chose to vocalize that at another time.

My mother paced the kitchen trying hard to avoid my interrogating eyes. She spoke lowly, "When I knew her, she was far from a deaconess. She was a drug dealer."

I was confused. "Michelle Camper? Who lives at 1445 Mulberry?"

Finally she looked at me. "You've been to her house?"

226

"So it's true. You know her address, so it must be true that Elton is my father."

"Nola, now isn't the time to discuss this. It's a very touchy subject for me."

"What's a touchy subject?" Walter entered the kitchen with an unlit cigar hanging in his mouth. He walked straight across and had his hand on the patio door.

"Touchy for you?" *The nerve.* "I'm just discovering that my father may or may not be my father after almost thirty years. All I'm asking is for the truth!"

My mother said nothing. She just looked at my father.

My blood boiled. I yelled loud enough to rock the house, "IS IT TRUE??"

"YES, IT'S TRUE!" my father roared.

"Walter—" My mother rubbed his arm.

"—Who do you think you are coming in here attacking your mother for something a monster did to create you? You're a bastard child who's lucky to be alive! You should've been aborted. You're an ingrate. A worthless piece of--"

"Enough!" That was the first time I've heard my mom yell at him.

"She's a moron for not questioning this sooner." He snarled at me, "Take a look in the mirror. Take a really close look at your skin, genius. You're not white."

I questioned my skin tone just once when I was younger. My mother assured me that everyone on her grandfather's father side tanned darker. That I took after them.

I swung around and grabbed the knife my mother was using. Filled with rage. Encompassed with thoughts like, *Kill him. Just kill him. He ruined you and Dominic. He deserves to die."*

I could taste the salty tears on my lips.

"Ha! She wants to end up in jail like her real father." My father was sweating. Even when he was afraid, he managed to be a jerk.

I moved in closer on in them. My eyes bounced back and forth from him to my mom—She deserved to go too.

My mother begged, "Nola. Please. Please put the knife down sweetie."

My father taunted me, "Now that you got it, you better use it!"

"WALTER SHUT UP! JUST SHUT UP!" My mother's face was red. Her eyes were daggers, and from the look on my father's face they stabbed him much worse than what the knife in my hand could have.

"Nola. I know you are angry. Dominic is gone and now this, but hurting us will only hurt yourself." She pressed her hands together. "Sweetheart. Please put the knife down."

Right then my father rushed me. The back of my head hit the tiled floor. He and I both gripping the knife, swinging it aimlessly. I was kicking and screaming. He was cramming his elbow into my chest, his knees thrusting into my abs. My mother was shrieking with horror, "Stop it! Stop it!"

I bit him. Sunk my teeth right into his forearm. And then he smacked me. His thick white hands felt like plywood to the left side of my face. I dropped the knife. As I held my jaw, I felt blood dripping on my thighs. *He stabbed me! I'm stabbed!* But, I could only feel the pain from my face. Not even a second later, I heard my father yelp in agony.

"It was an accident, Walter." My mother was holding the bloody knife.

***

"It was no accident." My mother whispered in my ear and patted my head.

I hopped off the hospital bed, grabbed my purse, and shoved in the script for ibuprofen that the ER doctor prescribed for my swollen face. I had nothing to say to her. Twenty-nine to thirty years was much too long to try to come to my defense.

My mother touched my arm. With beautiful pleading and desperate eyes she said, "Please say something."

"Did Elton really rape you? Don't lie to me. I already know I was conceived before any of that alleged rape happened. Walter may not know, but I know." I tore off my hospital gown and tossed it on the bed. "So, did he beat you up that night or did Walter?"

She said nothing. Just winced and sucked in her beautiful pouting lips, perhaps tasting the very fallacious statements she once fed a courtroom. She swung her beautiful silky jet-black hair over shoulder and rolled her eyes to the window as if the truth was out there, drifting in the wind.

I waited for the answer for five, maybe ten, minutes before I realized that I wasn't going to get one. I threw the strap of my Chanel maxi purse over my shoulder.

"Go be with your husband. They say he's four rooms down."

"Nola—"

"Did Elton Camper rape you? Answer that flat out. Did. He. Rape. You??"

"I couldn't get a divorce. I needed your father to help me through medical school."

"You are disgusting."

"I didn't want any of this to spiral out of control—'

"You are so freakin disgusting! Don't speak to me. Don't ever speak to me!"

***

I felt like I hit rock bottom when I checked into the very hotel Marley's bridesmaids used for the bridal shower. It was all I could afford. The concierge helped me lug all of my bags and boxes into the tiny hotel room. If I hadn't been in a rush to move out of my parents' house before they got home from the ER, I would have planned it better. At least found storage until I found an apartment. Anything was better than living in that house of lies. When the concierge left with a small tip balled in his fist, I plopped on the bed, slid off my sneakers, then got up to shut the shutters. I pulled out one of Dominic's trains from the box labeled Dom's Locomotives and then gripped it in my hand. I sobbed. I sobbed. I sobbed until I sobbed myself to sleep.

CHAPTER 40

"I've been calling you all day." He sounded agitated.

I said nothing. I just groaned.

"Are you still at the hotel?"

"I'm here," I mumbled. "I was asleep. Now My face feels like I was kicked by a baby elephant."

"Let me move you outta there and take care of you." Silas had been offering his help since I checked in two nights ago.

I declined each request. I wanted to be alone. "Nothing the ibuprofen can't fix."

He fought. "Let me do what a man is supposed to do and take care you."

"You're not my man."

There was silence. I thought he had hung up. Just as I was about to press the END button he spoke up. "I want to be your man. Allow me to be your man, Nola."

"You don't want me. I have nothing and I am nothing."

"Don't speak badly about yourself."

"I feel robbed. My identity is gone… I don't even know who I am. Dominic's life was taken from me. The opportunity to be a daddy's girl was stolen before I grew a heart. My happiness has been snatched."

"You are still alive, and so is your real father. Dominic was never yours to begin with, and you were never happy."

"Goodbye, Silas."

"No, hear me out. It's not too late to establish a relationship with Elton. Start that today. As far as Dominic goes, I know you called him your best friend but Im'ma be honest with you, Nola. He was your crutch. You were dependent on him. And the happiness you felt when he was alive, was actually his happiness borrowed. Now that he's gone, you can find out who you truly are. Every single day since Dom

231

passed you have woken up and been given a chance to live and start over. I know you know what the bible says about new mercy. Take advantage of that, Nola."

When I hung up with Silas, I couldn't get myself to fall back asleep. Too many thoughts were carousing in my mind. When the sun finally fell, and the moon lifted, I climbed out of bed and called Deaconess Michelle. Not only did she give me all the information I needed to reach Elton Camper, she helped me finish my New Member packet over the phone.

***

Deaconess Michelle didn't lie when she said our walk with Christ wasn't easy. It was the first day of August—Marley's wedding day—and I knew that on this day I wasn't walking with God at all. Otherwise, I wouldn't have gone to the church. I would have been in the hotel room highlighting scriptures and taking notes, or praying to God that He take away the yearning I felt for Ronnie.—It crept up on me that morning, and I allowed it drive me to the overflow parking lot of Worship Way.

Temptation grabbed me by the ankles and had me sneaking into the church, dodging guests – of which a bunch of them were sorors. And finally, it lead me through the doors of Ronnie's unlocked office.

"Thought I'd find you here." I may have startled him. He was in the mirror adjusting his bow tie.

It wasn't the look on his face, but how quickly he shut and locked the door that told me he was chary about me being in his office.

"What are you doing?" Ronnie looked at my clothes and sneakers. "Are you sick?"

I wasn't dressed in wedding attire, just gym shorts, a black tank, and flat hair. His first time seeing me dressed down this way.

"I miss you." I said impulsively. "My brother passed the day I last saw you. Ever since, if I wasn't mourning him, I was missing you."

"I am, truly, truly sorry for your lost. I empathized with you when I heard, and if you're still mourning your brother, I promise I will have the church pray for you. But Nola, now isn't the time for this. You need to go." Ronnie glanced down at his Movado. "The ceremony starts in a couple of minutes. I'll walk out first, and you just walk out a few minutes after me."

"You didn't miss me? You didn't think about me?" I tried looking into his eyes for truth, but his eyes were shifty. "Our friendship... that didn't mean anything?"

"Friendship shouldn't have happened to begin with, Nola. It wasn't my place, and I should've checked to see how Marley felt about it first. I apologize for my part of the confusion. Now, I don't mean to be rude, but I'm about to step out."

I hurried and wedged myself between him and door. I took his face into my hands and brought it down to mine. "Why are you doing this?"

"Nola. Move."

"Why...Why are you afraid to feel?"

His eyes locked with mine. That's when I kissed him. Seconds into, I felt him kiss me back as his full lips pressed ardently against mine. I threw my arms around his neck, and he picked me up by my legs. My back against his door. Takes zero time to pull zippers and lace to the side. And he swiftly entered. We were panting heavily, sucking on each other's lips, all self-control thrown out of the window. No cares were given.

And then he stopped. Gently let me down. Rubbed his head and shook it slowly. Just like that, the energy shifted from passion to shame, and we couldn't look at each other.

"This is the last time," he said.

I nodded.

"No more. For Marley's sake and mine... No more."

I nodded again.

He walked to his desk. His shoulder s slumped, his head hung low. "Excuse yourself," he had his hands resting on his desk. "I gotta... I need to repent."

I allowed myself out.

When I got back to my car, I spotted Marley climbing out of her limo. She looked absolutely stunning in her Pina Tornai gown and tiara. Her pregnant belly didn't draw any attention away from the gown and all of its immaculate beading and tulle skirt and train. She was so beautiful that a tear escaped and crept down my cheek.

***

I crawled back into the hotel bed feeling even emptier than when I left. I buried my face into the pillow and covered my head with blankets, somewhat trying to shield myself from God's conviction. When that didn't work, I felt compelled to strip myself completely naked, and I fell to the ground. Cried. Begged. Cried and begged God for forgiveness and that I'd be given the chance to see the sun rise again, so I could try to live righteous.

About an hour later, I got up feeling even closer to God than I did the day before.

CHAPTER 41

The next morning, I shifted uncomfortably in the pew. At first, I thought maybe Sharron told her pastor I was coming, and the pastor decided to preach for me. My palms grew sweaty, and my throat felt dry. It felt like she was talking about me. How else was it that in a sanctuary packed with people sitting shoulder to shoulder, that her pastor seemed to speaking directly to me about what I was currently going through? Then, I thought about it. Sharron had no idea I was coming. I had no idea I was coming. It was spur of the moment, and I was lucky enough to call her while she heading out of her door.

"Yeah, I'm on my way there now," she sounded happy that I decided to visit. "I'll text you the address and meet you in the parking lot!"

I picked up the bulletin and flipped to the page where that Sunday's topic would be found... just to make sure. "*Let it Go— Ephesians 4:31-32*" I fanned myself with the bulletin after it was confirmed that Sharron hadn't put in a request for me after all.

"God is waiting for you to realize that in order for you to come outta the storm you're in right now, and in order for you to experience the fullness of His glory, you gotta get rid of your *stuff*! Touch five people and tell them to get rid of their *stuff*." Everybody followed the pastor's command—except for me, I sat stiff absorbing her teaching, hooked by her elocution. As about seven people touched my shoulder, I felt my heart race with each touch.

***

I slurped my iced tea until the cup and straw made that bottom of the cup slurping noise. "On the way here, I thought about what your pastor was preaching and I think I wanna sell all of my shoes, bags, and even a couple of dresses."

Sharron side-eyed me while she chewed and swallowed FeliciTEA's signature tuna melt. "I don't think that's what she meant by *getting rid of your stuff*, Nola."

"I know exactly what she meant. Dropping resentment, bitterness, all that. But, this will be my fresh start. Some women cut their hair… I'm not doing that."

Sharron laughed, "Well I guess it's a good idea. Sell them on eBay and use the money to get outta that hotel."

"And, when I go back to my room, I'm gonna write a letter to my parents… Twenty-nine pages for each year of my life that they screwed up and twenty-nine pages for each year Elton had to serve."

"Stop. We don't know for sure if your mom lied. Technically she didn't confess."

I flagged away her comment. "*Anyway*… I'm not ready to see or speak to either of them yet, but I do wanna let them know I'm trying to forgive... I'm letting it go."

Sharron smiled and waved her hand. "Amen girl!"

"I'm gonna write a letter to Derrick, too. That'll be an extensive one. You know what, I'll even send a letter to Trav."

Sharron's eyes bulged.

"What the..? … WELL, LOOK AT GOD!"

CHAPTER 42

"She's pregnant."

"Congratulations."

"It's not mine."

"Must be a Victor thing."

"Her blood work came in yesterday." Derrick's eyes were now bloodshot red and watery. "She's HIV positive."

I almost lost my balance. I turned around and rested the crown of my head against the counter above my sink. It was about eleven o'clock on a Saturday morning. I knew it had to be something when Derrick called to say he was paying me a visit to check out my new spot. I had been living in my place for about two weeks now. Not only didn't he help me move in, he had been ignoring my phone calls and text messages since Dom passed, nor had he acknowledged the letter I sent to his email. I knew he wasn't coming because he genuinely wanted to see me. I just didn't think whatever it was would be of this magnitude. I reached for my favorite wine glass while Derrick continued.

"What will I say to mom and dad?... If I am...how can I cover this up?"

I had no answers. Just poured my Riesling.

"I haven't touched Alicia since the last time I started seeing Miguel again. I... I have never been tested... I don't know if it happened during the first time we started seeing each other..." Derrick looked like he was conversing with my ceiling. "I have to get out this situation. I have to...to move... move us away."

Then he looked at me. "Nola, you can't let them know anything if they wonder why I'm gone."

I took a gulp.

"Say something. I'm in despair."

"I don't have anything to say. And, I don't want anything to do with your drama."

"You are so cold hearted. Always have been, always will be." When Derrick fixed his lips to say something else, I stopped him.

"I don't want your negative energy in my place. Get out, Derrick. Get out and while you're at it go get tested."

Sharron was parking while Derrick was walking over to his Escalade. She watched him screech off, and then met me at my door with exuberant eyes.

"Was that your older brother? He is cuuuuuuuuute."

"Girl you don't want that. Trust me." I grabbed the newspapers and circulars she was carrying, and she followed me inside so we could clip coupons, something she got me into during the month I lived as a hotel resident.

Not only did Sharron become my coupon partner in crime, she became my prayer partner as well. Since I felt awkward about worshipping in Worship Way after all that had went down, I had been visiting Sharron's church instead. As a result, our friendship grew, and so did my relationship with Christ.

"I love what you're doing with this place. It's really coming together." She plopped on the sofa. "Told you you'd make a killing off eBay!"

"Most of those shoes and bags needed to go anyway. Fresh start. New beginnings of a frugal lifestyle." I sat the papers on the coffee table and moved a vase of multi-colored roses and a framed picture of Dominic that were sitting atop.

Sharron gushed, "Well! Those are beautiful."

"Silas of course." I gave Sharron the side eye. "I thought you weren't into flowers."

"I'm not, but girl, if this is something he always does, then it's good to see that God has given you EXACTLY what you've always wanted."

It was then that I remembered how much I longed for the kind of affection that Silas had been showering me all along. The flowers for absolutely any occasion, especially made-up ones. The phone calls just to hear my voice, the visits to shower me with attention. I was so distracted by the idea of having Ronnie that I hadn't noticed this. On top that, just recently I sent him into friend-zone, without warning, after I vowed celibacy until marriage.

"So how you like it here so far?" Sharron busted into my train of thoughts.

I shrugged my shoulders. "It's cool I guess. Other than the small tub…. And, there's always a few ants in the kitchen…. Oh, and, I hate that the cabinets behind the mirrors are so flimsy."

She laughed. "That's pretty normal for $750 a month. At least the neighborhood isn't bad at all. You wouldn't survive my hood."

"This is true." I felt blessed and knew that God was on my side when I found the apartment just less ten minutes down the road from my parents' development. The complex was pretty quiet and mostly occupied with families who had small children and people who travelled for work often.

Sharron glanced down at the wrist watch. "Speaking of my neighborhood, I wanna take you somewhere when we finish this."

***

While riding in the car with Sharron, I decided to shoot Silas a text. I wanted to see him. Talk to him about my revelation. I silently prayed that it wasn't too late. *What if he had moved on… finally tired of me jerking his feelings around?*

Me: Where are you?

Silas: Rehoboth. Why?

Me:I need to see you.

Silas: Would have to wait… fixing the beach house for Pastor.

***

"We're here."

Sharron turned off her car and hopped out. I followed her inside a recreation building. She gave me a quick a tour. There were two gyms, about four classrooms, an area for dance, locker rooms and bathrooms, and outside there was a pool. As we dipped in and out of each room, the middle to high school aged kids would swarm around Sharron, giving her hugs, high-fives, updating her on their eventful week, and so forth. I stood off to the side in awe. They loved her. I could see it on their faces, and from the way she interacted with them, I could see that each and every one of those children held a special place in her heart. After the tour and introductions to the other staff, we walked back to the front desk.

"So this is my job. The RFTS Club."   Sharron handed me their brochure. "Reach For The Stars Club. It's a place for where the education, talents, and self-esteem of troubled youth could be enriched, embraced, and empowered. How you like it?"

"I love it. I think it's perfect." I flipped through the brochure thinking about how cool it would have been for Dominic to have a place like this to retreat to and socialize. There were plenty of schools for people with neurodevelopmental disorders, but there were hardly any recreational clubs for them.

"I'm glad you love it, because it's mine." Sharron smiled big.

"Really?" I playfully slapped her on the shoulder with the brochure. "That's amazing, girl!"

"It was my mother's first, but she passed earlier this year and left it to me. I wanna open more in different cities and states."

"Go for it!"

"That's not all I want… I want us to do it together. I'm offering you part ownership."

My eyes bulged. "Is this a prank?"

"Absolutely not! Follow me." Sharron led me into an office that was behind the front desk. *Her office.* There were two desks—hers which was decorated with tons of pictures, and miniature plants. The other desk was completely bare aside from the desktop computer. We sat at her desk and she began presenting me with her business plans. The more she spoke, the more I grew convinced that this wasn't a prank. In fact, her tone of voice changed and she even sounded professional. She was a true boss, although she was dressed in yoga pants, a t-shirt, and sneakers, and I never knew it. "I have ideas, Nola - BIG ideas that keep me up at night. And, I want you to help me."

"Why me? We just reunited. And, anyway you've seen with your own eyes how financially irresponsible I used to be. Why would you trust me?"

"Okay, two reasons." Sharron folded her hands on top of her desk and looked directly into my eyes. "The first one because I want to. I told you, you blessed me, and I'm gonna bless you. The second reason is because God said so. You see that desk over there. I bought it knowing exactly the kind of person I wanted to fill that seat. She has sincere passion for the misunderstood and challenged. She can see the beauty, strength, and intelligence within them that most cannot. She's patient with them, deeply compassionate... does this sound like anyone you know?"

I nodded. My body grew chills... But pleasant chills... The chills you get when things began to make sense and dots connect, and the picture becomes clear.

Sharron continued, "Well, I had no idea *WHO* this person was going to be so I held about thirty interviews until I finally gave up. I got so frustrated and handed it over to God. I prayed myself to sleep that night, and the next morning the Holy Spirit laid it on my heart to relax, take a drive, and treat myself to the finest cup of tea. When have you ever seen me with a cup of FeliciTEA's?"

I laughed. "Never."

"When I saw you sitting there, I thought it could be God sent. When we chatted, and from the way you spoke about Dominic, I knew so. That passion you had for Dominic could very well be your calling." Sharron opened her hands. "I believe that this is for you. I believe that everything… *everything…* that you have gone through within the past couple of years, up until now, was designed by God to bring you where you are today. The same goes for me, too."

"I was such a train wreck."

"Me too!"

I smiled. "He's putting us on the right track." I closed my eyes. I could see and hear Dominic telling me to *Push hard. Pull hard. Chug hard, like a train.* I opened my eyes.

"I wanna do it… just let me pray about it."

CHAPTER 43

I got a chance to have a two-hour and thirty-minute prayer and praise session with God, all the way down to Silas's beach house in Rehoboth, De.

I pulled one of his numbers – a pop-up – because I didn't want to wait. I needed him to know how I felt right away. When Sharron dropped me back to my place, I showered, threw on a shorts and tank outfit from H&M, and flat sandals from Macy's—simplistic being my new and affordable style—and I hopped in my Range to hit the highway.

Parking at the beach was a headache. It was as if everyone decided to wrap up August there, and I wound up having to park a few blocks away. The excitement however, had me power walking. I was catching my breath when I knocked on the front door.

"Hello." A pretty, slim, and tall woman opened the door. She was dressed in a bikini top with a towel wrapped around her waist. Her hair was damp and pulled into a pony.

My heart stopped. I Froze. *It was too late*.

"Can I help you?" The woman raised her eyebrow.

Behind her, Silas came into view. "Sofia, who is it?" He got closer. His shirt was off. Both of them looking like I just interrupted their afternoon tryst. "Nola! What are you doing here?"

I took off running. Silas ran after me and caught me at the corner. He held my arm.

"I'm sorry." I couldn't look at him. "I shouldn't have popped up on you like that." I tried to get him to release me.

He refused to let go. "Why didn't you tell me you were coming?"

"Silas, it's cool. Let go of me and go back to your girl."

"She's not my girl."

"Your fling."

"She's not a fling."

"Let go!"

He released me. "She's the pastor's lady friend."

I threw up my hands and shook my head. "Wait…what? He has a woman? That fast. Already?"

"You sound like you have a problem with it."

"I don't!" *half-false.* "But, why the hell are you half naked with Pastor Ronnie's woman?"

Silas laughed.

"It's funny??"

"You're funny!" Silas backed up as if he were saying I needed a better look at him. "I'm working, and covered in paint. I told you I was fixing it. Pastor and Sofia were just coming from the boardwalk when you knocked."

I threw my hands in my face, trying to process that Ronnie had a girl now – not just any girl. She looked gorgeous, young, tall, and smiled brightly. She was most likely the one he told me about in the park.

"It's his vacation, and he brought her yesterday. I don't blame him. She's alright. Kinda nice… Marley introduced them. I think she works at her job or something like that. "

I didn't need to hear anymore. I wasn't jealous either, which was a huge testament that my feelings towards the pastor had dissolved. I just wasn't interested in Ronnie at all anymore—just by the fact that he moved on.

"Anyway..." I stepped closer and looked up at him. He smiled. His red hair glowed against the sun. "…I didn't come here to talk about Pastor Ronnie or his girl."

"Is that right?"

"I came here to talk about you and me."

Silas nodded, but his reaction wasn't at all like how I expected it. The way I pictured it driving down, he was supposed to wrap his arms around me, squeeze me, lift me up, and take my lips into his and then whisper, "Finally" or something romantically cheesy like that. Instead, his posture shifted and he stepped back a bit.

"You don't know what you want, Nola. I think you're confused."

I shook my head. "I figured it out."

"I think you need to chill. Focus on you and your relationship with Christ."

"You moved on."

"That's not it."

"You have a girl now, too? What--she's on her way? If you moved on, then say that you moved on. Don't down play it and push me off on God."

"I'm single." Silas stuffed his hands in his pocket and shrugged. "I got things I need to work on. These past couple of months I realized that God isn't through with me. It's stuff in my past that's effecting me today. I can't bring that into no relationship."

I said nothing.

"You need work, too."

"Don't tell me what I need," I snapped.

Silas lifted his hands, "I'm just telling you what I've learned since knowing you. You're empty."

"I'm going home."

I started to walk off. Silas stopped me. "That void can't be filled with nobody but God, Nola. I'm telling you."

I had no comment to that. There was too much to take in, so much for one day. And now, I had to prepare for a two-hour drive home, alone with my thoughts. "I'll text you to let you know I made it home safe, Silas."

CHAPTER 44

I was afraid to come to the chapter meeting now that all my dirty laundry had been aired. I missed the first two months of the meetings because of this. I knew I'd come back eventually, present them with the new and improved Nola Victor, but I feared the unexpected. Would my sorors still love me? Would my presence still light up the room?

I was a bit late, so the tapping sounds of my Jessica Simpson booties were all that could be heard as I walked across the lobby and through the conference room doors.

"Heyyyy good to see you soror!" Our hostess rose from the behind the table and embraced me with a warm hug, and gentle rub on my back. Just like that, I felt welcomed. Accepted as if word hadn't gotten out about the chaos I had caused Marley over the summer. I sat at a table in the back, engaged in small chatter and jokes with sorors who patted my hands and smiled with their eyes as they'd always done. Just like that, I felt glad I came. Sorority sisterhood is powerful. They'll love you unconditionally like family, if not more. They'll be disappointed in you, you may let them down, but breaking the bond was about as easy as moving a mountain.

An hour later, President Gabrielle started with the closing remarks.

"As we know, Soror Marley is on bed rest with Hyperemesis Gravidarum." *This was news to me.* "Because of all of your donations, we were able to make this beautiful care package."

She pointed to an oversized wicker basket filled with bath and body products, other spa essentials, candles and magazines, all wrapped in cellophane. Our sorors clapped and "awwwed."

President Gabrielle looked at me. "Nola, you wouldn't mind dropping this off to her place?"

All eyes were on me. I nervously twirled my hair with my index finger. She took advantage of my hesitation.

"Ok, good. Thanks Nola." President Gabrielle gave me a knowing smile. "Sorors this concludes our chapter meeting."

***

"I know you had sex with my father on my wedding day."

I stood frozen, clutching the basket.

"So don't come in here unless you're gonna keep it real…. Put the basket on my dresser." Marley pointed across from her. I followed her direction. "Greg!"

Greg appeared from the living room. "Yes, baby?"

"Could you open the basket for me? I wanna see what's in it." Greg shuffled to the dresser. Marley looked at me. "Sit down."

She pointed to chair by her bed. I hesitated. I wasn't about to get cozy next to her after she just shot me with that statement as soon as I entered her bedroom.

"I won't bite, Nola. Sit down. It's the least you could do."

I sat.

Greg showed Marley all the contents of the basket one-by-one. Marley's eyes lit up. Even while she was sick, she glowed. Her skin looked flawless and smooth, her hair full and healthy, and her cheeks were rouge—enamored and filled with gratitude.

"Awwww. I love my sorors."

After displaying the gifts, Greg excused himself. Marley looked at me. "I'm sorry about Dominic. I cried for days… I went to the funeral."

"Thank you. I appreciate that."

For the first time ever, I felt intimated and nervous about being in her presence. "And you look gorgeous. You carry pregnancy beautifully."

It was the first time I've ever given Marley a well-deserved compliment. She beamed and rubbed her basketball-sized belly.

"Thank you, Nola."

Her smile brought me ease. "I don't want to hold you up, but I just wanna let you know that I'm sorry. I apologize for ever taking advantage of our friendship" I swallowed hard. "And, I apologize for… your father."

"I can't believe y'all had sex." Marley shook her head but laughed. "I mean, you shoulda saw his face when he told me. Poor man, felt horrible."

"This… is pretty uncomfortable … to talk about…"

"I had forgiven you a while ago, Nola. Anyway, my father has moved on, and he is happy. Sophia is great. He's great. And I'm feeling great because of it. It's in the past, and the both of you are grown. You guys have your own sins to deal with, and I have my own. That's what I needed to learn."

I breathed. "Thank you."

There was a pause for what seemed like a few minutes, and then she said, "We may never be as close as we were, but that shouldn't stop you from worshiping at Worship Way. Come back to our church, Nola. It's your home, too."

I sighed. "I miss it."

"Then come back."

I nodded.

"Thanks for bringing the basket soror Nola. Tell Silas I said hello when you go to our church tomorrow."

***

I left Marley's in time to get to the Deaconess's place. She wanted me there by noon.

BEEEEEEEEP! BEEEEEEEEEEP!

"Hold on. I'm coming, I'm coming." She descended down her porch steps looking fly and stylish as usual. She pinched my cheek when she hopped in on passenger side of my Range.

"How's my beautiful granddaughter?"

I laughed. "Stop it… you're so silly."

"I'm just happy that God brought you here. You know that was nothing but Him."

"Amen to that!" I waved my hand.

My grandmother sighed, "You ready?"

My purity ring flickered as I gripped the stirring wheel. I inhaled and exhaled, then smiled.

"Lord knows I'm ready."

"Good." She smiled back. "Elton is anxious to meet you."

ABOUT THE AUTHOR

J. Jakée is a living example of transformation and she's currently resting in the palms of her Potter's hand. She is a freelance and ghost writer, an editor, a motivator and encourager by nature, and a mother to an adorable prince. At 29, she self-published *Beautiful Liar*, the debut novel to the *Sisterly Relations* series.

Jakée worships at Mt. Pleasant Baptist Church in Twin Oaks, PA, and she is in the process of obtaining a certification in Biblical Counseling. Jakée belongs to the first Black Greek letter sorority, Alpha Kappa Alpha Sorority, Inc., and she's also a faithful Partner in Hope for St. Jude Children's Research Hospital.

For more information about J. Jakée and future projects, please visit AuthorJJakee.com

Blessed by God, so that I may be a blessing to others

www.ingramcontent.com/pod-product-compliance
Lightning Source LLC
Chambersburg PA
CBHW020754250626
47155CB00003B/1073